James Thomson

The Works of James Thomson - With his Last Corrections and Improvements

Volume the First

James Thomson

The Works of James Thomson - With his Last Corrections and Improvements
Volume the First

ISBN/EAN: 9783337107369

Printed in Europe, USA, Canada, Australia, Japan

Cover: Foto ©Andreas Hilbeck / pixelio.de

More available books at **www.hansebooks.com**

CASTLE·OF·INDOLENCE

THE

BRITANNIA

JAMES
THOMSON
ÆTAT. XLVI.

J. Paton delin .

T. Cook sculp .

THE
WORKS
OF
JAMES THOMSON.

WITH HIS LAST

CORRECTIONS AND IMPROVEMENTS.

IN THREE VOLUMES COMPLETE.

TO WHICH IS PREFIXED

THE LIFE OF THE AUTHOR,
By PATRICK MURDOCH, D.D. F.R.S.

VOLUME THE FIRST.

LONDON:
PRINTED BY A. STRAHAN;
For J. Rivington and Sons, T. Payne and Sons, S. Crowder,
T. Longman, B. Law, G. G. J. and J. Robinson, T. Cadell,
J. Nichols, R. Baldwin, W. Goldsmith, W. Stuart, J. Murray,
J. White, W. Lowndes. W. Bent, S. Hayes, G. and T. Wilkie,
D. Ogilvy, and Scatcherd and Whitaker.
MDCCLXXXVIII.

TO THE

KING'S MOST EXCELLENT MAJESTY,

THIS COMPLETE EDITION OF
THE WORKS OF JAMES THOMSON,

WHO WAS
PARTICULARLY HONOURED WITH
THE FAVOUR AND PATRONAGE OF
HIS MAJESTY'S ROYAL PARENTS;

AND WHOSE STRAINS
HAVE BEEN AUSPICIOUSLY PROPHETIC
OF THE PRESENT GLORIOUS REIGN;

IS,
WITH THE MOST PROFOUND HUMILITY,
INSCRIBED AND DEDICATED,

BY
HIS MAJESTY'S
MOST DUTIFUL SUBJECT
AND SERVANT,

PATRICK MURDOCH.

A 3

vII

CONTENTS

OF THE

FIRST VOLUME.

———————

A 4

viii   C O N T E N T S.

AN
ACCOUNT

OF THE

LIFE AND WRITINGS

OF

Mr. JAMES THOMSON.

IT is commonly faid, that the life of a good
writer is beft read in his works: which can
fcarce fail to receive a peculiar ti   om his
temper, manners, and habits; th   guifhing
character of his mind, his ruling paffion, at leaft,
will there appear undifguifed. But however juft
this obfervation may be; and although we might
fafely reft Mr. *Thomfon*'s fame, as a good man, as
well as a man of genius, on this fole footing; yet
the defire which the Public always fhews of being
more particularly acquainted with the hiftory of
an eminent author, ought not to be difappointed;
as it proceeds not from mere curiofity, but chiefly
from affection and gratitude to thofe by whom
they have been entertained and inftructed.

To give fome account of a deceafed friend is often a piece of juftice likewife, which ought not to be refufed to his memory: to prevent or efface the impertinent fictions which officious Biographers are fo apt to collect and propagate. And we may add, that the circumftances of an author's life will fometimes throw the beft light upon his writings; inftances whereof we fhall meet with in the following pages.

Mr. *Thomfon* was born at *Ednam*, in the fhire of *Roxburgh*, on the 11th of *September*, in the year 1700. His father, minifter of that place, was but little known beyond the narrow circle of his co-prefbyters, and to a few gentlemen in the neighbourhood; but highly refpected by them, for his piety, and his diligence in the paftoral duty: as appeared afterwards in their kind offices to his widow and orphan family.

The Reverend Meffrs. *Riccarton* and *Gufthart* particularl⬤⬤⬤⬤moft affectionate and friendly part in all th⬤⬤⬤rns. The former, a man of uncommon⬤⬤ration and good tafte, had very early difcovered, through the rudenefs of young *Thomfon*'s puerile effays, a fund of genius well deferving culture and encouragement. He undertook therefore, with the father's approbation, the chief direction of his ftudies, furnifhed him with the proper books, corrected his performances; and was daily rewarded with the pleafure of feeing his labour fo happily employed.

The other reverend gentleman, Mr. *Gufthart*, who is ftill living *, one of the minifters of *Edin-*

* 1762.

burgh, and senior of the Chapel Royal, was no less serviceable to Mrs. *Thomson* in the management of her little affairs; which, after the decease of her husband, burdened as she was with a family of nine children, required the prudent counsels and assistance of that faithful and generous friend.

Sir *William Bennet* likewise, well known for his gay humour and ready poetical wit, was highly delighted with our young poet, and used to invite him to pass the summer vacation at his country seat: a scene of life which Mr. *Thomson* always remembered with particular pleasure. But what he wrote during that time, either to entertain Sir *William* and Mr. *Riccarton,* or for his own amusement, he destroyed every new year's day; committing his little pieces to the flames, in their due order; and crowning the solemnity with a copy of verses, in which were humorously recited the several grounds of their condemnation.

After the usual course of school e   un-der an able master at *Jedburgh,* Mr.   was sent to the Univerfity of *Edinburgh.* But in the second year of his admission, his studies were for some time interrupted by the death of his father; who was carried off so suddenly, that it was not possible for Mr. *Thomson,* with all the diligence he could use, to receive his last blessing. This affected him to an uncommon degree; and his relations still remember some extraordinary instances of his grief and filial duty on that occasion.

Mrs. *Thomson,* whose maiden name was *Hume,* and who was co-heiress of a small estate in the

country, did not fink under this misfortune. She
confulted her friend Mr. *Gufbart*; and having, by
his advice, mortgaged her moiety of the farm, re-
paired with her family to *Edinburgh*; where fhe
lived in a decent frugal manner, till her favourite
fon had not only finifhed his academical courfe,
but was even diftinguifhed and patronifed as a man
of genius. She was, herfelf, a perfon of uncommon natural endowments; poffeffed of every focial
and domeftic virtue; with an imagination, for
vivacity and warmth, fcarce inferior to her fon's,
and which raifed her devotional exercifes to a pitch
bordering on enthufiafm.

But whatever advantage Mr. *Thomfon* might de-
rive from the complexion of his parent, it is certain he owed much to a religious education; and
that his early acquaintance with the facred writings
contributed greatly to that *fublime*, by which his
work will be for ever diftinguifhed. In his firft
piece *afons*, we fee him at once affume the
majefom of an Eaftern writer; feizing the
grand images as they rife, clothing them in his
own expreffive language, and preferving, through-
out, the grace, the variety, and the dignity which
belong to a juft compofition; unhurt by the ftiff-
nefs of formal method.

About this time, the ftudy of poetry was become general in *Scotland*, the beft *Englifb* authors
being univerfally read, and imitations of them
attempted. *Addifon* had lately difplayed the beauties of *Milton*'s immortal work; and his remarks
on it, together with Mr. *Pope*'s celebrated *Effay*,

had opened the way to an acquaintance with the beft poets and critics.

But the moft learned critic is not always the beft judge of poetry; tafte being a gift of nature, the want of which, *Ariftotle* and *Boffu* cannot fupply; nor even the ftudy of the beft originals, when the reader's faculties are not *tuned in a certain confonance* to thofe of the poet: and this happened to be the cafe with certain learned gentlemen, into whofe hands a few of Mr. *Thomfon*'s firft eſſays had fallen. Some inaccuracies of ftyle, and thofe luxuriancies which a young writer can hardly avoid, lay open to their cavils and cenfure ; fo far indeed they might be competent judges: but the fire and enthufiafm of the poet had entirely efcaped their notice. Mr. *Thomfon*, however, confcious of his own ftrength, was not difcouraged by this treatment; efpecially as he had fome friends on whofe judgment he could better rely, and who thought very differently of his performances. On from that time, he began to turn his views towards *London*; where works of genius may always expect a candid reception and due encouragement; and an accident foon after entirely determined him to try his fortune there.

The divinity chair at *Edinburgh* was then filled by the reverend and learned Mr. *Hamilton*; a gentleman univerfally refpected and beloved; and who had particularly endeared himfelf to the young divines under his care, by his kind offices, his candor and affability. Our author had attended his lectures for about a year, when there was prescribed to him for the subject of an exercise, a psalm, in which the power and majesty of God are celebrated. Of this psalm he gave a paraphrase and illustration, as the nature of the exercise required; but in a style so highly poetical as surprised the whole audience. Mr. *Hamilton*, as his custom was, complimented the orator upon his performance, and pointed out to the students the most masterly striking parts of it; but at last, turning to Mr. *Thomson*, he told him, smiling, that if he thought of being useful in the ministry, he must keep a stricter rein upon his imagination, and express himself in language more intelligible to an ordinary congregation.

This gave Mr. *Thomson* to understand, that his expectations from the study of theology might be very precarious; even though the *Church* had been more his free choice than probably it was. So that having, soon after, received some encouragement from a lady of quality, a friend of his mother's, then in *London*, he quickly prepared himself for his journey. And although this encouragement ended in nothing beneficial, it served for the present as a good pretext, to cover the imprudence of committing himself to the wide world, unfriended and unpatronised, and with the slender stock of money he was then possessed of.

But his merit did not long lie concealed. Mr. *Forbes*, afterwards Lord President of the Session, then attending the service of Parliament, having seen a specimen of Mr. *Thomson*'s poetry in *Scotland*, received him very kindly, and recommended

him to fome of his friends: particularly to Mr.
Aikman, who lived in great intimacy with many
perfons of diftinguifhed rank and worth.   This
gentleman, from a connoiffeur in painting, was
become a profeffed painter; and his tafte being no
lefs juft and delicate in the kindred art of defcrip-
tive poetry, than in his own, no wonder that he
foon conceived a friendfhip for our author.   What
a warm return he met with, and how Mr. *Thomfon*
was affected by his friend's premature death, appears in the copy of verfes which he wrote on that
occafion.

In the mean time, our author's reception, where-
ever he was introduced, emboldened him to rifque
the publication of his *Winter:* in which, as himfelf
was a mere novice in fuch matters, he was kindly
affifted by Mr. *Mallet*, then private tutor to his
Grace the Duke of *Montrofe*, and his brother the
Lord *George Graham*, fo well known afterwards as
an able and gallant fea officer.   To Mr. *Mallet* he
likewife owed his firft acquaintance with féveral of
the wits of that time; an exact information of their
characters, perfonal and poetical, and how they
ftood affected to each other.

The Poem of *Winter*, publifhed in *March* 1726,
was no fooner read than univerfally admired; thofe
only excepted who had not been ufed to feel, or to
look for, any thing in poetry, beyond a *point* of
fatirical or epigrammatic wit, a fmart *antithefis*
richly trimmed with rhyme, or the foftnefs of an
elegiac complaint.   To fuch his manly claffical fpirit
could not readily recommend itfelf; till after a

more attentive perufal, they had got the better of
their prejudices, and either acquired or affected a
truer tafte. A few others ftood aloof, merely becaufe they had long before fixed the articles of
their poetical creed, and refigned themfelves to
an abfolute defpair of ever feeing any thing new
and original. Thefe were fomewhat mortified to
find their notions difturbed by the appearance of a
poet, who feemed to owe nothing but to nature
and his own genius. But, in a fhort time, the
applaufe became unanimous; every one wondering how fo many pictures, and pictures fo familiar, fhould have moved them but faintly to what
they felt in his defcriptions. His digreffions too,
the overflowings of a tender benevolent heart,
charmed the reader no lefs; leaving him in doubt,
whether he fhould more admire the *Poet*, or love
the *Man*.

From that time Mr. *Thomfon*'s acquaintance was
courted by all men of tafte; and feveral ladies of
high rank and diftinction became his declared
patroneffes: the Countefs of *Hertford*, Mifs *Drelin-
court*, afterwards Vifcountefs *Primrofe*, Mrs. *Stanley*,
and others. But the chief happinefs which his
Winter procured him was, that it brought him
acquainted with Dr. *Rundle*, afterwards Lord
Bifhop of *Derry:* who, upon converfing with Mr.
Thomfon, and finding in him qualities greater ftill,
and of more value, than thofe of a poet, received
him into his intimate confidence and friendfhip;
promoted his character every where; introduced
him to his great friend the Lord Chancellor *Tal-*

bot; and; fome years after, when the eldeft fon of that nobleman was to make his *tour* of travelling, recommended Mr. *Thomfon* as a proper companion for him. His affection and gratitude to Dr. *Rundle*, and his indignation at the treatment that worthy prelate had met with, are finely expreffed in his poem to the memory of Lord *Talbot*. The true caufe of that undeferved treatment has been fecreted from the Public, as well as the dark *manœuvres* that were employed: but Mr. *Thomfon*, who had accefs to the beft information, places it to the account of

> ———Slanderous zeal, and politics infirm,
> Jealous of worth.———

Meanwhile, our poet's chief care had been, in return for the public favour, to finifh the plan which their wifhes laid out for him; and the expectations which his *Winter* had raifed, were fully fatisfied by the fucceffive publication of the other *Seafons:* of *Summer*, in the year 1727; of *Spring*, in the beginning of the following year; and of *Autumn*, in a quarto edition of his works, printed in 1730.

In that edition, the *Seafons* are placed in their natural order; and crowned with that inimitable *Hymn*, in which we view them in their beautiful fucceffion, as *one whole*, the *immediate* effect of infinite *Power* and *Goodnefs*. In imitation of the Hebrew Bard, all nature is called forth to do homage to the Creator, and the reader is left enraptured in filent adoration and praife.

VOL. I.   a

Befides thefe, and his tragedy of *Sophonifba*, written and acted with applaufe, in the year 1729, Mr. *Thomfon* had, in 1727, publifhed his poem to the memory of Sir *Ifaac Newton*, then lately deceafed; containing a deferved encomium of that incomparable man, with an account of his chief difcoveries; fublimely poetical; and yet fo juft, that an ingenious foreigner, the Count *Algarotti*, takes a line of it for the text of his philofophical dialogues, *Il Neutonianifmo per le dame:* this was in part owing to the affiftance he had of his friend Mr. *Gray*, a gentleman well verfed in the *Newtonian Philofophy*, who, on that occafion, gave him a very exact, though general, abftract of its principles.

That fame year, the refentment of our merchants, for the interruption of their trade by the *Spaniards* in *America*, running very high, Mr. *Thomfon* zealoufly took part in it; and wrote his poem *Britannia*, to roufe the nation to revenge. And although this piece is the lefs read that its fubject was but accidental and temporary; the fpirited generous fentiments that enrich it, can never be out of feafon: they will at leaft remain a monument of that love of his country, that *devotion to the Public*, which he is ever inculcating as the perfection of virtue, and which none ever felt more pure, or more intenfe, than himfelf.

Our author's poetical ftudies were now to be interrupted, or rather improved, by his attendance on the Honourable Mr. *Charles Talbot* in his

travels. A delightful tafk indeed! endowed as
that young nobleman was by nature, and accom-
plifhed by the care and example of the beft of
fathers, in whatever could adorn humanity: graceful of perfon, elegant in manners and addrefs,
pious, humane, generous; with an exquifite tafte
in all the finer arts.

  With this amiable companion and friend, Mr.
Thomfon vifited moft of the courts and capital cities
of Europe; and returned with his views greatly en-
larged; not of exterior nature only, and the works
of art, but of human life and manners, of the
conftitution and policy of the feveral ftates, their
connexions, and their religious inftitutions. How
particular and judicious his obfervations were, we
fee in his poem of Liberty, begun foon after his
return to England. We fee, at the fame time, to
what a high pitch his love of his country was
raifed, by the comparifons he had all along been
making of our happy well-poifed government with
thofe of other nations. To infpire his fellow-fubjects
with the like fentiments; and to fhew them by
what means the precious freedom we enjoy may
be preferved, and how it may be abufed or loft; he
employed two years of his life in compofing that
noble work: upon which, confcious of the im-
portance and dignity of the fubject, he valued himfelf more than upon all his other writings.

  While Mr. Thomfon was writing the Firft Part
of Liberty, he received a fevere fhock, by the death
of his noble friend and fellow-traveller: which
was foon followed by another that was feverer

ftill, and of more general concern; the death of
Lord *Talbot* himfelf; which Mr. *Thomfon* fo pa-
thetically and fo juftly laments in the poem dedicated to his memory.   In him the nation faw
itfelf deprived of an uncorrupted patriot, the faithful guardian of their rights, on whofe wifdom and
integrity they had founded their hopes of relief
from many tedious vexations: and Mr. *Thomfon*,
befides his fhare in the general mourning, had to
bear all the affliction which a heart like his could
feel, for the perfon whom, of all mankind, he moft
revered and loved.   At the fame time, he found
himfelf, from an eafy competency, reduced to a
ftate of precarious dependence, in which he paffed
the remainder of his life; excepting only the two
laft years of it, during which he enjoyed the place
of Surveyor-General of the *Leeward Iflands*, procured for him by the generous friendfhip of my
Lord *Lyttelton*.

Immediately upon his return to *England* with
Mr. *Talbot*, the Chancellor had made him his Se-
cretary of Briefs; a place of little attendance,
fuiting his retired indolent way of life, and equal
to all his wants.   This place fell with his patron;
and although the noble Lord, who fucceeded to
Lord *Talbot* in office, kept it vacant for fome time,
probably till Mr. *Thomfon* fhould apply for it, he
was fo difpirited, and fo liftlefs to every concern
of that kind, that he never took one ftep in the
affair: a neglect which his beft friends greatly
blamed in him.

Yet could not his genius be depreffed, or his temper hurt, by this reverfe of fortune. He re-fumed, with time, his ufual chearfulnefs, and never abated one article in his way of living; which, though fimple, was genial and elegant. The profits arifing from his works were not inconfiderable; his tragedy of *Agamemnon*, acted in 1738, yielded a good fum; Mr. *Millar* was always at hand, to anfwer, or even to prevent his demands; and he had a friend or two befides, whofe hearts, he knew, were not contracted by the ample fortunes they had acquired; who would, of themfelves, interpofe, if they faw any occafion for it.

But his chief dependance, during this long interval, was on the protection and bounty of his Royal Highnefs FREDERIC Prince of *Wales*; who, upon the recommendation of Lord *Lyttelton*, then his chief favourite, fettled on him a handfome allowance. And afterwards, when he was introduced to his Royal Highnefs, that excellent prince, who truly was what Mr. *Thomfon* paints him, *the friend of mankind and of merit*, received him very gracioufly, and ever after honoured him with many marks of particular favour and confidence. A circumftance, which does equal honour to the patron and the poet, ought not here to be omitted; that my Lord *Lyttelton*'s recommendation came altogether unfolicited, and long before Mr. *Thomfon* was perfonally known to him.

It happened, however, that the favour of his Royal Highnefs was in one inftance of fome prejudice to our author; in the refufal of a licence for his tragedy of *Edward* and *Eleonora*, which he had prepared for the ftage in the year 1739. The reader may fee that this play contains not a line which could juftly give offence; but the miniftry, ftill fore from certain pafquinades, which had lately produced the ftage-act; and as little fatisfied with fome parts of the prince's political conduct, as he was with their management of the public affairs; would not rifque the reprefentation of a piece written under his eye, and, they might probably think, by his command.

This refufal drew after it another; and in a way which, as it is related, was rather ludicrous. Mr. *Paterfon*, a companion of Mr. *Thomfon*, afterwards his *deputy* and then his *fucceffor* in the general-furveyorfhip, ufed to write out fair copies for his friend, when fuch were wanted for the prefs or for the ftage. This gentleman likewife courted the tragic mufe; and had taken for his fubject, the ftory of *Arminius* the *German* hero. But his play, guiltlefs as it was, being prefented for a licence, no fooner had the *cenfor* caft his eyes on the hand-writing in which he had feen *Edward* and *Eleonora*, than he cried out, Away with it! and the author's profits were reduced to what his bookfeller could afford for a tragedy in diftrefs.

Mr. *Thomfon*'s next dramatic performance was the *Mafque* of *Alfred*; written, jointly with Mr. *Mallet*, by command of the Prince of *Wales*, for the entertainment of his Royal Highnefs's court, at his fummer-refidence. This piece, with fome alterations, and the mufic new, has been fince

brought upon the ſtage by Mr. *Mallet;* but the
edition we give is from the *original,* as it was acted
at *Clifden,* in the year 1740, on the birth-day of
her Royal Highneſs the Princeſs *Auguſta.*

In the year 1745, his *Tancred* and *Sigiſmunda,*
taken from the novel in *Gil Blas,* was performed
with applauſe; and from the deep romantic diſtreſs
of the lovers, continues to draw crowded houſes.
The ſucceſs of this piece was indeed enſured from
the firſt by Mr. *Garrick* and Mrs. *Cibber,* their appearing in the principal characters; which they
heighten and adorn with all the magic of their
never-failing art.

He had, in the mean time, been finiſhing his
Caſtle of Indolence, in two *Cantos.* It was, at firſt,
little more than a few detached ſtanzas, in the
way of raillery on himſelf, and on ſome of his
friends, who would reproach him with indolence;
while he thought them, at leaſt, as indolent as
himſelf. But he ſaw very ſoon, that the ſubject
deſerved to be treated more ſeriouſly, and in a form
fitted to convey one of the moſt important moral
leſſons.

The *ſtanza* which he uſes in this work is that
of *Spenſer,* borrowed from the *Italian* poets; in
which he thought rhymes had their proper place,
and were even graceful: the compaſs of the ſtanza
admitting an agreeable variety of final ſounds;
while the ſenſe of the poet is not cramped or cut
ſhort, nor yet too much dilated: as muſt often
happen, when it is parcelled out into rhymed
couplets; the uſual meaſure indeed of our *elegy*

and *fatire*; but which always weakens the higher poetry, and, to a true ear, will fometimes give it an air of the *burlefque*.

This was the laft piece Mr. *Thomfon* himfelf publifhed; his tragedy of *Coriolanus* being only prepared for the theatre, when a fatal accident robbed the world of one of the beft men, and beft poets, that lived in it.

He had always been a timorous horfeman; and more fo, in a road where numbers of giddy or unfkilful riders are continually paffing: fo that when the weather did not invite him to go by water, he would commonly walk the diftance between *London* and *Richmond*, with any acquaintance that offered; with whom he might chat and reft himfelf, or perhaps dine, by the way. One fummer evening, being alone, in his walk from town to *Hammerfmith*, he had overheated himfelf, and in that condition, imprudently took a boat to carry him to *Kew*; apprehending no bad confequence from the chill air on the river, which his walk to his houfe, at the upper end of *Kew-lane*, had always hitherto prevented. But, now, the cold had fo feized him, that next day he found himfelf in a high fever, fo much the more to be dreaded that he was of a full habit. This, however, by the ufe of proper medicines, was removed, fo that he was thought to be out of danger: till the fine weather having tempted him to expofe himfelf once more to the evening dews, his fever returned with violence, and with fuch fymptoms as left no hopes of a cure. Two days had paffed before his relapfe was known in town; at laft Mr. *Mitchell* and Mr. *Reid*, with Dr. *Armftrong*, being informed of it, pofted out at midnight to his affiftance: but alas! came only to endure a fight of all others the moft fhocking to nature, the laft agonies of their beloved friend. This lamented death happened on the 27th day of *Auguft*, 1748.

His teftamentary executors were, the Lord *Lyttelton*, whofe care of our poet's fortune and fame ceafed not with his life; and Mr. *Mitchell*, a gentleman equally noted for the truth and conftancy of his private friendfhips, and for his addrefs and fpirit as a public minifter. By their united intereft, the orphan play of *Coriolanus* was brought on the ftage to the beft advantage: from the profits of which, and the fale of manufcripts, and other effects, all demands were duly fatisfied, and a handfome fum remitted to his fifters. My Lord *Lyttelton*'s prologue to this piece was admired as one of the beft that had ever been *written:* the beft *fpoken* it certainly was. The fympathizing audience faw that, *then* indeed, Mr. *Quin* was *no actor*; that the tears he fhed, were thofe of real friendfhip and grief.

Mr. *Thomfon*'s remains were depofited in the church of *Richmond*, under a plain ftone, without any infcription: nor did his brother poets at all exert themfelves on the occafion, as they had lately done for one who had been the terror of poets all his lifetime. This filence furnifhed matter to one of his friends for an excellent fatirical epigram, which we are forry we cannot give the reader. Only one gentleman, Mr. *Collins*, who had lived fome time at *Richmond*, but forfook it when Mr. *Thomfon* died, wrote an Ode to his memory. This, for the dirgelike melancholy it breathes, and the warmth of affection that feems to have dictated it, we fhall fubjoin to the prefent account.

Our author himfelf hints, fomewhere in his works, that his exterior was not the moft pro-mifing; his make being rather robuft than grace-ful: though it is known that in his youth he had been thought handfome. His worft appearance was, when you faw him walking alone, in a thoughtful mood: but let a friend accoft him, and enter into converfation, he would inftantly brighten into a moft amiable afpect, his features no longer the fame, and his eye darting a peculiar animated fire. The cafe was much alike in company; where, if it was mixed, or very numerous, he made but an indifferent figure: but with a few felect friends, he was open, fprightly, and entertaining. His wit flowed freely, but pertinently, and at due intervals, leaving room for every one to contribute his fhare. Such was his extreme fenfibility, fo perfect the harmony of his organs with the fenti-ments of his mind, that his looks always an-nounced, and half expreffed, what he was about to fay; and his voice correfponded exactly to the manner and degree in which he was affected. This fenfibility had one inconvenience attending it, that it rendered him the very worft reader of good poetry: a *fonnet*, or a copy of tame verfes, he could manage pretty well; or even improve them in the reading: but a paſſage of *Virgil*, *Milton*, or *Shakeſpeare*, would ſometimes quite oppreſs him, that you could hear little elſe than ſome ill-articulated ſounds, riſing as from the bottom of his breaſt.

He had improved his taſte upon the beſt originals, ancient and modern; but could not bear to write what was not ſtrictly his own, what had not more immediately ſtruck his imagination, or touched his heart: ſo that he is not in the leaſt concerned in that queſtion about the *merit* or *demerit* of *imitators*. What he borrows from the ancients, he gives us in an avowed faithful paraphraſe or tranſlation; as we ſee in a few paſſages taken from *Virgil*, and in that beautiful picture from *Pliny* the elder, where the courſe, and gradual increaſe, of the *Nile* are figured by the ſtages of man's life.

The autumn was his favourite ſeaſon for poetical compoſition, and the deep ſilence of the night, the time he commonly choſe for ſuch ſtudies; ſo that he would often be heard walking in his library, till near morning, humming over, in his way, what he was to correct and write out next day.

The amuſements of his leiſure hours were civil and natural hiſtory, voyáges, and the relations of travellers, the moſt authentic he could procure: and, had his ſituation favoured it, he would certainly have excelled in gardening, agriculture, and every rural improvement and exerciſe. Although he performed on no inſtrument, he was paſſionately fond of mufic, and would fometimes liften a full hour at his window to the nightingales in *Richmond* gardens. While abroad, he had been greatly delighted with the regular *Italian* drama, fuch as *Metaſtaſio* writes; as it is there heightened by the charms of the beſt voices and inſtruments; and looked upon our theatrical entertainments as, in one refpeēt, naked and imperfeēt, when compared with the *ancient*, or with thofe of *Italy*; wiſhing fometimes that a *chorus*, at leaſt, and a better *recitative*, could be introduced.

Nor was his taſte lefs exquiſite in the arts of *painting, ſculpture,* and *architeēture.* In his travels he had feen all the moſt celebrated monuments of antiquity, and the beſt produētions of modern art; and ſtudied them fo minutely, and with fo true a judgment, that in fome of his defcriptions, in the poem of *Liberty,* we have the maſter-pieces there mentioned placed in a ſtronger light perhaps than if we faw them with our eyes; at leaſt more juſtly delineated than in any other account extant: fo fuperior is a natural taſte of the *grand* and *beautiful,* to the traditional leſſons of a common *virtuofo.* His colleētion of prints, and fome drawings from the antique, are now in the poſſeſſion of his friend Mr. *Gray* of *Richmond-Hill.*

As for his more diſtinguiſhing qualities of *mind* and *heart,* they are better reprefented in his writings, than they can be by the pen of any biographer. There, his love of mankind, of his country and friends; his devotion to the *Supreme Being,* founded on the moſt elevated and juſt concep-

tions of his operations and providence, fhine out
in every page. So unbounded was his tendernefs
of heart, that it took in even the brute creation:
judge what it muft have been towards his own
fpecies. He is not indeed known, through his
whole life, to have given any perfon one moment's
pain, by his writings or otherwife. He took no
part in the poetical fquabbles which happened in
his time; and was refpected and left undifturbed
by both fides. He would even refufe to take
offence when he juftly might; by interrupting any
perfonal ftory that was brought him, with fome
jeft, or fome humorous apology for the offender.
Nor was he ever feen ruffled or difcompofed, but
when he read or heard of fome flagrant inftance
of injuftice, oppreffion, or cruelty: then, indeed,
the ftrongeft marks of horror and indignation were
vifible in his countenance.

Thefe amiable virtues, this divine temper of
mind, did not fail of their due reward. His friends
loved him with an enthufiaftic ardor, and lamented
his untimely fate in the manner that is ftill frefh
in every one's memory; the beft and greateft men
of his time honoured him with their friendfhip
and protection; the applaufe of the Public attended every appearance he made; the actors, of whom
the more eminent were his friends and admirers,
grudging no pains to do juftice to his tragedies.
At prefent indeed, if we except *Tancred*, they are
feldom called for; the fimplicity of his plots, and
the models he worked after, not fuiting the reign-
ing tafte, nor the impatience of an *Englifh* theatre.

They may hereafter come to be in vogue: but we hazard no comment or conjecture upon them, or upon any part of Mr. *Thomson*'s works; neither need they any defence or apology, after the reception they have had at home, and in the foreign languages into which they have been tranflated. We fhall only fay, that, to judge from the imitations of his *manner*, which have been following him clofe, from the very firft publication of *Winter*, he feems to have fixed no inconfiderable æra of the *Englifh* poetry.

O D E

ON THE

DEATH of Mr. THOMSON.

By Mr. COLLINS.

[The fcene of the following ftanzas is fuppofed to
lie on the *Thames* near *Richmond*.]

IN yonder grave a Druid lies
 Where flowly winds the ftealing wave!
The year's beft fweets fhall duteous rife
 To deck its Poet's fylvan grave!

In yon deep bed of whifpering reeds
 His airy harp* fhall now be laid,
That he, whofe heart in forrow bleeds,
 May love thro' life the foothing fhade.

Then maids and youths fhall linger here,
 And while its founds at diftance fwell,
Shall fadly feem in Pity's ear,
 To hear the Woodland Pilgrim's knell.

Remembrance oft fhall haunt the fhore
 When Thames in fummer wreaths is dreft,
And oft fufpend the dafhing oar
 To bid his gentle fpirit reft!

* The harp of ÆOLUS, of which fee a defcription in the
CASTLE OF INDOLENCE.

And oft as Eafe and Health retire
   To breezy lawn, or foreft deep,
The friend fhall view yon whitening fpire *,
   And 'mid the varied landfcape weep.

But Thou, who own'ft that earthy bed,
   Ah! what will every dirge avail?
Or tears, which Love and Pity fhed
   That mourn beneath the gliding fail!

Yet lives there one, whofe heedlefs eye
   Shall fcorn thy pale fhrine glimm'ring near?
With him, fweet bard, may Fancy die,
   And Joy defert the blooming year.

But thou, lorn ftream, whofe fullen tide
   No fedge-crown'd Sifters now attend,
Now waft me from the green hill's fide
   Whofe cold turf hides the buried friend!

And fee the fairy valleys fade,
   Dun Night has veil'd the folemn view!
Yet once again, dear parted fhade,
   Meek Nature's Child, again adieu!

The genial meads affign'd to blefs
   Thy life, fhall mourn thy early doom,
Their hinds, and fhepherd-girls fhall drefs
   With fimple hands thy rural tomb.

Long, long, thy ftone, and pointed clay,
   Shall melt the mufing Briton's eyes,
O! vales, and wild woods, fhall he fay,
   In yonder grave Your Druid lies!

* RICHMOND Church.

Dodd del.   T. Cook sculp

SPRING.

Published as the Act directs Jan.ᵗ 1ˢᵗ 1778 by Thoˢ. Cadell in the Strand.

S P R I N G.

B

THE ARGUMENT.

The fubjeƈt propofed. Infcribed to the Countefs of HARTFORD. The
Seafon is defcribed as it affeƈts the various parts of Nature, afcending
from the lower to the higher; with digreffions arifing from the fubjeƈt. Its influence on inanimate Matter, on Vegetables, on brute
Animals, and laft on Man; concluding with a diffuafive from the
wild and irregular paffion of Love, oppofed to that of a pure and
happy kind.

· S P R I N G.

COME, gentle Spring, ethereal Mildnefs, come,
  And from the bofom of yon dropping cloud,
While mufic wakes around, veil'd in a fhower
Of fhadowing rofes, on our plains defcend.

  O Hartford, fitted or to fhine in courts
With unaffected grace, or walk the plain
With innocence and meditation join'd
In foft affemblage, liften to my fong,
Which thy own Seafon paints; when Nature all
Is blooming and benevolent, like thee.

  And fee where furly Winter paffes off,
Far to the north, and calls his ruffian blafts:
His blafts obey, and quit the howling hill,   —
The fhatter'd foreft, and the ravag'd vale;
While fofter gales fucceed, at whofe kind touch,
Diffolving fnows in livid torrents loft,
The mountains lift their green heads to the fky.

  As yet the trembling year is unconfirm'd,   —
And Winter oft at eve refumes the breeze,
Chills the pale morn, and bids his driving fleets
Deform the day delightlefs: fo that fcarce
The bittern knows his time, with bill ingulpht
To fhake the founding marfh; or from the fhore

THE ARGUMENT.

The fubject propofed. Infcribed to the Countefs of HARTFORD. The
Seafon is defcribed as it affects the various parts of Nature, afcending
from the lower to the higher; with digreffions arifing from the fubject. Its influence on inanimate Matter, on Vegetables, on brute
Animals, and laft on Man; concluding with a diffuafive from the
wild and irregular paffion of Love, oppofed to that of a pure and
happy kind.

· S P R I N G.

COME, gentle Spring, ethereal Mildnefs, come,
   And from the bofom of yon dropping cloud,
While mufic wakes around, veil'd in a fhower
Of fhadowing rofes, on our plains defcend.
   O Hartford, fitted or to fhine in courts
With unaffected grace, or walk the plain
With innocence and meditation join'd
In foft affemblage, liften to my fong,
Which thy own Seafon paints; when Nature all
Is blooming and benevolent, like thee.
   And fee where furly Winter paffes off,
Far to the north, and calls his ruffian blafts:
His blafts obey, and quit the howling hill,   ——.
The fhatter'd foreft, and the ravag'd vale;
While fofter gales fucceed, at whofe kind touch,
Diffolving fnows in livid torrents loft,
The mountains lift their green heads to the fky.
   As yet the trembling year is unconfirm'd,   ——
And Winter oft at eve refumes the breeze,
Chills the pale morn, and bids his driving fleets
Deform the day delightlefs: fo that fcarce
The bittern knows his time, with bill ingulpht
To fhake the founding marfh; or from the fhore

The plovers when to fcatter o'er the heath,
And fing their wild notes to the liftening wafte.

    At laft from *Aries* rolls the bounteous fun,
And the bright *Bull* receives him.   Then no more
Th' expanfive atmofphere is cramp'd with cold;
But, full of life and vivifying foul,   .
Lifts the light clouds fublime, and fpreads them thin,
Fleecy and white, o'er all-furrounding heaven.

    Forth fly the tepid airs; and unconfin'd,
Unbinding earth, the moving foftnefs ftrays.
Joyous, th' impatient hufbandman perceives
Relenting Nature, and his lufty fteers
Drives from their ftalls, to where the well-us'd plough
Lies in the furrow, loofened from the froft.
There, unrefufing, to the harnefs'd yoke
They lend their fhoulder, and begin their toil,
Chear'd by the fimple fong and foaring lark.
Meanwhile incumbent o'er the fhining fhare
The mafter leans, removes th' obftructing clay,
Winds the whole work, and fidelong lays the glebe.

    White thro' the neighbouring fields the fower ftalks,
With meafur'd ftep; and liberal throws the grain
Into the faithful bofom of the ground:
The harrow follows harfh, and fhuts the fcene.

    Be gracious, HEAVEN! for now laborious Man
Has done his part.   Ye foftering breezes, blow!
Ye foftening dews, ye tender fhowers defcend!
And temper all, thou world-reviving fun,
Into the perfect year! Nor ye who live
In luxury and eafe, in pomp and pride,
Think thefe loft themes unworthy of your ear:
Such themes as thefe the *rural* MARO fung
To wide-imperial ROME, in the full height
Of elegance and tafte, by GREECE refin'd.

In ancient times, the facred plough employ'd
The kings, and awful fathers of mankind: ———
And fome, with whom compar'd your infect-tribes
Are but the beings of a fummer's day,
Have held the fcale of empire, rul'd the ftorm
Of mighty war; then, with unwearied hand,
Difdaining little delicacies, feiz'd
The plough, and greatly independent liv'd.

Ye generous BRITONS, venerate the plough;
And o'er your hills, and long withdrawing vales,
Let Autumn fpread his treafures to the fun,
Luxuriant and unbounded: as the fea,
Far thro' his azure turbulent domain,
Your empire owns, and from a thoufand fhores
Wafts all the pomp of life into your ports;
So with fuperior boon may your rich foil,
Exuberant, Nature's better bleffings pour
O'er every land, the naked nations clothe,
And be th' exhauftlefs granary of a world!

Nor only thro' the lenient air this change,
Delicious, breathes; the penetrative fun,
His force deep-darting to the dark retreat ———
Of vegetation, fets the fteaming *Power*
At large, to wander o'er the vernant earth,
In various hues; but chiefly thee, gay *Green!*
Thou fmiling Nature's univerfal robe!
United light and fhade! where the fight dwells
With growing ftrength, and ever-new delight.

From the moift meadow to the withered hill,
Led by the breeze, the vivid verdure runs,
And fwells, and deepens, to the cherifh'd eye,
The hawthorn whitens; and the juicy groves
Put forth their buds, unfolding by degrees,
Till the whole leafy foreft ftands difplay'd,

In full luxuriance to the fighing gales;
Where the deer ruftle thro' the twining brake,
And the birds fing conceal'd.   At once array'd
In all the colours of the flufhing year,
By Nature's fwift and fecret-working hand,
The garden glows, and fills the liberal air
With lavifh fragrance; while the promis'd fruit
Lies yet a little embryo, unperceiv'd,
Within its crimfon folds.   Now from the town
Buried in fmoke, and fleep, and noifome damps,
Oft let me wander o'er the dewy fields,
Where frefhnefs breathes, and dafh the trembling drops
From the bent bufh, as thro' the verdant maze
Of fweet-briar hedges I purfue my walk;
Or tafte the fmell of dairy; or afcend
Some eminence, Augusta, in thy plains,
And fee the country, far diffus'd around,
One boundlefs blufh, one white-empurpled fhower
Of mingled bloffoms; where the raptur'd eye
Hurries from joy to joy, and, hid beneath
The fair profufion, yellow Autumn fpies:
    If, brufh'd from *Ruffian* wilds, a cutting gale
Rife not, and fcatter from his humid wings
The clammy mildew; or, dry-blowing, breathe
Untimely froft; before whofe baleful blaft
The full-blown Spring thro' all her foliage fhrinks,
Joylefs and dead, a wide-dejected wafte.
For oft, engender'd by the hazy north,
Myriads on myriads, infect armies warp
Keen in the poifon'd breeze; and wafteful eat,
Thro' buds and bark, into the blackened core,
Their eager way.   A feeble race! yet oft
The facred fons of vengeance; on whofe courfe
Corrofive famine waits, and kills the year.

To check this plague the fkilful farmer chaff,
And blazing ftraw, before his orchard burns;
Till, all involv'd in fmoke, the latent foe
From every cranny fuffocated falls:
Or fcatters o'er the blooms the pungent duft
Of pepper, fatal to the frofty tribe:
Or, when th' envenom'd leaf begins to curl,
With fprinkled water drowns them in their neft;
Nor, while they pick them up with bufy bill,
The little trooping birds unwifely fcares.

Be patient, fwains; thefe cruel-feeming winds
Blow not in vain. Far hence they keep reprefs'd
Thofe deep'ning clouds on clouds, furcharg'd with rain,
That o'er the vaft *Atlantic* hither borne,
In endlefs train, would quench the fummer-blaze,
And, chearlefs, drown the crude unripened year.

The north-eaft fpends his rage; he now fhut up
Within his iron cave, th' effufive fouth
Warms the wide air, and o'er the void of heaven
Breathes the big clouds with vernal fhowers diftent.
At firft a dufky wreath they feem to rife,
Scarce ftaining ether; but by fwift degrees,
In heaps on heaps, the doubling vapour fails
Along the loaded fky, and mingling deep
Sits on th' horizon round a fettled gloom:
Not fuch as wintry-ftorms on mortals fhed,
Oppreffing life; but lovely, gentle, kind,
And full of every hope and every joy,
The wifh of Nature. Gradual finks the breeze
Into a perfect calm; that not a breath
Is heard to quiver thro' the clofing woods,
Or ruftling turn the many twinkling leaves
Of afpin tall. Th' uncurling floods, diffus'd
In glaffy breadth, feem thro' delufive lapfe

Forgetful of their courſe. 'Tis ſilence all,
And pleaſing expeȼtation.   Herds and flocks
Drop the dry ſprig, and mute-imploring eye
The falling verdure.   Huſh'd in ſhort ſuſpenſe,
The plumy people ſtreak their wings with oil,
To throw the lucid moiſture trickling off;
And wait th' approaching ſign to ſtrike, at once,
Into the general choir.   Even mountains, vales,
And foreſts ſeem, impatient, to demand
The promis'd ſweetneſs.   Man ſuperior walks
Amid the glad creation, muſing praiſe,
And looking lively gratitude.   At laſt,
The clouds conſign their treaſures to the fields;
And, ſoftly ſhaking on the dimpled pool
Preluſive drops, let all their moiſture flow,
In large effuſion, o'er the freſhened world.
The ſtealing ſhower is ſcarce to patter heard,
By ſuch as wander thro' the foreſt walks,
Beneath the umbrageous multitude of leaves.
But who can hold the ſhade, while Heaven deſcends
In univerſal bounty, ſhedding herbs,
And fruits, and flowers; on Nature's ample lap?
Swift fancy fir'd anticipates their growth;
And, while the milky nutriment diſtils,
Beholds the kindling country colour round.

   Thus all day long the full-diſtended clouds
Indulge their genial ſtores, and well-ſhower'd earth
Is deep enrich'd with vegetable life;
Till, in the weſtern ſky, the downward ſun
Looks out, effulgent, from amid the fluſh
Of broken clouds, gay-ſhifting to his beam.
The rapid radiance inſtantaneous ſtrikes
Th' illumin'd mountain, thro' the foreſt ſtreams,
Shakes on the floods, and in a yellow miſt,

Far fmoking o'er th' interminable plain,
In twinkling myriads lights the dewy gems.
Moift, bright, and green, the landfkip laughs around.
Full fwell the woods; their very mufic wakes,
Mix'd in wild concert with the warbling brooks
Increas'd, the diftant bleatings of the hills,
And hollow lows refponfive from the vales,
Whence blending all the fweetened zephyr fprings.
Mean time refracted from yon eaftern cloud,
Beftriding earth, the grand ethereal bow
Shoots up immenfe; and every hue unfolds,
In fair proportion running from the red,
To where the violet fades into the fky.
Here, awful NEWTON, the diffolving clouds
Form, fronting on the fun, thy fhowery prifm;
And to the fage-inftructed eye unfold
The various twine of light, by thee difclos'd
From the white mingling maze.   Not fo the boy;
He wondering views the bright enchantment bend,
Delightful, o'er the radiant fields, and runs
To catch the falling glory; but amaz'd
Beholds th' amufive arch before him fly,
Then vanifh quite away.   Still night fucceeds,
A foftened fhade, and faturated earth
Awaits the morning-beam, to give to light,
Rais'd thro' ten thoufand different plaftic tubes,
The balmy treafures of the former day.
   Then fpring the living herbs, profufely wild,
O'er all the deep-green earth, beyond the power
Of botanift to number up their tribes:
Whether he fteals along the lonely dale,
In filent fearch; or thro' the foreft, rank
With what the dull incurious weeds account,
Burfts his blind way; or climbs the mountain-rock,

Fir'd by the nodding verdure of its brow.
With fuch a liberal hand has Nature flung
Their feeds abroad, blown them about in winds,
Innumerous mix'd them with the nurfing mold,
The moiftening current, and prolific rain.

But who their virtues can declare? who pierce,
With vifion pure, into thefe fecret ftores
Of health, and life, and joy? the food of Man,
While yet he liv'd in innocence, and told
A length of golden years; unflefh'd in blood,
A ftranger to the favage arts of life,
Death, rapine, carnage, furfeit, and difeafe;
The lord, and not the tyrant, of the world.

The firft frefh dawn then wak'd the gladdened race
Of uncorrupted Man, nor blufh'd to fee
The fluggard fleep beneath its facred beam:
For their light flumbers gently fum'd away;
And up they rofe as vigorous as the fun,
Or to the culture of the willing glebe,
Or to the chearful tendance of the flock.
Meantime the fong went round; and dance and fport,
Wifdom and friendly talk, fucceffive, ftole
Their hours away: while in the rofy vale
Love breath'd his infant fighs, from anguifh free,
And full replete with blifs; fave the fweet pain,
That inly thrilling, but exalts it more.
Nor yet injurious act, nor furly deed,
Was known among thofe happy fons of HEAVEN;
For reafon and benevolence were law.
Harmonious Nature too look'd fmiling on.
Clear fhone the fkies, cool'd with eternal gales,
And balmy fpirit all.   The youthful fun
Shot his beft rays, and ftill the gracious clouds
Drop'd fatnefs down; as o'er the fwelling mead,

The herds and flocks, commixing, play'd fecure.
This when, emergent from the gloomy wood,
The glaring lion faw, his horrid heart
Was meekened, and he join'd his fullen joy.
For mufic held the whole in perfect peace:
Soft figh'd the flute: the tender voice was heard,
Warbling the varied heart; the woodlands round
Apply'd their quire; and winds and waters flow'd
In confonance. Such were thofe prime of days.
    But now thofe white unblemifh'd manners, whence
The fabling poets took their golden age,
Are found no more amid thefe iron times,
Thefe dregs of life! Now the diftemper'd mind
Has loft that concord of harmonious powers,
Which forms the foul of happinefs; and all
Is off the poife within: the paffions all
Have burft their bounds; and reafon half extinct,
Or impotent, or elfe approving, fees
The foul diforder. Senfelefs, and deform'd,
Convulfive anger ftorms at large; or pale,
And filent, fettles into fell revenge.
Bafe envy withers at another's joy,
And hates that excellence it cannot reach.
Defponding fear, of feeble fancies full,
Weak and unmanly, loofens every power.
Even love itfelf is bitternefs of foul,
A penfive anguifh pining at the heart;
Or, funk to fordid intereft, feels no more
That noble wifh, that never cloy'd defire,
Which, felfifh joy difdaining, feeks alone
To blefs the dearer object of its flame.
Hope fickens with extravagance; and grief,
Of life impatient, into madnefs fwells;
Or in dead filence waftes the weeping hours.

Thefe, and a thoufand mixt emotions more,
From ever-changing views of good and ill,
Form'd infinitely various, vex the mind
With endlefs ftorm: whence, deeply rankling, grows
The partial thought, a liftlefs unconcern,
Cold, and averting from our neighbour's good;
Then dark difguft, and hatred, winding wiles,
Coward deceit, and ruffian violence:
At laft, extinct each focial feeling, fell
And joylefs inhumanity pervades
And petrifies the heart. Nature difturb'd
Is deem'd, vindictive, to have chang'd her courfe.

Hence, in old dufky time, a deluge came:
When the deep-cleft difparting orb, that arch'd
The central waters round, impetuous rufh'd,
With univerfal burft, into the gulph,
And o'er the high-pil'd hills of fractur'd earth
Wide dafh'd the waves, in undulation vaft;
Till, from the center to the ftreaming clouds,
A fhorelefs ocean tumbled round the globe.

The Seafons fince have, with feverer fway,
Opprefs'd a broken world: the Winter keen
Shook forth his wafte of fnows; and Summer fhot
His peftilential heats. Great Spring, before,
Green'd all the year; and fruits and bloffoms blufh'd,
In focial fweetnefs, on the felf-fame bough.
Pure was the temperate air; an even calm
Perpetual reign'd, fave what the zephyrs bland
Breath'd o'er the blue expanfe: for then nor ftorms
Were taught to blow, nor hurricanes to rage;
Sound flept the waters; no fulphureous glooms
Swell'd in the fky, and fent the lightning forth;
While fickly damps, and cold autumnal fogs,
Hung not, relaxing, on the fprings of life.

But now, of turbid elements the fport,
From clear to cloudy toft, from hot to cold,
And dry to moift, with inward-eating change,
Our drooping days are dwindled down to nought,
Their period finifh'd ere 'tis well begun.

  And yet the wholefome herb neglected dies;
Though with the pure exhilarating foul
Of nutriment and health, and vital powers,
Beyond the fearch of art, 'tis copious bleft.
For, with hot ravine fir'd, enfanguin'd Man
Is now become the lion of the plain,
And worfe. The wolf, who from the nightly fold
Fierce drags the bleating prey, ne'er drunk her milk,
Nor wore her warming fleece: nor has the fteer,
At whofe ftrong cheft the deadly tyger hangs,
E'er plow'd for him. They too are temper'd high,
With hunger ftung and wild neceffity,
Nor lodges pity in their fhaggy breaft.
But *Man*, whom Nature form'd of milder clay,
With every kind emotion in his heart,
And taught alone to weep; while from her lap
She pours ten thoufand delicacies, herbs,
And fruits, as numerous as the drops of rain
Or beams that gave them birth: fhall he, fair form!
Who wears fweet fmiles, and looks erect on Heaven,
E'er ftoop to mingle with the prowling herd,
And dip his tongue in gore? The beaft of prey,
Blood-ftain'd, deferves to bleed: but you, ye flocks,
What have ye done; ye peaceful people, what,
To merit death? you, who have given us milk
In lufcious ftreams, and lent us your own coat
Againft the winter's cold? And the plain ox,
That harmlefs, honeft, guilelefs animal,
In what has he offended? he, whofe toil,

Patient and ever ready, clothes the land
With all the pomp of harveſt; ſhall he bleed,
And ſtruggling groan beneath the cruel hands
Even of the clown he feeds? and that, perhaps,
To ſwell the riot of th' autumnal feaſt,
Won by his labour? Thus the feeling heart
Would tenderly ſuggeſt: but 'tis enough,
In this late age, adventurous, to have touch'd
Light on the numbers of the *Samian* ſage.
High HEAVEN forbids the bold preſumptuous ſtrain,
Whoſe wiſeſt will has fix'd us in a ſtate
That muſt not yet to pure perfection riſe.

   Now when the firſt foul torrent of the brooks,
Swell'd with the vernal rains, is ebb'd away,
And, whitening, down their moſſy-tinctur'd ſtream
Deſcends the billowy foam: now is the time,
While yet the dark-brown water aids the guile,
To tempt the trout. The well-diſſembled fly,
The rod fine-tapering with elaſtic ſpring,
Snatch'd from the hoary ſteed the floating line,
And all thy ſlender watery ſtores prepare.
But let not on thy hook the tortur'd worm,
Convulſive, twiſt in agonizing folds;
Which, by rapacious hunger ſwallowed deep,
Gives, as you tear it from the bleeding breaſt
Of the weak helpleſs uncomplaining wretch,
Harſh pain and horror to the tender hand.

   When with his lively ray the potent ſun
Has pierc'd the ſtreams, and rous'd the finny race,
Then, iſſuing chearful, to thy ſport repair;
Chief ſhould the weſtern breezes curling play,
And light o'er ether bear the ſhadowy clouds.
High to their fount, this day, amid the hills,
And woodlands warbling round, trace up the brooks;

The next purſue their rocky-channel'd maze,
Down to the river, in whoſe ample wave
Their little naiads love to ſport at large.
Juſt in the dubious point, where with the pool
Is mix'd the trembling ſtream, or where it boils
Around the ſtone, or from the hollow'd bank
Reverted plays in undulating flow,
There throw, nice-judging, the deluſive fly;
And as you lead it round in artful curve,
With eye attentive mark the ſpringing game.
Strait as above the ſurface of the flood
They wanton riſe, or urg'd by hunger leap,
Then fix, with gentle twitch, the barbed hook:
Some lightly toſſing to the graſſy bank,
And to the ſhelving ſhore ſlow-dragging ſome,
With various hand proportion'd to their force.
If yet too young, and eaſily deceiv'd,
A worthleſs prey ſcarce bends your pliant rod,
Him, piteous of his youth and the ſhort ſpace
He has enjoy'd the vital light of Heaven,
Soft diſengage, and back into the ſtream
The ſpeckled captive throw. But ſhould you lure
From his dark haunt, beneath the tangled roots
Of pendant trees, the monarch of the brook,
Behoves you then to ply your fineſt art.
Long time he, following cautious, ſcans the fly;
And oft attempts to ſeize it, but as oft
The dimpled water ſpeaks his jealous fear.
At laſt, while haply o'er the ſhaded ſun
Paſſes a cloud, he deſperate takes the death,
With ſullen plunge. At once he darts along,
Deep-ſtruck, and runs out all the lengthened line;
Then ſeeks the fartheſt ooze, the ſheltering weed,
The cavern'd bank, his old ſecure abode;

And flies aloft, and flounces round the pool,
Indignant of the guile.   With yielding hand,
That feels him ftill, yet to his furious courfe
Gives way, you, now retiring, following now
Acrofs the ftream, exhauft his idle rage:
Till floating broad upon his breathlefs fide,
And to his fate abandon'd, to the fhore
You gaily drag your unrefifting prize.
    Thus pafs the temperate hours; but when the fun
Shakes from his noon-day throne the fcattering clouds,
Even fhooting liftlefs languor thro' the deeps;
Then feek the bank where flowering elders crowd,
Where fcatter'd wild the lily of the vale
Its balmy effence breathes, where cowflips hang
The dewy head, where purple violets lurk,
With all the lowly children of the fhade:
Or lie reclin'd beneath yon fpreading afh,
Hung o'er the fteep; whence, borne on liquid wing,
The founding culver fhoots; or where the hawk,
High, in the beetling cliff, his airy builds.
There let the claffic page thy fancy lead
Thro' rural fcenes; fuch as the *Mantuan* fwain
Paints in the matchlefs harmony of fong.
Or catch thyfelf the landfkip, gliding fwift
Athwart imagination's vivid eye:
Or by the vocal woods and waters lull'd,
And loft in lonely mufing, in the dream,
Confus'd, of carelefs folitude, where mix
Ten thoufand wandering images of things,
Soothe every guft of paffion into peace;
All but the fwellings of the foften'd heart,
That waken, not difturb, the tranquil mind.
    Behold yon breathing profpect bids the Mufe
Throw all her beauty forth.   But who can paint

Like Nature? Can imagination boaſt,
Amid .its gay creation, hues like hers?
Or can it mix them with that matchleſs ſkill,
And loſe them in each other, as appears
In every bud that blows? If fancy then
Unequal fails beneath the pleaſing taſk,
Ah what ſhall language do? ah where find words
Ting'd with ſo many colours; and whoſe power,
To life approaching, may perfume my lays
With that fine oil, thoſe aromatic gales,
That inexhauſtive flow continual round?
   Yet, tho' ſucceſsleſs, will the toil delight.
Come then, ye virgins and ye youths, whoſe hearts
Have felt the raptures of refining love;
And thou, AMANDA, come, pride of my ſong!
Form'd by the Graces, lovelineſs itſelf!
Come with thoſe downcaſt eyes, ſedate and ſweet,
Thoſe looks demure, that deeply pierce the ſoul,
Where, with the light of thoughtful reaſon mix'd,
Shines lively fancy and the feeling heart:
O come! and while the roſy-footed May
Steals bluſhing on, together let us tread
The morning dews, and gather in their prime
Freſh-blooming flowers, to grace thy braided hair,
And thy lov'd boſom that improves their ſweets.
   See, where the winding vale its laviſh ſtores,
Irriguous, ſpreads. See, how the lily drinks
The latent rill, ſcarce oozing thro' the graſs,
Of growth luxuriant; or the humid bank,
In fair profuſion, decks. Long let us walk,
Where the breeze blows from yon extended field
Of bloſſom'd beans. *Arabia* cannot boaſt
A fuller gale of joy, than, liberal, thence
Breathes thro' the ſenſe, and takes the raviſh'd ſoul.
   VOL. I.   C

Nor is the mead unworthy of thy foot,
Full of freſh verdure, and unnumber'd flowers,
The negligence of *Nature*, wide, and wild;
Where, undiſguis'd by mimic *Art*, ſhe ſpreads
Unbounded beauty to the roving eye.
Here their delicious taſk the fervent bees,
In ſwarming millions, tend: around, athwart,
Thro' the ſoft air, the buſy nations fly,
Cling to the bud, and, with inſerted tube,
Suck its pure eſſence, its ethereal ſoul;
And oft, with bolder wing, they ſoaring dare
The purple heath, or where the wild thyme grows,
And yellow load them with the luſcious ſpoil.
  At length the finiſh'd garden to the view
Its viſtas opens, and its alleys green.
Snatch'd thro' the verdant maze, the hurried eye
Diſtracted wanders; now the bowery walk
Of covert cloſe, where ſcarce a ſpeck of day
Falls on the lengthen'd gloom, protracted ſweeps:
Now meets the bending ſky; the river now
Dimpling along, the breezy ruffled lake,
The foreſt darkening round, the glittering ſpire,
Th' ethereal mountain, and the diſtant main.
But why ſo far excurſive? when at hand,
Along theſe bluſhing borders, bright with dew,
And in yon mingled wilderneſs of flowers,
Fair-handed Spring unboſoms every grace;
Throws out the ſnow-drop, and the crocus firſt;
The daiſy, primroſe, violet darkly blue,
And polyanthus of unnumber'd dyes;
The yellow wall-flower, ſtain'd with iron brown;
And laviſh ſtock that ſcents the garden round:
From the ſoft wing of vernal breezes ſhed,
Anemonies; auriculas, enrich'd

With ſhining meal o'er all their velvet leaves;
And full ranunculas, of glowing red.
Then comes the tulip-race, where Beauty plays
Her idle freaks; from family diffus'd
To family, as flies the father-duſt,
The varied colours run; and, while they *break*
On the charm'd eye, th' exulting floriſt marks,
With ſecret pride, the wonders of his hand.
No gradual bloom is wanting; from the bud,
Firſt-born of Spring, to Summer's muſky tribes:
Nor hyacinths, of pureſt virgin white,
Low-bent, and bluſhing inward; nor jonquils,
Of potent fragrance ; nor Narciſſus fair,
As o'er the fabled fountain hanging ſtill;
Nor broad carnations, nor gay-ſpotted pinks;
Nor, ſhower'd from every buſh, the damaſk-roſe.
Infinite numbers, delicacies, ſmells,
With hues on hues expreſſion cannot paint,
The breath of Nature, and her endleſs bloom.

 Hail, SOURCE OF BEING! UNIVERSAL SOUL
Of Heaven and earth! ESSENTIAL PRESENCE, hail!
To THEE I bend the knee; to THEE my thoughts,
Continual, climb; who, with a maſter-hand,
Haſt the great whole into perfection touch'd.
By THEE the various vegetative tribes,
Wrapt in a filmy net, and clad with leaves,
Draw the live ether, and imbibe the dew:
By THEE diſpos'd into congenial ſoils,
Stands each attractive plant, and ſucks, and ſwells
The juicy tide; a twining maſs of tubes.
At THY command the vernal ſun awakes
The torpid ſap, detruded to the root
By wintry winds; that now in fluent dance,

C 2

And lively fermentation, mounting, ſpreads
All this innumerous-coloured ſcene of things.
　　As riſing from the vegetable world
My theme aſcends, with equal wing aſcend,
My panting Muſe; and hark, how loud the woods
Invite you forth in all your gayeſt trim.
Lend me your ſong, ye nightingales! oh pour
The mazy-running ſoul of melody
Into my varied verſe! while I deduce,
From the firſt note the hollow cuckoo ſings,
The ſymphony of Spring, and touch a theme
Unknown to fame, *the Paſſion of the groves.*
　　When firſt the ſoul of love is ſent abroad,
Warm thro' the vital air, and on the heart
Harmonious ſeizes, the gay troops begin,
In gallant thought, to plume the painted wing;
And try again the long-forgotten ſtrain,
At firſt faint-warbled.　But no ſooner grows
The ſoft infuſion prevalent, and wide,
Than, all alive, at once their joy o'erflows
In muſic unconfin'd.　Up-ſprings the lark,
Shrill-voic'd, and loud, the meſſenger of morn;
Ere yet the ſhadows fly, he mounted ſings
Amid the dawning clouds, and from their haunts
Calls up the tuneful nations.　Every copſe
Deep-tangled, tree irregular, and buſh
Bending with dewy moiſture, o'er the heads
Of the coy quiriſters that lodge within,
Are prodigal of harmony.　The thruſh
And wood-lark, o'er the kind-contending throng
Superior heard, run thro' the ſweeteſt length
Of notes; when liſtening *Philomela* deigns
To let them joy, and purpoſes, in thought

Elate, to make her night excel their day.
The black-bird whiſtles from the thorny brake;
The mellow bullfinch anſwers from the grove:
Nor are the linnets, o'er the flowering furze
Pour'd out profuſely, ſilent. Join'd to theſe
Innumerous ſongſters, in the freſhening ſhade
Of new-ſprung leaves, their modulations mix
Mellifluous. The jay, the rook, the daw,
And each harſh pipe, diſcordant heard alone,
Aid the full concert : while the ſtock-dove breathes
A melancholy murmur thro' the whole.
　'Tis love creates their melody, and all
This waſte of muſic is the voice of love;
That even to birds, and beaſts, the tender arts
Of pleaſing teaches. Hence the gloſſy kind
Try every winning way inventive love
Can dictate, and in courtſhip to their mates
Pour forth their little ſouls. Firſt, wide around,
With diſtant awe, in airy rings they rove,
Endeavouring by a thouſand tricks to catch
The cunning, conſcious, half-averted glance
Of their regardleſs charmer. Should ſhe ſeem
Softening the leaſt approvance to beſtow,
Their colours burniſh, and by hope inſpir'd,
They briſk advance; then, on a ſudden ſtruck,
Retire diſorder'd; then again approach;
In fond rotation ſpread the ſpotted wing,
And ſhiver every feather with deſire.
　Connubial leagues agreed, to the deep woods
They haſte away, all as their fancy leads,
Pleaſure, or food, or ſecret ſafety prompts;
That NATURE's *great command* may be obey'd:
Nor all the ſweet ſenſations they perceive
Indulg'd in vain. Some to the holly-hedge

Neſtling repair, and to the thicket ſome;
Some to the rude protection of the thorn
Commit their feeble offspring : the cleft tree
Offers its kind concealment to a few,
Their food its inſects, and its moſs their neſts.
Others apart far in the graſſy dale,
Or roughening waſte, their humble texture weave.
But moſt in woodland ſolitudes delight,
In unfrequented glooms, or ſhaggy banks,
Steep, and divided by a babbling brook,
Whoſe murmurs ſoothe them all the live-long day,
When by kind duty fix'd.   Among the roots
Of hazel, pendant o'er the plaintive ſtream,
They frame the firſt foundation of their domes;
Dry ſprigs of trees, in artful fabric laid,
And bound with clay together.   Now 'tis nought
But reſtleſs hurry thro' the buſy air,
Beat by unnumber'd wings.   The ſwallow ſweeps
The ſlimy pool, to build his hanging houſe
Intent.   And often, from the careleſs back
Of herds and flocks a thouſand tugging bills
Pluck hair and wool; and oft, when unobſerv'd,
Steal from the barn a ſtraw : till ſoft and warm,
Clean, and complete, their habitation grows.
    As thus the patient dam aſſiduous ſits,
Not to be tempted from her tender taſk,
Or by ſharp hunger, or by ſmooth delight,
Tho' the whole looſened Spring around her blows,
Her ſympathizing lover takes his ſtand
High on th' opponent bank, and ceaſeleſs ſings
The tedious time away; or elſe ſupplies
Her place a moment, while ſhe ſudden flits
To pick the ſcanty meal.   Th' appointed time
With pious toil fulfill'd, the callow young,

SPRING.

Warm'd and expanded into perfect life,
Their brittle bondage break, and come to light,
A helpless family, demanding food
With constant clamour: O what passions then,
What melting sentiments of kindly care,
On the new parents seize! Away they fly
Affectionate, and undesiring bear
The most delicious morsel to their young;
Which equally distributed, again
The search begins. Even so a gentle pair,
By fortune sunk, but form'd of generous mold,
And charm'd with cares beyond the vulgar breast,
In some lone cott amid the distant woods,
Sustain'd alone by providential HEAVEN,
Oft, as they weeping eye their infant train,
Check their own appetites, and give them all.

Nor toil alone they scorn: exalting love,
By the great FATHER OF THE SPRING inspir'd,
Gives instant courage to the *fearful* race,
And to the *simple* art. With stealthy wing,
Should some rude foot their woody haunts molest,
Amid a neighbouring bush they silent drop,
And whirring thence, as if alarm'd, deceive
Th' unfeeling school-boy. Hence, around the head
Of wandering swain, the white-wing'd plover wheels
Her sounding flight, and then directly on
In long excursion skims the level lawn,
To tempt him from her nest. The wild-duck, hence,
O'er the rough moss, and o'er the trackless waste
The heath-hen flutters, pious fraud! to lead
The hot pursuing spaniel far astray.

Be not the Muse asham'd, here to bemoan
Her brothers of the grove, by tyrant Man
Inhuman caught, and in the narrow cage

From liberty confin'd, and boundlefs air.
Dull are the pretty flaves, their plumage dull,
Ragged, and all its brightening luftre loft;
Nor is that fprightly wildnefs in their notes,
Which, clear and vigorous, warbles from the beech.
O then, ye friends of love and love-taught fong,
Spare the foft tribes, this barbarous art forbear;
If on your bofom innocence can win,
Mufic engage, or piety perfuade.
    But let not chief the nightingale lament
Her ruin'd care, too delicately fram'd
To brook the harfh confinement of the cage.
Oft when, returning with her loaded bill,
Th' aftonifh'd mother finds a vacant neft,
By the hard hand of unrelenting clowns
Robb'd, to the ground the vain provifion falls;
Her pinions ruffle, and low-drooping fcarce
Can bear the mourner to the poplar fhade;
Where, all abandon'd to defpair, fhe fings
Her forrows thro' the night; and, on the bough,
Sole-fitting, ftill at every dying fall
Takes up again her lamentable ftrain
Of winding woe; till, wide around, the woods
Sigh to her fong, and with her wail refound.
    But now the feather'd youth their former bounds,
Ardent, difdain; and, weighing oft their wings,
Demand the free poffeffion of the fky:
This one glad office more, and then diffolves
Parental love at once, now needlefs grown.
Unlavifh *Wifdom* never works in vain.
'Tis on fome evening, funny, grateful, mild,
When nought but balm is breathing thro' the woods,
With yellow luftre bright, that the new tribes
Vifit the fpacious heavens, and look abroad

On Nature's common, far as they can fee,
Or wing, their range and pafture.   O'er the boughs
Dancing about, ftill at the giddy verge
Their refolution fails ; their pinions ftill,
In loofe libration ftretch'd, to truft the void
Trembling refufe: till down before them fly
The parent-guides, and chide, exhort, command,
Or pufh them off.   The furging air receives
Its plumy burden; and their felf-taught wings
Winnow the waving element.   On ground
Alighted, bolder up again they lead,
Farther and farther on, the lengthening flight;
Till vanifh'd every fear, and every power
Rous'd into life and action, light in air
Th' acquitted parents fee their foaring race,
And once rejoicing never know them more.

　　High from the fummit of a craggy cliff,
Hung o'er the deep, fuch as amazing frowns
On utmoft * *Kilda*'s fhore, whofe lonely race
Refign the fetting fun to *Indian* worlds,
The royal eagle draws his vigorous young,
Strong-pounc'd, and ardent with paternal fire.
Now fit to raife a kingdom of their own,
He drives them from his fort, the towering feat,
For ages, of his empire; which, in peace,
Unftain'd he holds, while many a league to fea
He wings his courfe, and preys in diftant ifles.

　　Should I my fteps turn to the rural feat,
Whofe lofty elms, and venerable oaks,
Invite the rook, who high amid the boughs,
In early Spring, his airy city builds,
And ceafelefs caws amufive; there, well-pleas'd,

* The fartheft of the weftern iflands of Scotland.

I might the various polity furvey
Of the mixt houfhold kind.   The careful hen
Calls all her chirping family around,
Fed and defended by the fearlefs cock;
Whofe breaft with ardour flames, as on he walks,
Graceful, and crows defiance.   In the pond,
The finely-checker'd duck, before her train,
Rows garrulous.   The ftately-failing fwan
Gives out his fnowy plumage to the gale;
And, arching proud his neck, with oary feet
Bears forward fierce, and guards his ofier-ifle,
Protective of his young.   The turkey nigh,
Loud-threatening, reddens; while the peacock fpreads
His every-colour'd glory to the fun,
And fwims in radiant majefty along.
O'er the whole homely fcene, the cooing dove
Flies thick in amorous chace, and wanton rolls
The glancing eye, and turns the changeful neck.
    While thus the gentle tenants of the fhade
Indulge their purer loves, the rougher world
Of brutes, below, rufh furious into flame,
And fierce defire.   Thro' all his lufty veins
The bull, deep-fcorch'd, the raging paffion feels.
Of pafture fick, and negligent of food,
Scarce feen, he wades among the yellow broom,
While o'er his ample fides the rambling fprays
Luxuriant fhoot; or thro' the mazy wood
Dejected wanders, nor th' inticing bud
Crops, tho' it preffes on his carelefs fenfe.
And oft, in jealous madning fancy wrapt,
He feeks the fight; and, idly-butting, feigns
His rival gor'd in every knotty trunk.
Him fhould he meet, the bellowing war begins:
Their eyes flafh fury; to the hollow'd earth,

Whence the fand flies, they mutter bloody deeds,
And groaning deep, th' impetuous battle mix:
While the fair heifer, balmy-breathing, near,
Stands kindling up their rage. The trembling fteed,
With this hot impulfe feiz'd in every nerve,
Nor heeds the rein, nor hears the founding thong;
Blows are not felt; but toffing high his head,
And by the well-known joy to diftant plains
Attracted ftrong, all wild he burfts away;
O'er rocks, and woods, and craggy mountains flies;
And, neighing, on the aërial fummit takes
Th' exciting gale; then, fteep-defcending, cleaves
The headlong torrents foaming down the hills,
Even where the madnefs of the ftraiten'd ftream
Turns in black eddies round: fuch is the force
With which his frantic heart and finews fwell.

Nor undelighted by the boundlefs Spring
Are the broad monfters of the foaming deep:
From the deep ooze and gelid cavern rous'd,
They flounce and tumble in unwieldy joy.
Dire were the ftrain, and diffonant, to fing
The cruel raptures of the favage kind:
How by this flame their native wrath fublim'd,
They roam, amid the fury of their heart,
The far-refounding wafte in fiercer bands,
And growl their horrid loves. But this the theme
I fing, enraptur'd, to the BRITISH FAIR,
Forbids, and leads me to the mountain-brow,
Where fits the fhepherd on the graffy turf,
Inhaling, healthful, the defcending fun.
Around him feeds his many-bleating flock,
Of various cadence; and his fportive lambs,
This way and that convolv'd, in frifkful glee,
Their frolicks play. And now the fprightly race

Invites them forth; when fwift, the fignal given,
They ftart away, and fweep the maffy mound
That runs around the hill; the rampart once
Of iron war, in ancient barbarous times,
When difunited BRITAIN ever bled,
Loft in eternal broil: ere yet fhe grew
To this deep-laid indiffoluble ftate,
Where *Wealth* and *Commerce* lift their golden heads;
And o'er our labours, *Liberty* and *Law*,
Impartial, watch; the wonder of a world!
     What is this *mighty Breath*, ye fages, fay,
That, in a powerful language, felt not heard,
Inftructs the fowls of heaven; and thro' their breaft
Thefe arts of love diffufes? What, but GOD?
Infpiring GOD! who boundlefs Spirit all,
And unremitting Energy, pervades,
Adjufts, fuftains, and agitates the whole.
He ceafelefs works *alone*; and yet *alone*
Seems not to work: with fuch perfection fram'd
Is this complex ftupendous fcheme of things.
But, tho' conceal'd, to every purer eye
Th' informing Author in his works appears:
Chief, lovely Spring, in thee, and thy foft fcenes,
The SMILING GOD is feen; while water, earth,
And air atteft his bounty; which exalts
The brute creation to this finer thought,
And annual melts their undefigning hearts
Profufely thus in tendernefs and joy.
     Still let my fong a nobler note affume,
And fing th' infufive force of Spring on Man;
When heaven and earth, as if contending, vye
To raife his being, and ferene his foul.
Can he forbear to join the general fmile
Of Nature? Can fierce paffions vex his breaft,

While every gale is peace, and every grove
Is melody? Hence! from the bounteous walks
Of flowing Spring, ye fordid fons of earth,
Hard, and unfeeling of another's woe;
Or only lavifh to yourfelves; away!
But come, ye generous minds, in whofe wide thought,
Of all his works, CREATIVE BOUNTY burns
With warmeft beam; and on your open front
And liberal eye, fits, from his dark retreat
Inviting modeft Want. Nor, till invok'd
Can reftlefs goodnefs wait; your active fearch
Leaves no cold wintry corner unexplor'd;
Like filent-working HEAVEN, furprifing oft
The lonely heart with unexpected good.
For you the roving fpirit of the wind
Blows Spring abroad; for you the teeming.clouds
Defcend in gladfome plenty o'er the world;
And the fun fheds his kindeft rays for you,
Ye flower of human race! In thefe green days,
Reviving Sicknefs lifts her languid head;
Life flows afrefh; and young-ey'd Health exalts
The whole creation round. Contentment walks
The funny glade, and feels an inward blifs
Spring o'er his mind, beyond the power of kings
To purchafe. Pure ferenity apace
Induces thought, and contemplation ftill.
By fwift degrees the love of Nature works,
And warms the bofom; till at laft fublim'd
To rapture, and enthufiaftic heat,
We feel the prefent DEITY, and tafte
The joy of GOD to fee a happy world!
    Thefe are the facred feelings of thy heart,
Thy heart inform'd by reafon's purer ray,
O LYTTELTON, the friend! thy paffions thus

And meditations vary, as at large,
Courting the Mufe, thro' *Hagley Park* thou ftrayeft;
Thy *Britifh Tempe!* There along the dale,
With woods o'er-hung, and fhagg'd with moſſy rocks,
Whence on each hand the gufhing waters play,
And down the rough cafcade white-dafhing fall,
Or gleam in lengthened vifta thro' the trees,
You filent fteal; or fit beneath the fhade
Of folemn oaks, that tuft the fwelling mounts
Thrown graceful round by Nature's carelefs hand,
And penfive liften to the various voice
Of rural peace: the herds, the flocks, the birds,
The hollow-whifpering breeze, the plaint of rills,
That, purling down amid the twifted roots
Which creep around, their dewy murmurs fhake
On the footh'd ear. From thefe abftracted oft,
You wander thro' the philofophic world;
Where in bright train continual wonders rife,
Or to the curious or the pious eye.
And oft, conducted by hiftoric truth,
You tread the long extent of backward time:
Planning, with warm benevolence of mind,
And honeft zeal unwarp'd by party-rage,
BRITANNIA's weal; how from the venal gulph
To raife her virtue, and her arts revive.
Or, turning thence thy view, thefe graver thoughts
The Mufes charm: while, with fure tafte refin'd,
You draw th' infpiring breath of ancient fong;
Till nobly rifes, emulous, thy own.
Perhaps thy lov'd LUCINDA fhares thy walk,
With foul to thine attun'd. Then Nature all
Wears to the lover's eye a look of love;
And all the tumult of a guilty world,
Toft by ungenerous paffions, finks away.

The tender heart is animated peace;
And as it pours its copious treafures forth,
In varied converfe, foftening every theme,
You, frequent-paufing, turn, and from her eyes,
Where meekened fenfe, and amiable grace,
And lively fweetnefs dwell, enraptur'd, drink
That namelefs fpirit of ethereal joy,
Unutterable happinefs! which love,
Alone, beftows, and on a *favour'd few*.
Meantime you gain the height, from whofe fair brow
The burfting profpect fpreads immenfe around:
And fnatch'd o'er hill and dale, and wood and lawn,
And verdant field, and darkening heath between,
And villages embofom'd foft in trees,
And fpiry towns by furging columns mark'd
Of houfhold fmoak, your eye excurfive roams:
Wide-ftretching from the *Hall*, in whofe kind haunt
The *Hofpitable Genius* lingers ftill,
To where the broken landfkip, by degrees,
Afcending, roughens into rigid hills;
O'er which the *Cambrian* mountains, like far clouds
That fkirt the blue horizon, dufky rife.
    Flufh'd by the fpirit of the genial year,
Now from the virgin's cheek a frefher bloom
Shoots, lefs and lefs, the live carnation round;
Her lips blufh deeper fweets; fhe breathes of youth;
The fhining moifture fwells into her eyes,
In brighter flow; her wifhing bofom heaves,
With palpitations wild; kind tumults feize
Her veins, and all her yielding foul is love.
From the keen gaze her lover turns away,
Full of the dear exftatic power, and fick
With fighing languifhment. Ah then, ye fair!
Be greatly cautious of your fliding hearts:

Dare not th' infectious figh; the pleading look,
Downcaft, and low, in meek fubmiffion dreft,
But full of guile.   Let not the fervent tongue,
Prompt to deceive, with adulation fmooth,
Gain on your purpos'd will.   Nor in the bower,
Where woodbinds flaunt, and rofes fhed a couch,
While Evening draws her crimfon curtains round,
Truft your foft minutes with betraying Man.

    And let th' afpiring youth beware of love,
Of the fmooth glance beware; for 'tis too late,
When on his heart the torrent-foftnefs pours.
Then wifdom proftrate lies, and fading fame
Diffolves in air away; while the fond foul,
Wrapt in gay vifions of unreal blifs,
Still paints th' illufive form; the kindling grace;
Th' inticing fmile; the modeft-feeming eye,
Beneath whofe beauteous beams, belying heaven,
Lurk fearchlefs cunning, cruelty, and death:
And ftill falfe-warbling in his cheated ear,
Her fyren voice, enchanting, draws him on
To guileful fhores, and meads of fatal joy.

    Even prefent, in the very lap of love
Inglorious laid; while mufic flows around,
Perfumes, and oils, and wine, and wanton hours;
Amid the rofes fierce Repentance rears
Her fnaky creft: a quick-returning pang
Shoots thro' the confcious heart; where honour ftill,
And great defign, againft the oppreffive load
Of luxury, by fits, impatient heave.

    But abfent, what fantaftic woes arous'd,
Rage in each thought, by reftlefs mufing fed,
Chill the warm cheek, and blaft the bloom of life?
Neglected fortune flies; and fliding fwift,
Prone into ruin, fall his fcorn'd affairs.

'Tis nought but gloom around: the darkened fun
Lofes his light. The rofy-bofom'd Spring
To weeping Fancy pines; and yon bright arch,
Contracted, bends into a dufky vault.
All Nature fades extinct; and fhe alone
Heard, felt, and feen, poffeffes every thought,
Fills every fenfe, and pants in every vein.
Books are but formal dulnefs, tedious friends:
And fad amid the focial band he fits,
Lonely, and unattentive. From his tongue
Th' unfinifh'd period falls: while, borne away
On fwelling thought, his wafted fpirit flies
To the vain bofom of his diftant fair;
And leaves the femblance of a lover, fix'd
In melancholy fite, with head declin'd,
And love-dejected eyes. Sudden he ftarts,
Shook from his tender trance, and reftlefs runs
To glimmering fhades, and fympathetic glooms;
Where the dun umbrage o'er the falling ftream,
Romantic, hangs; there thro' the penfive dufk
Strays, in heart-thrilling meditation loft,
Indulging all to love: or on the bank
Thrown, amid drooping lilies, fwells the breeze
With fighs unceafing, and the brook with tears.
Thus in foft anguifh he confumes the day,
Nor quits his deep retirement, till the Moon
Peeps thro' the chambers of the fleecy eaft,
Enlightened by degrees, and in her train
Leads on the gentle hours; then forth he walks,
Beneath the trembling languifh of her beam,
With foftened foul, and wooes the bird of eve
To mingle woes with his: or while the world
And all the fons of Care lie hufh'd in fleep,

Affociates with the midnight fhadows drear;
And, fighing to the lonely taper, pours
His idly-tortur'd heart into the page,
Meant for the moving meffenger of love;
Where rapture burns on rapture, every line
With rifing frenzy fir'd. But if on bed
Delirious flung, fleep from his pillow flies.
All night he toffes, nor the balmy power
In any pofture finds; till the grey morn
Lifts her pale luftre on the paler wretch,
Exanimate by love: and then perhaps
Exhaufted Nature finks a while to reft,
Still interrupted by diftracted dreams,
That o'er the fick imagination rife,
And in black colours paint the mimic fcene.
Oft with th' enchantrefs of his foul he talks;
Sometimes in crowds diftrefs'd; or if retir'd
To fecret winding flower-enwoven bowers,
Far from the dull impertinence of Man,
Juft as he, credulous, his endlefs cares
Begins to lofe in blind oblivious love,
Snatch'd from her yielded hand, he knows not how,
Thro' forefts huge, and long untravel'd heaths
With defolation brown, he wanders wafte,
In night and tempeft wrapt: or fhrinks aghaft,
Back, from the bending precipice; or wades
The turbid ftream below, and ftrives to reach
The farther fhore; where fuccourlefs, and fad,
She with extended arms his aid implores;
But ftrives in vain: borne by th' outrageous flood
To diftance down, he rides the ridgy wave,
Or whelm'd beneath the boiling eddy finks.

Thefe are the charming agonies of love,
Whofe mifery delights.   But thro' the heart
Should jealoufy its venom once diffufe,
'Tis then delightful mifery no more,
But agony unmix'd, inceffant gall,
Corroding every thought, and blafting all
Love's paradife.   Ye fairy profpects, then,
Ye beds of rofes, and ye bowers of joy,
Farewel! Ye gleamings of departed peace,
Shine out your laft! the yellow-tinging plague
Internal vifion taints, and in a night
Of livid gloom imagination wraps.
Ah then! inftead of love-enlivened cheeks,
Of funny features, and of ardent eyes
With flowing rapture bright, dark looks fucceed,
Suffus'd and glaring with untender fire;
A clouded afpect, and a burning cheek,
Where the whole poifon'd foul, malignant, fits,
And frightens love away.   Ten thoufand fears
Invented wild, ten thoufand frantic views
Of horrid rivals, hanging on the charms
For which he melts in fondnefs, eat him up
With fervent anguifh, and confuming rage.
In vain reproaches lend their idle aid,
Deceitful pride, and refolution frail,
Giving falfe peace a moment.   Fancy pours,
Afrefh, her beauties on his bufy thought,
Her firft endearments twining round the foul,
With all the witchcraft of enfnaring love.
Straight the fierce ftorm involves his mind anew,
Flames thro' the nerves, and boils along the veins;
While anxious doubt diftracts the tortur'd heart:
For even the fad affurance of his fears

Were eafe to what he feels. Thus the warm youth,
Whom love deludes into his thorny wilds,
Thro' flowery-tempting paths, or leads a life
Of fevered rapture, or of cruel care;
His brighteft flames extinguifh'd all, and all
His lively moments running down to wafte.

But happy they! the happieft of their kind!
Whom gentler ftars unite, and in one fate
Their hearts, their fortunes, and their beings blend.
'Tis not the coarfer tie of human laws,
Unnatural oft, and foreign to the mind,
That binds their peace, but harmony itfelf,
Attuning all their paffions into love;
Where friendfhip full-exerts her fofteft power,
Perfect efteem enlivened by defire
Ineffable, and fympathy of foul;
Thought meeting thought, and will preventing will,
With boundlefs confidence: for nought but love
Can anfwer love, and render blifs fecure.
Let him, ungenerous, who, alone intent
To blefs himfelf, from fordid parents buys
The loathing virgin, in eternal care,
Well-merited, confume his nights and days:
Let barbarous nations, whofe inhuman love
Is wild defire, fierce as the funs they feel;
Let eaftern tyrants, from the light of Heaven
Seclude their bofom-flaves, meanly poffefs'd
Of a mere, lifelefs, violated form:
While thofe whom love cements in holy faith,
And equal tranfport, free as Nature live,
Difdaining fear. What is the world to them,
Its pomp, its pleafure, and its nonfenfe all!
Who in each other clafp whatever fair

High fancy forms, and lavifh hearts can wifh;
Something than beauty dearer, fhould they look
Or on the mind, or mind-illumin'd face;
Truth, goodnefs, honour, harmony, and love,
The richeft bounty of indulgent HEAVEN.
Meantime a fmiling offspring rifes round,
And mingles both their graces. By degrees,
The human bloffom blows; and every day,
Soft as it rolls along, fhews fome new charm,
The father's luftre, and the mother's bloom.
Then infant reafon grows apace, and calls
For the kind hand of an affiduous care.
Delightful tafk! to rear the tender thought,
To teach the young idea how to fhoot,   — — —
To pour the frefh inftruction o'er the mind,
To breathe th' enlivening fpirit, and to fix
The generous purpofe in the glowing breaft.
Oh fpeak the joy! ye, whom the fudden tear
Surprizes often, while you look around,
And nothing ftrikes your eye but fights of blifs,
All various Nature preffing on the heart:
An elegant fufficiency, content,
Retirement, rural quiet, friendfhip, books,
Eafe and alternate labour, ufeful life,
Progreffive virtue, and approving HEAVEN.
Thefe are the matchlefs joys of virtuous love;
And thus their moments fly. The Seafons thus,
As ceafelefs round a jarring world they roll,
Still find them happy; and confenting SPRING
Sheds her own rofy garland on their heads:
Till evening comes at laft, ferene and mild;
When after the long vernal day of life,

Enamour'd more, as more remembrance fwells
With many a proof of recollected love,
Together down they fink in focial fleep;
Together freed, their gentle fpirits fly
To fcenes where love and blifs immortal reign.

SUMMER.

THE ARGUMENT.

The fubject propofed. Invocation. Addrefs to Mr. DODINGTON.
An introductory reflection on the motion of the heavenly bodies;
whence the fucceffion of the feafons. As the face of Nature in this
feafon is almoft uniform, the progrefs of the poem is a defcription
of a fummer's day. The dawn. Sun-rifing. 'Hymn to the fun.
Forenoon. Summer infects defcribed. Hay-making. Sheep-
fhearing. Noon-day. A woodland retreat. Groupe of herds and
flocks. A folemn grove: how it affects a contemplative mind. A
cataract, and rude fcene. View of Summer in the torrid zone.
Storm of thunder and lightning. A tale. The ftorm over, a ferene
afternoon. Bathing. Hour of walking. Tranfition to the profpect
of a rich well-cultivated country; which introduces a panegyric on
GREAT BRITAIN. Sun-fet. Evening. Night. Summer meteors.
A comet. The whole concluding with the praife of philofophy.

Dodd del.

T. Cook sculp.

SUMMER.

Published as the Act directs Jan.ʸ 1.ᵗ 1778, by Tho.ˢ Cadell in the Strand.

S U M M E R.

F ROM brightening fields of ether fair difclos'd,
Child of the Sun, refulgent SUMMER comes,
In pride of youth, and felt thro' Nature's depth:
He comes attended by the fultry *hours*,
And ever-fanning *breezes*, on his way;
While, from his ardent look, the turning SPRING
Averts her blufhful face; and earth, and fkies,
All-fmiling, to his hot dominion leaves.

Hence, let me hafte into the mid-wood fhade,
Where fcarce a fun-beam wanders thro' the gloom;
And on the dark-green grafs, befide the brink
Of haunted ftream, that by the roots of oak
Rolls o'er the rocky channel, lie at large,
And fing the glories of the circling year.

Come, *Infpiration!* from thy hermit-feat,
By mortal feldom found: may Fancy dare,
From thy fix'd ferious eye, and raptur'd glance
Shot on furrounding Heaven, to fteal one look
Creative of the Poet, every power
Exalting to an ecftafy of foul.

And thou, my youthful Mufe's early friend,
In whom the human graces all unite:
Pure light of mind, and tendernefs of heart;

Genius, and wifdom; the gay focial fenfe,
By decency chaftis'd; goodnefs and wit,
In feldom-meeting harmony combin'd;
Unblemifh'd honour, and an active zeal
For BRITAIN's glory, Liberty, and Man:
O DODINGTON! attend my rural fong,
Stoop to my theme, infpirit every line,
And teach me to deferve thy juft applaufe.

    With what an awful world-revolving power
Were firft the unwieldy planets launch'd along
Th' illimitable void! Thus to remain,
Amid the flux of many thoufand years,
That oft has fwept the toiling race of Men,
And all their labour'd monuments away,
Firm, unremitting, matchlefs, in their courfe;
To the kind-temper'd change of night and day,
And of the feafons ever ftealing round,
Minutely faithful: Such TH' ALL-PERFECT HAND!
That pois'd, impels, and rules the fteady WHOLE.

    When now no more th' alternate *Twins* are fir'd,
And *Cancer* reddens with the folar blaze,
Short is the doubtful empire of the night;
And foon, obfervant of approaching day,
The meek-ey'd Morn appears, mother of dews,
At firft faint-gleaming in the dappled eaft:
Till far o'er ether fpreads the widening glow;
And, from before the luftre of her face,
White break the clouds away. With quickened ftep,
Brown Night retires: young Day pours in apace,
And opens all the lawny profpect wide.
The dripping rock, the mountain's mifty top
Swell on the fight, and brighten with the dawn.
Blue, thro' the dufk, the fmoaking currents fhine;
And from the bladed field the fearful hare

Limps, awkward: while along the foreſt-glade
The wild deer trip, and often turning gaze
At early paſſenger. · Muſic awakes
The native voice of undiſſembled joy;
And thick around the woodland hymns ariſe.
Rous'd by the cock, the ſoon-clad ſhepherd leaves
His moſſy cottage, where with *Peace* he dwells;
And from the crowded fold, in order, drives
His flock, to taſte the verdure of the morn.

 Falſely luxurious, will not Man awake;
And, ſpringing from the bed of ſloth, enjoy
The cool, the fragrant, and the ſilent hour,
To meditation due and ſacred ſong?
For is there aught in ſleep can charm the wiſe?
To lie in dead oblivion, loſing half
The fleeting moments of too ſhort a life;
Total extinction of th' enlightened ſoul!
Or elſe to feveriſh vanity alive,
Wildered, and toſſing thro' diſtemper'd dreams?
Who would in ſuch a gloomy ſtate remain
Longer than Nature craves; when every Muſe
And every blooming pleaſure wait without,
To bleſs the wildly-devious morning-walk?

 But yonder comes the powerful King of Day,
Rejoicing in the eaſt. The leſſening cloud,
The kindling azure, and the mountain's brow
Illum'd with fluid gold, his near approach
Betoken glad. Lo! now, apparent all,
Aſlant the dew-bright earth, and coloured air,
He looks in boundleſs majeſty abroad;
And ſheds the ſhining day, that burniſh'd plays
On rocks, and hills, and towers, and wandering ſtreams,
High-gleaming from afar. Prime chearer Light!
Of all material beings firſt, and beſt!

Efflux divine! Nature's refplendent robe!
Without whofe vefting beauty all were wrapt
In uneffential gloom; and thou, O Sun!
Soul of furrounding worlds! in whom beft feen
Shines out thy Maker! may I fing of thee?

'Tis by thy fecret, ftrong, attractive force,
As with a chain indiffoluble bound,
Thy Syftem rolls entire: from the far bourne
Of utmoft *Saturn*, wheeling wide his round
Of thirty years; to *Mercury*, whofe difk
Can fcarce be caught by philofophic eye,
Loft in the near effulgence of thy blaze.

Informer of the planetary train!
Without whofe quickening glance their cumbrous orbs
Were brute unlovely mafs, inert and dead,
And not, as now, the green abodes of life!
How many forms of being wait on thee!
Inhaling fpirit; from th' unfettered mind,
By thee fublim'd, down to the daily race,
The mixing myriads of thy fetting beam.

The vegetable world is alfo thine,
Parent of *Seafons!* who the pomp precede
That waits thy throne, as thro' thy vaft domain,
Annual, along the bright ecliptic road,
In world-rejoicing ftate, it moves fublime.
Mean-time, th' expecting nations, circled gay
With all the various tribes of foodful earth,
Implore thy bounty, or fend grateful up
A common hymn: while, round thy beaming car,
High-feen, the *Seafons* lead, in fprightly dance
Harmonious knit, the rofy-finger'd *Hours*,
The *Zephyrs* floating loofe, the timely *Rains*,
Of bloom ethereal the light-footed *Dews*,
And foftened into joy the furly *Storms*.

Thefe, in fucceffive turn, with lavifh hand,
| Shower every beauty, every fragrance fhower, |
Herbs, flowers, and fruits; till, kindling at thy touch,
From land to land is flufh'd the vernal year.
  Nor to the furface of enlivened earth,
Graceful with hills and dales, and leafy woods,
Her liberal treffes, is thy force confin'd:
But, to the bowel'd cavern darting deep,
The mineral kinds confefs thy mighty power.
Effulgent, hence the veiny marble fhines;
Hence Labour draws his tools; hence burnifh'd War
Gleams on the day; the nobler works of Peace
Hence blefs mankind, and generous Commerce binds
The round of nations in a golden chain.
  The unfruitful rock itfelf, impregn'd by thee,
In dark retirement forms the lucid ftone.
The lively Diamond drinks thy pureft rays,
Collected light, compact; that, polifh'd bright,
And all its native luftre let abroad,
Dares, as it fparkles on the fair one's breaft,
With vain ambition emulate her eyes.
At thee the Ruby lights its deepening glow,
And with a waving radiance inward flames.
From thee the Sapphire, folid ether, takes
Its hue cerulean; and, of evening tinct,
The purple-ftreaming Amethyft is thine.
With thy own fmile the, yellow Topaz burns.
Nor deeper verdure dyes the robe of Spring,
When firft fhe gives it to the fouthern gale,
Than the green Emerald fhows.   But, all combin'd,
Thick thro' the whitening Opal play thy beams;
Or, flying feveral from its furface, form
A trembling variance of revolving hues,
As the fite varies in the gazer's hand.

The very dead creation, from thy touch,
Aſſumes a mimic life. By thee refin'd,
In brighter mazes the relucent ſtream
Plays o'er the mead. The precipice abrupt,
Projecting horror on the blackened flood,
Softens at thy return. The deſart joys
Wildly, thro' all his melancholy bounds.
Rude ruins glitter; and the briny deep,
Seen from ſome pointed promontory's top,
Far to the blue horizon's utmoſt verge,
Reſtleſs, reflects a floating gleam. But this,
And all the much-tranſported Muſe can ſing,
Are to thy beauty, dignity, and uſe,
Unequal far; great delegated ſource
Of light, and life, and grace, and joy below!

How ſhall I then attempt to ſing of HIM!
Who, LIGHT HIMSELF, in uncreated light
Inveſted deep, dwells awfully retir'd
From mortal eye, or angel's purer ken;
Whoſe ſingle ſmile has, from the firſt of time,
Fill'd, overflowing, all thoſe lamps of Heaven,
That beam for ever thro' the boundleſs ſky:
But, ſhould he hide his face, th' aſtoniſh'd ſun,
And all th' extinguiſh'd ſtars, would looſening reel
Wide from their ſpheres, and Chaos come again.

And yet was every faultering tongue of Man,
ALMIGHTY FATHER! ſilent in thy praiſe,
Thy Works themſelves would raiſe a general voice,
Even in the depth of ſolitary woods
By human foot untrod; proclaim thy power,
And to the quire celeſtial THEE reſound,
Th' eternal cauſe, ſupport, and end of all!

To me be Nature's volume broad-diſplay'd;
And to peruſe its all-inſtructing page,

Or, haply catching infpiration thence,
Some eafy paffage, raptur'd, to tranflate,
My fole delight; as thro' the falling glooms
Penfive I ftray, or with the rifing dawn
On Fancy's eagle-wing excurfive foar.

Now, flaming up the heavens, the potent fun
Melts into limpid air the high-rais'd clouds,
And morning fogs, that hovered round the hills
In party-colour'd bands; till wide unveil'd
The face of Nature fhines, from where earth feems,
Far-ftretch'd around, to meet the bending fphere.

Half in a blufh of cluftering rofes loft,
Dew-dropping *Coolnefs* to the fhade retires;
There, on the verdant turf, or flowery bed,
By gelid founts and carelefs rills to mufe;
While tyrant *Heat*, difpreading thro' the fky,
With rapid fway, his burning influence darts
On Man, and beaft, and herb, and tepid ftream.

Who can unpitying fee the flowery race,
Shed by the morn, their new-flufh'd bloom refign,
Before the parching beam? So fade the fair,
When fevers revel thro' their azure veins.
But one, the lofty follower of the fun,
Sad when he fets, fhuts up her yellow leaves,
Drooping all night; and, when he warm returns,
Points her enamour'd bofom to his ray.

Home, from his morning tafk, the fwain retreats;
His flock before him ftepping to the fold:
While the full-udder'd mother lows around
The chearful cottage, then expecting food,
The food of innocence, and health! The daw,
The rook and magpie, to the grey-grown oaks
That the calm village in their verdant arms,
Sheltering, embrace, direct their lazy flight;

Where on the mingling boughs they fit embower'd,
All the hot noon, till cooler hours arife.
Faint. underneath, the houfhold fowls convene;
And, in a corner of the buzzing fhade,
The houfe-dog, with the vacant greyhound, lies,
Out-ftretch'd, and fleepy. In his flumbers one
Attacks the nightly thief, and one exults
O'er hill and dale; till, wakened by the wafp,
They ftarting fnap. Nor fhall the Mufe difdain
To let the little noify fummer-race
Live in her lay, and flutter thro' her fong:
Not mean tho' fimple; to the fun ally'd,
From him they draw their animating fire.

Wak'd by his warmer ray, the reptile young
Come wing'd abroad; by the light air upborn,
Lighter, and full of foul. From every chink,
And fecret corner, where they flept away
The wintry ftorms; or rifing from their tombs,
To highen life; by myriads, forth at once,
Swarming they pour; of all the vary'd hues
Their beauty-beaming parent can difclofe.
Ten thoufand forms! ten thoufand different tribes!
People the blaze. To funny waters fome
By fatal inftinct fly; where on the pool
They, fporti/e, wheel; or, failing down the ftream,
Are fnatch'd immediate by the quick-ey'd trout,
Or darting falmon. Thro' the green-wood glade
Some love to ftray; there lodg'd, amus'd and fed,
In the frefh leaf. Luxurious, others make
The meads their choice, and vifit every flower,
And every latent herb: for the fweet tafk,
To propagate their kinds, and where to wrap,
In what foft beds, their young yet undifclos'd,
Employs their tender care. Some to the houfe,

The fold, and dairy, hungry, bend their flight;
Sip round the pail, or taſte the curdling cheeſe:
Oft, inadvertent, from the milky ſtream
They meet their fate; or, weltering in the bowl,
With powerleſs wings around them wrapt, expire.
    But chief to heedleſs flies the window proves
A conſtant death; where, gloomily retir'd,
The villain ſpider lives, cunning, and fierce,
Mixture abhorr'd! Amid a mangled heap
Of carcaſſes, in eager watch he ſits,
O'erlooking all his waving ſnares around.
Near the dire cell the dreadleſs wanderer oft
Paſſes, as oft the ruffian ſhows his front;
The prey at laſt enſnar'd, he dreadful darts,
With rapid glide, along the leaning line;
And, fixing in the wretch his cruel fangs,
Strikes backward grimly pleas'd: the fluttering wing,
And ſhriller ſound declare extreme diſtreſs,
And aſk the helping hoſpitable hand.
    Reſounds the living ſurface of the ground:
Nor undelightful is the ceaſeleſs hum,
To him who muſes thro' the woods at noon;
Or drowſy ſhepherd, as he lies reclin'd,
With half-ſhut eyes, beneath the floating ſhade
Of willows grey, cloſe-crowding o'er the brook.
    Gradual, from theſe what numerous kinds deſcend,
Evading even the microſcopic eye!
Full Nature ſwarms with life; one wondrous maſs
Of animals, or atoms organiz'd,
Waiting the *vital Breath*, when PARENT-HEAVEN
Shall bid his ſpirit blow. The hoary fen,
In putrid ſteams, emits the living cloud
Of peſtilence. Thro' ſubterranean cells,
Where ſearching ſun-beams ſcarce can find a way,

Earth animated heaves. The flowery leaf
Wants not its foft inhabitants. Secure,
Within its winding citadel, the ftone
Holds multitudes. But chief the foreft-boughs,
That dance unnumber'd to the playful breeze,
The downy orchard, and the melting pulp
Of mellow fruit, the namelefs nations feed
Of evanefcent infects. Where the pool
Stands mantled o'er with green, invifible,
Amid the floating verdure millions ftray.
Each liquid too, whether it pierces, footbs,
Inflames, refrefhes, or exalts the tafte,
With various forms abounds. Nor is the ftream
Of pureft cryftal, nor the lucid air,
Tho' one tranfparent vacancy it feems,
Void of their unfeen people. Thefe, conceal'd
By the kind art of forming HEAVEN, efcape
The groffer eye of Man: for, if the worlds
In worlds inclos'd fhould on his fenfes burft,
From cates ambrofial, and the nectar'd bowl,
He would abhorrent turn; and in dead night,
When filence fleeps o'er all, be ftunn'd with noife.

    Let no prefuming impious railer tax
CREATIVE WISDOM, as if aught was form'd
In vain, or not for admirable ends.
Shall little haughty ignorance pronounce
His works unwife, of which the fmalleft part
Exceeds the narrow vifion of her mind?
As if upon a full proportion'd dome,
On fwelling columns heav'd, the pride of art!
A critic-fly, whofe feeble ray fcarce fpreads
An inch around, with blind prefumption bold,
Should dare to tax the ftructure of the whole.
    And lives the Man, whofe univerfal eye

Has 'fwept at once th' unbounded fcheme of things;
Mark'd their dependance fo, and firm accord,
As with unfaultering accent to conclude
That *This* availeth nought? Has any feen
The mighty chain of beings, leffening down
From INFINITE PERFECTION to the brink
Of dreary *Nothing*, defolate abyfs!
From which aftonifh'd thought, recoiling, turns?
Till then alone let zealous praife afcend,
And hymns of holy wonder, to that POWER,
Whofe wifdom fhines as lovely on our minds,
As on our fmiling eyes his fervant-fun.

Thick in yon ftream of light, a thoufand ways,
Upward, and downward, thwarting, and convolv'd,
The quivering nations fport; till, tempeft-wing'd,
Fierce Winter fweeps them from the face of day.
Even fo luxurious Men, unheeding, pafs
An idle fummer life in fortune's fhine,
A feafon's glitter! Thus they flutter on
From toy to toy, from vanity to vice;
Till, blown away by death, oblivion comes
Behind, and ftrikes them from the book of life.

Now fwarms the village o'er the jovial mead:
The ruftic youth, brown with meridian toil,
Healthful and ftrong; full as the fummer-rofe
Blown by prevailing funs, the ruddy maid,
Half naked, fwelling on the fight, and all
Her kindled graces burning o'er her cheek.
Even ftooping age is here; and infant-hands
Trail the long rake, or, with the fragrant load
O'ercharg'd, amid the kind oppreffion roll.
Wide flies the tedded grain; all in a row
Advancing broad, or wheeling round the field,
They fpread their breathing harveft to the fun,

That throws refreſhful round a rural ſmell:
Or, as they rake the green-appearing ground,
And drive the duſky wave along the mead,
The ruſſet hay-cock riſes thick behind,
In order gay.   While heard from dale to dale,
Waking the breeze, reſounds the blended voice
Of happy labour, love, and ſocial glee.
    Or ruſhing thence, in one diffuſive band,
They drive the troubled flocks, by many a dog
Compell'd, to where the mazy-running brook
Forms a deep pool; this bank abrupt and high,
And That fair ſpreading in a pebbled ſhore.
Urg'd to the giddy brink, much is the toil,
The clamour much, of men, and boys, and dogs,
Ere the ſoft fearful people to the flood
Commit their woolly ſides.   And oft the ſwain,
On ſome impatient ſeizing, hurls them in:
Embolden'd then, nor heſitating more,
Faſt, faſt, they plunge amid the flaſhing wave,
And panting labour to the fartheſt ſhore.
Repeated this, till deep the well-waſh'd fleece
Has drunk the flood, and from his lively haunt
The trout is baniſh'd by the ſordid ſtream;
Heavy, and dripping, to the breezy brow
Slow move the harmleſs race: where, as they ſpread
Their ſwelling treaſures to the ſunny ray,
Inly diſturb'd, and wondering what this wild
Outrageous tumult means, their loud complaints
The country fill; and, toſs'd from rock to rock,
Inceſſant bleatings run around the hills.
At laſt, of ſnowy white, the gathered flocks
Are in the wattled pen innumerous preſs'd,
Head above head: and, rang'd in luſty rows
The ſhepherds ſit, and whet the ſounding ſhears.

The houfewife waits to roll her fleecy ftores,
With all her gay-dreft maids attending round.
One, chief, in gracious dignity enthron'd,
Shines o'er the reft, the paftoral queen, and rays
Her fmiles, fweet-beaming, on her fhepherd-king;
While the glad circle round them yield their fouls
To feftive mirth, and wit that knows no gall.
Meantime, their joyous tafk goes on apace:
Some mingling ftir the melted tar, and fome,
Deep on the new-fhorn vagrant's heaving fide,
To ftamp his mafter's cypher ready ftand;
Others the unwilling wether drag along;
And, glorying in his might, the fturdy boy
Holds by the twifted horns th' indignant ram.
Behold where bound, and of its robe bereft,
By needy Man, that all-depending lord,
How meek, how patient, the mild creature lies!
What foftnefs in its melancholy face,
What dumb complaining innocence appears!
Fear not, ye gentle tribes, 'tis not the knife
Of horrid flaughter that is o'er you wav'd;
No, 'tis the tender fwain's well-guided fhears,
Who having now, to pay his annual care,
Borrowed your fleece, to you a cumbrous load,
Will fend you bounding to your hills again.
    A fimple fcene! yet hence BRITANNIA fees
Her folid grandeur rife: hence fhe commands
Th' exalted ftores of every brighter clime,
The treafures of the Sun without his rage:
Hence, fervent all, with culture, toil, and arts,
Wide glows her land: her dreadful thunder hence
Rides o'er the waves fublime, and now, even now,
Impending hangs o'er Gallia's humbled coaft;
Hence rules the circling deep, and awes the world.

'Tis raging Noon; and, vertical, the Sun
Darts on the head direct his forceful rays.
O'er heaven and earth, far as the ranging eye
Can fweep, a dazzling deluge reigns; and all
From pole to pole is undiftinguifh'd blaze.
In vain the fight, dejected to the ground,
Stoops for relief; thence hot-afcending fteams
And keen reflection pain.   Deep to the root
Of vegetation parch'd, the cleaving fields
And flippery lawn an arid hue difclofe,
Blaft Fancy's bloom, and wither even the Soul.
Echo no more returns the chearful found
Of fharpening fcythe: the mower finking heaps
O'er him the humid hay, with flowers perfum'd;
And fcarce a chirping grafs-hopper is heard
'Thro' the dumb mead.   Diftrefsful Nature pants.
The very ftreams look languid from afar;
Or, thro' th' unfhelter'd glade, impatient, feem
To hurl into the covert of the grove.

　　All-conquering Heat, oh intermit thy wrath!
And on my throbbing temples potent thus
Beam not fo fierce! Inceffant ftill you flow,
And ftill another fervent flood fucceeds,
Pour'd on the head profufe.   In vain I figh,
And reftlefs turn, and look around for Night;
Night is far off; and hotter hours approach.
Thrice happy he! who on the funlefs fide
Of a romantic mountain, foreft-crown'd,
Beneath the whole collected fhade reclines:
Or in the gelid caverns, woodbine-wrought,
And frefh bedew'd· with ever-fpouting ftreams,
Sits coolly calm; while all the world without,
Unfatisfied, and fick, toffes in noon.
Emblem inftructive of the virtuous Man,

Who keeps his temper'd mind serene, and pure,
And every paffion aptly harmoniz'd,
Amid a jarring world with vice inflam'd.
  Welcome, ye fhades! ye bowery thickets, hail!
Ye lofty pines! ye venerable oaks!
Ye afhes wild, refounding o'er the fteep!
Delicious is your fhelter to the foul,
As to the hunted hart the fallying fpring,
Or ftream full-flowing, that his fwelling fides
Laves, as he floats along the herbag'd brink.
Cool, thro' the nerves, your pleafing comfort glides;
The heart beats glad; the frefh expanded eye
And ear refume their watch; the finews knit;
And life fhoots fwift thro' all the lightened limbs.
  Around th' adjoining brook, that purls along
The vocal grove, now fretting o'er a rock,
Now fcarcely moving thro' a reedy pool,
Now ftarting to a fudden ftream, and now
Gently diffus'd into a limpid plain;
A various groupe the herds and flocks compofe,
Rural confufion! On the graffy bank
Some ruminating lie; while others ftand
Half in the flood, and often bending fip
The circling furface. In the middle droops
The ftrong laborious ox, of honeft front,
Which incompos'd he fhakes; and from his fides
The troublous infects lafhes with his tail,
Returning ftill. Amid his fubjects fafe,
Slumbers the monarch fwain; his carelefs arm
Thrown round his head, on downy mofs fuftain'd;
Here laid his fcrip, with wholefome viands fill'd;
There, liftening every noife, his watchful dog.
  Light fly his flumbers, if perchance a flight
Of angry gad-flies faften on the herd;

That ſtartling ſcatters from the ſhallow brook,
In ſearch of laviſh ſtream. Toſſing the foam,
They ſcorn the keeper's voice, and ſcour the plain,
Thro' all the bright ſeverity of noon;
While, from their labouring breaſts, a hollow moan
Proceeding, runs low-bellowing round the hills.

Oft in this ſeaſon too the horſe, provok'd,
While his big ſinews full of ſpirits ſwell,
Trembling with vigour, in the heat of blood,
Springs the high fence; and, o'er the field effus'd,
Darts on the gloomy flood, with ſtedfaſt eye,
And heart eſtranged to fear: his nervous cheſt,
Luxuriant, and erect, the ſeat of ſtrength!
Bears down th' oppoſing ſtream: quenchleſs his thirſt;
He takes the river at redoubled draughts;
And with wide noſtrils, ſnorting, ſkims the wave.

Still let me pierce into the midnight depth
Of yonder grove, of wildeſt largeſt growth:
That, forming high in air a woodland quire,
Nods o'er the mount beneath. At every ſtep,
Solemn, and ſlow, the ſhadows blacker fall,
And all is awful liſtening gloom around.

Theſe are the haunts of Meditation, theſe
The ſcenes where ancient bards th' inſpiring breath,
Extatic, felt; and, from this world retir'd,
Convers'd with angels, and immortal forms,
On gracious errands bent: to ſave the fall
Of virtue ſtruggling on the brink of vice;
In waking whiſpers, and repeated dreams,
To hint pure thought, and warn the favour'd ſoul
For future trials fated to prepare;
To prompt the poet, who devoted gives
His muſe to better themes; to ſoothe the pangs
Of dying worth, and from the patriot's breaſt

(Backward to mingle in detefted war,
But foremoft when engag'd) to turn the death;
And numberlefs fuch offices of love
Daily, and nightly, zealous to perform.

 Shook fudden from the bofom of the fky,
A thoufand fhapes or glide athwart the dufk,
Or ftalk majeftic on. Deep-rous'd, I feel
A facred terror, a fevere delight,
Creep thro' my mortal frame; and thus, methinks,
A voice, than human more, th' abftracted ear
Of fancy ftrikes. " Be not of us afraid,
" Poor kindred Man! thy fellow-creatures, we
" From the fame PARENT-POWER our beings drew,
" The fame our Lord, and laws, and great purfuit.
" Once fome of us, like thee, thro' ftormy life,
" Toil'd, tempeft-beaten, ere we could attain
" This holy calm, this harmony of mind,
" Where purity and peace immingle charms.
" Then fear not us; but with refponfive fong,
" Amid thefe dim receffes, undifturb'd
" By noify folly and difcordant vice,
" Of Nature fing with us, and Nature's GOD.
" Here frequent, at the vifionary hour,
" When mufing midnight reigns or filent noon,
" Angelic harps are in full concert heard,
" And voices chaunting from the wood-crown'd hill,
" The deepening dale, or inmoft fylvan glade:
" A privilege beftow'd by us, alone,
" On Contemplation, or the hallow'd ear
" Of Poet, fwelling to feraphic ftrain."
 And art thou, STANLEY *, of that facred band?
Alas, for us too foon! Tho' rais'd above

---

* A young lady, well known to the author, who died at the age of
eighteen, in the year 1738.

The reach of human pain, above the flight
Of human joy; yet, with a mingled ray
Of fadly pleas'd remembrance, muft thou feel
A mother's love, a mother's tender woe:
Who feeks thee ftill, in many a former fcene;
Seeks thy fair form, thy lovely beaming eyes,
Thy pleafing converfe, by gay lively fenfe
Infpir'd: where moral wifdom mildly fhone,
Without the toil of art; and virtue glow'd,
In all her fmiles, without forbidding pride.
But, O thou beft of parents! wipe thy tears;
Or rather to PARENTAL NATURE pay
The tears of grateful joy, who for a while
Lent thee this younger felf, this opening bloom
Of thy enlightened mind and gentle worth.
Believe the Mufe: the wintry blaft of death
Kills not the buds of virtue; no, they fpread,
Beneath the heavenly beam of brighter funs,
Thro' endlefs ages, into higher powers.
    Thus up the mount, in airy vifion rapt,
I ftray, regardlefs whither; till the found
Of a near fall of water every fenfe   [back,
Wakes from the charm of thought: fwift-fhrinking
I check my fteps, and view the broken fcene.
    Smooth to the fhelving brink a copious flood
Rolls fair, and placid; where collected all,
In one impetuous torrent, down the fteep
It thundering fhoots, and fhakes the country round.
At firft, an azure fheet, it rufhes broad;
Then whitening by degrees, as prone it falls,
And from the loud-refounding rocks below
Dafh'd in a cloud of foam, it fends aloft
A hoary mift, and forms a ceafelefs fhower.
Nor can the tortur'd wave here find repofe:

But, raging ſtill amid the ſhaggy rocks,
Now flaſhes o'er the ſcatter'd fragments, now
Aſlant the hollow channel rapid darts;
And falling faſt from gradual ſlope to ſlope,
With wild infraćted courſe, and leſſened roar,
It gains a ſafer bed, and ſteals, at laſt,
Along the mazes of the quiet vale.
 Invited from the cliff, to whoſe dark brow
He clings, the ſteep-aſcending eagle ſoars,
With upward pinions thro' the flood of day;
And, giving full his boſom to the blaze,
Gains on the ſun; while all the tuneful race,
Smit by afflićtive noon, diſorder'd droop,
Deep in the thicket; or, from bower to bower
Reſponſive, force an interrupted ſtrain.
The ſtock-dove only thro' the foreſt cooes,
Mournfully hoarſe; oft ceaſing from his plaint,
Short interval of weary woe! again
The ſad idea of his murder'd mate,
Struck from his ſide by ſavage fowler's guile,
Acroſs his fancy comes; and then reſounds
A louder ſong of ſorrow thro' the grove.
 Beſide the dewy border let me ſit,
All in the freſhneſs of the humid air;
There in that hollowed rock, groteſque and wild,
An ample chair moſs-lin'd, and over head
By flowering umbrage ſhaded; where the bee
Strays diligent, and with th' extraćted balm
Of fragrant wood-bine loads his little thigh.
 Now, while I taſte the ſweetneſs of the ſhade,
While Nature lies around deep-lull'd in Noon,
Now come bold *Fancy*, ſpread a daring flight,
And view the wonders of the *torrid Zone:*

Climes unrelenting! with whose rage compar'd,
Yon blaze is feeble, and yon skies are cool.
   See, how at once the bright-effulgent sun,
Rising direct, swift chases from the sky
The short-liv'd twilight; and with ardent blaze
Looks gaily fierce thro' all the dazzling air:
He mounts his throne; but kind before him sends,
Issuing from out the portals of the morn,
The *general Breeze* *, to mitigate his fire,
And breathe refreshment on a fainting world.
Great are the scenes, with dreadful beauty crown'd
And barbarous wealth, that see, each circling year,
Returning suns and *double seasons* † pass:
Rocks rich in gems, and mountains big with mines,
That on the high equator ridgy rise,
Whence many a bursting stream auriferous plays:
Majestic woods, of every vigorous green,
Stage above stage, high waving o'er the hills;
Or to the far horizon wide diffus'd,
A boundless deep immensity of shade.
Here lofty trees, to ancient song unknown,
The noble sons of potent heat and floods
Prone-rushing from the clouds, rear high to Heaven
Their thorny stems, and broad around them throw
Meridian gloom. Here, in eternal prime,
Unnumber'd fruits of keen delicious taste

---

* Which blows constantly between the tropics from the east, or the collateral points, the north-east and south-east: caused by the pressure of the rarefied air on that before it, according to the diurnal motion of the sun from east to west.

† In all climates between the tropics, the sun, as he passes and repasses in his annual motion, is twice a-year vertical, which produces this effect.

And vital fpirit, drink amid the cliffs,
And burning fands that bank the fhrubby vales,
Redoubled day, yet in their rugged coats
A friendly juice to cool its rage contain.
  Bear me, *Pomona!* to thy citron groves;
To where the lemon and the piercing lime,
With the deep orange, glowing thro' the green,
Their lighter glories blend.   Lay me reclin'd
Beneath the fpreading tamarind that fhakes,
Fann'd by the breeze, its fever-cooling fruit.
Deep in the night the maffy locuft fheds,
Quench my hot limbs; or lead me thro' the maze,
Embowering endlefs, of the *Indian* fig;
Or thrown at gayer eafe, on fome fair brow,
Let me behold, by breezy murmurs cool'd,
Broad o'er my head the verdant cedar wave,
And high palmetos lift their graceful fhade.
O ftretch'd amid thefe orchards of the fun,
Give me to drain the cocoa's milky bowl,
And from the palm to draw its frefhening wine!
More bounteous far than all the frantic juice
Which *Bacchus* pours.   Nor, on its flender twigs
Low-bending, be the full pomegranate fcorn'd;
Nor, creeping thro' the woods, the gelid race
Of berries.   Oft in humble ftation dwells
Unboaftful worth, above faftidious pomp.
Witnefs, thou beft Anâna, thou the pride
Of vegetable life, beyond whate'er
The poets imag'd in the golden age:
Quick let me ftrip thee of thy tufty coat,
Spread thy ambrofial ftores, and feaft with *Jove!*
  From thefe the profpect varies.   Plains immenfe
Lie ftretch'd below, interminable meads,
And vaft favannahs, where the wandering eye,

Unfixt, is in a verdant ocean loft.
Another *Flora* there, of bolder hues,
And richer fweets, beyond our garden's pride,
Plays o'er the fields, and fhowers with fudden hand
Exuberant fpring: for oft thefe valleys fhift
Their green-embroider'd robe to fiery brown,
And fwift to green again, as fcorching funs,
Or ftreaming dews and torrent rains, prevail.
    Along thefe lonely regions, where retir'd,
From little fcenes of art, great *Nature* dwells
In awful folitude, and nought is feen
But the wild herds that own no mafter's ftall,
Prodigious rivers roll their fat'ning feas:
On whofe luxuriant herbage, half-conceal'd,
Like a fallen cedar, far diffus'd his train,
Cas'd in green fcales, the crocodile extends.
The flood difparts: behold! in plaited mail,
Behemoth * rears his head.   Glanc'd from his fide,
The darted fteel in idle fhivers flies:
He fearlefs walks the plain, or feeks the hills;
Where, as he crops his varied fare, the herds,
In widening circle round, forget their food,
And at the harmlefs ftranger wondering gaze.
    Peaceful, beneath primeval trees, that caft
Their ample fhade o'er *Niger*'s yellow ftream,
And where the *Ganges* rolls his facred wave;
Or mid the central depth of blackening woods,
High-rais'd in folemn theatre around,
Leans the huge elephant: wifeft of brutes!
O truly wife! with gentle might endow'd,
Tho' powerful, not deftructive! Here he fees
Revolving ages fweep the changeful earth,

* The Hippopotamus, or river-horfe.

And empires rife and fall; regardlefs he
Of what the never-refting race of Men
Projeſt: thrice happy! could he 'fcape their guile,
Who mine, from cruel avarice, his fteps;
Or with his towery grandeur fwell their ftate,
The pride of kings! or elfe his ftrength pervert,
And bid him rage amid the mortal fray,
Aftonifh'd at the madnefs of mankind.

Wide o'er the winding umbrage of the floods,
Like vivid bloffoms glowing from afar,
Thick-fwarm the brighter birds. For Nature's hand,
That with a fportive vanity has deck'd
The plumy nations, there her gayeft hues
Profufely pours. But, if fhe bids them fhine,
Array'd in all the beauteous beams of day,
Yet frugal ftill, fhe humbles them in fong *.
Nor envy we the gaudy robes they lent
Proud *Montezuma's* realm, whofe legions caft
A boundlefs radiance waving on the fun,
While Philomel is ours; while in our fhades,
Thro' the foft filence of the liftening night,
The fober-fuited fongftrefs trills her lay.

But come, my *Mufe*, the defart-barrier burft,
A wild expanfe of lifelefs fand and fky:
And, fwifter than the toiling caravan,
Shoot o'er the vale of *Sennar*; ardent climb
The *Nubian* mountains, and the fecret bounds
Of jealous *Abyffinia* boldly pierce.
Thou art no ruffian, who beneath the mafk
Of focial commerce com'ft to rob their wealth;
No *holy Fury* thou, blafpheming HEAVEN,

* In all the regions of the torrid zone, the birds, though more
beautiful in their plumage, are obferved to be lefs melodious than ours.

With confecrated fteel to ftab their peace,
And thro' the land, yet red from civil wounds,
To fpread the purple tyranny of *Rome.*
Thou, like the harmlefs bee, may'ft freely range,
From mead to mead bright with exalted flowers,
From jafmine grove to grove, may'ft wander gay,
Thro' palmy fhades and aromatic woods,
That grace the plains, inveft the peopled hills,
And up the more than Alpine mountains wave.
There on the breezy fummit, fpreading fair,
For many a league; or on ftupendous rocks,
That from the fun-redoubling valley lift,
Cool to the middle air, their lawny tops;
Where palaces, and fanes, and villas rife;
And gardens fmile around, and cultur'd fields;
And fountains gufh; and carelefs herds and flocks
Securely ftray; a world within itfelf,
Difdaining all affault: there let me draw
Ethereal foul, there drink reviving gales,
Profufely breathing from the fpicy groves,
And vales of fragrance; there at diftance hear
The roaring floods, and cataracts, that fweep
From difembowel'd earth the virgin gold;
And o'er the varied landfkip, reftlefs, rove,
Fervent with life of every fairer kind:
A land of wonders! which the fun ftill eyes
With ray direct, as of the lovely realm
Inamour'd, and delighting there to dwell. ___
   How chang'd the fcene! In blazing height of noon,
The fun, opprefs'd, is plung'd in thickeft gloom.
Still Horror reigns, a dreary twilight round,
Of ftruggling night and day malignant mix'd.
For to the hot equator crowding faft,
Where, highly rarefy'd, the yielding air

Admits their ſtream, inceſſant vapours roll,
Amazing clouds on clouds continual heap'd;
Or whirl'd tempeſtuous by the guſty wind,
Or ſilent borne along, heavy, and ſlow,
With the big ſtores of ſteaming oceans charg'd.
Meantime, amid theſe upper ſeas, condens'd
Around the cold aërial mountain's brow,
And by conflicting winds together daſh'd,
The Thunder holds his black tremendous throne:
From cloud to cloud the rending Lightnings rage;
Till, in the furious elemental war
Diſſolv'd, the whole precipitated maſs
Unbroken floods and ſolid torrents pours.

    The treaſures theſe, hid from the bounded ſearch
Of ancient knowledge; whence, with annual pomp,
Rich king of floods! o'erflows the ſwelling *Nile*.
From his two ſprings, in *Gojam*'s ſunny realm,
Pure-welling out, he thro' the lucid lake
Of fair *Dambea* rolls his infant-ſtream.
There, by the Naiads nurs'd, he ſports away
His playful youth, amid the fragrant iſles,
That with unfading verdure ſmile around.
Ambitious, thence the manly river breaks;
And gathering many a flood, and copious fed
With all the mellowed treaſures of the ſky,
Winds in progreſſive majeſty along:
Thro' ſplendid kingdoms now devolves his maze,
Now wanders wild o'er ſolitary tracts
Of life-deſerted ſand; till, glad to quit
The joyleſs deſart, down the *Nubian* rocks
From thundering ſteep to ſteep, he pours his urn,
And *Egypt* joys beneath the ſpreading wave.

    His brother *Niger* too, and all the floods
In which the full-form'd maids of *Afric* lave

Their jetty limbs; and all that from the tract
Of woody mountains ftretch'd thro' gorgeous *Ind*
Fall on *Cormandel's* coaft, or *Malabar*;
From *Menam's* * orient ftream, that nightly fhines
With infect-lamps, to where Aurora fheds
On *Indus'* fmiling banks the rofy fhower:
All, at this bounteous feafon, ope their urns,
And pour untoiling harveft o'er the land.

   Nor lefs thy world, COLUMBUS, drinks, refrefh'd,
The lavifh moifture of the melting year.
Wide o'er his ifles, the branching *Oronoque*
Rolls a brown deluge; and the native drives
To dwell aloft on life-fufficing trees,
At once his dome, his robe, his food, and arms.
Swell'd by a thoufand ftreams, impetuous hurl'd
From all the roaring *Andes*, huge defcends
The mighty *Orellana* †.   Scarce the Mufe
Dares ftretch her wing o'er this enormous mafs
Of rufhing water; fcarce fhe dares attempt
The fea-like *Plata*; to whofe dread expanfe,
Continuous depth, and wondrous length of courfe,
Our floods are rills.   With unabated force,
In filent dignity they fweep along,
And traverfe realms unknown, and blooming wilds,
And fruitful defarts, worlds of folitude,
Where the fun fmiles and feafons teem in vain,
Unfeen, and unenjoy'd.   Forfaking thefe,
O'er peopled plains they fair-diffufive flow,
And many a nation feed, and circle fafe,
In their foft bofom, many a happy ifle;

   * The river that runs through *Siam*; on whofe banks, a vaft multitude of thofe infects called *Fire-flies* make a beautiful appearance in the night.

   † The river of the Amazons.

The feat of blamelefs *Pan*, yet undifturb'd
By chriftian crimes and *Europe*'s cruel fons.
Thus pouring on they proudly feek the deep,
Whofe vanquifh'd tide, recoiling from the fhock,
Yields to the liquid weight of half the globe;
And Ocean trembles for his green domain.
    But what avails this wondrous wafte of wealth?
This gay profufion of luxurious blifs?
This pomp of Nature? what their balmy meads,
Their powerful herbs, and *Ceres* void of pain?
By vagrant birds difpers'd, and wafting winds,
What their unplanted fruits? what the cool draughts,
Th' ambrofial food, rich gums, and fpicy health,
Their forefts yield? Their toiling infects what,
Their filky pride, and vegetable robes?
Ah! what avail their fatal treafures, hid
Deep in the bowels of the pitying earth,
Golconda's gems, and fad *Potofi*'s mines;
Where dwelt the gentleft children of the fun?
What all that *Afric*'s golden rivers roll,
Her odorous woods, and fhining ivory ftores?
Ill-fated race! the foftening arts of Peace,
Whate'er the humanizing Mufes teach;
The godlike wifdom of the temper'd breaft;
Progreffive truth, the patient force of thought;
Inveftigation calm, whofe filent powers
Command the world; the Light that leads to HEAVEN;
Kind equal rule, the government of laws,
And all-protecting FREEDOM, which alone
Suftains the name and dignity of Man:
Thefe are not theirs. The parent-fun himfelf
Seems o'er this world of flaves to tyrannize;
And, with oppreffive ray, the rofeat bloom
Of beauty blafting, gives the gloomy hue,

And feature grofs: or worfe, to ruthlefs deeds,
Mad jealoufy, blind rage, and fell revenge,
Their fervid fpirit fires. Love dwells not there,
The foft regards, the tendernefs of life,
The heart-fhed tear, th' ineffable delight
Of fweet humanity: thefe court the beam
Of milder climes; in felfifh fierce defire,
And the wild fury of voluptuous fenfe,
There loft. The very brute creation there
This rage partakes, and burns with horrid fire.
  Lo! the green ferpent, from his dark abode,
Which even Imagination fears to tread,
At noon forth-iffuing, gathers up his train
In orbs immenfe, then, darting out anew,
Seeks the refrefhing fount; by which diffus'd,
He throws his folds; and while, with threatning tongue,
And deathful jaws erect, the monfter curls
His flaming creft, all other thirft appall'd,
Or fhivering flies, or check'd at diftance ftands,
Nor dares approach. But ftill more direful he,
The fmall clofe-lurking minifter of fate,
Whofe high-concocted venom thro' the veins
A rapid lightning darts, arrefting fwift
The vital current. Form'd to humble Man,
This child of vengeful Nature! There, fublim'd
To fearlefs luft of blood, the favage race
Roam, licens'd by the fhading hour of guilt,
And foul mifdeed, when the pure day has fhut
His facred eye) The tyger darting fierce
Impetuous on the prey his glance has doom'd:
The lively-fhining leopard, fpeckled o'er
With many a fpot, the beauty of the wafte;
And, fcorning all the taming arts of Man,
The keen hyena, felleft of the fell.

Thefe, rufhing from th' inhofpitable woods
Of *Mauritania,* or the tufted ifles,
That verdant rife amid the *Lybian* wild,
Innumerous glare around their fhaggy king,
Majeftic, ftalking o'er the printed fand;
And, with imperious and repeated roars,
Demand their fated food. The fearful flocks
Crowd near the guardian fwain; the nobler herds,
Where, round their lordly bull, in rural eafe,
They ruminating lie, with horror hear
The coming rage. Th' awakened village ftarts;
And to her fluttering breaft the mother ftrains
Her thoughtlefs infant. From the *Pyrate's* den,
Or ftern *Morocco's* tyrant fang efcap'd,
The wretch half-wifhes for his bonds again:
While, uproar all, the wildernefs refounds,
From *Atlas* eaftward to the frighted *Nile.*

Unhappy he! who from the firft of joys,
Society, cut off, is left alone
Amid this world of death. Day after day,
Sad on the jutting eminence he fits,
And views the main that ever toils below;
Still fondly forming in the fartheft verge,
Where the round ether mixes with the wave,
Ships, dim-difcovered, dropping from the clouds;
At evening, to the fetting fun he turns
A mournful eye, and down his dying heart
Sinks helplefs; while the wonted roar is up,
And hifs continual thro' the tedious night.
Yet here, even here, into thefe black abodes
Of monfters, unappall'd, from ftooping *Rome,*
And guilty *Cæfar,* LIBERTY retir'd,
Her CATO following thro' *Numidian* wilds:
Difdainful of *Campania's* gentle plains,

And all the green delights *Aufonia* pours;
When for them fhe muft bend the fervile knee,
And fawning take the fplendid robber's boon.

    Nor ftop the terrors of thefe regions here.
Commiffion'd demons oft, angels of wrath,
Let loofe the raging elements.   Breath'd hot,
From all the boundlefs furnace of the fky,
And the wide glittering wafte of burning fand,
A fuffocating wind the pilgrim fmites
With inftant death.   Patient of thirft and toil,
Son of the defart! even the camel feels,
Shot thro' his wither'd heart, the fiery blaft.
Or from the black-red ether, burfting broad,
Sallies the fudden whirlwind.   Strait the fands,
Commov'd around, in gathering eddies play:
Nearer and nearer ftill they darkening come;
Till, with the general all-involving ftorm
Swept up, the whole continuous wilds arife;
And by their noon-day fount dejected thrown,
Or funk at night in fad difaftrous fleep,
Beneath defcending hills, the caravan
Is buried deep.   In *Cairo*'s crowded ftreets
Th' impatient merchant, wondering, waits in vain,
And *Mecca* faddens at the long delay.

    But chief at fea, whofe every flexile wave
Obeys the blaft, the aërial tumult fwells.
In the dread ocean, undulating wide,
Beneath the radiant line that girts the globe,
The circling Typhon *, whirl'd from point to point,
Exhaufting all the rage of all the fky,
And dire Ecnephia * reign.   Amid the heavens,

---

   * *Typhon* and *Ecnephia*, names of particular ftorms or hurricanes, known only between the tropics.

Falfely ferene, deep in a cloudy * fpeck
Comprefs'd, the mighty tempeft brooding dwells:
Of no regard, fave to the fkilful eye,
Fiery and foul, the fmall prognoftic hangs
Aloft, or on the promontory's brow
Mufters its force. A faint deceitful calm,
A fluttering gale, the demon fends before,
To tempt the fpreading fail. Then down at once,
Precipitant, defcends a mingled mafs
Of roaring winds, and flame, and rufhing floods.
In wild amazement fix'd the failor ftands.
Art is too flow: by rapid fate opprefs'd,
His broad-wing'd veffel drinks the whelming tide,
Hid in the bofom of the black abyfs.
With fuch mad feas the daring GAMA † fought,
For many a day, and many a dreadful night,
Inceffant, lab'ring round the *ftormy Cape*;
By bold ambition led, and bolder thirft
Of gold. For then from ancient gloom emerg'd
The rifing world of trade: the *Genius*, then,
Of navigation, that, in hopelefs floth,
Had flumber'd on the vaft Atlantic deep,
For idle ages, ftarting, heard at laft
The LUSITANIAN PRINCE ‡; who, HEAV'N-infpir'd,
To love of ufeful glory rous'd mankind,
And in unbounded Commerce mix'd the world.
  Increafing ftill the terrors of thefe ftorms,
His jaws horrific arm'd with threefold fate,

* Called by failors the *Ox-eye*, being in appearance at firft no bigger.
† VASCO DE GAMA, the firft who failed round *Africa*, by the *Cape of Good Hope*, to the *Eaft Indies*.
‡ DON HENRY, third fon to *John* the Firft, king of *Portugal*. His ftrong genius to the difcovery of new countries was the chief fource of all the modern improvements in navigation.

F 4

Here dwells the direful fhark. Lur'd by the fcent
Of fteaming crowds, of rank difeafe, and death,
Behold! he rufhing cuts the briny flood,
Swift as the gale can bear the fhip along;
And, from the partners of that cruel trade,
Which fpoils unhappy *Guinea* of her fons,
Demands his fhare of prey; demands themfelves.
The ftormy fates defcend: one death involves
Tyrants and flaves; when ftrait, their mangled limbs
Crafhing at once, he dyes the purple feas   .
With gore, and riots in the vengeful meal.

   When o'er this world, by equinoctial rains
Flooded immenfe, looks out the joylefs fun,
And draws the copious fteam: from fwampy fens,
Where putrefaction into life ferments,
And breathes deftructive myriads; or from woods,
Impenetrable fhades, receffes foul,
In vapours rank and blue corruption wrapt,
Whofe gloomy horrors yet no defperate foot
Has ever dar'd to pierce; then, wafteful, forth
Walks the dire *Power* of peftilent difeafe.
A thoufand hideous fiends her courfe attend,
Sick Nature blafting, and to heartlefs woe,
And feeble defolation, cafting down
The towering hopes and all the pride of Man.
Such as, of late, at *Carthagena* quench'd
The BRITISH fire. You, gallant VERNON, faw
The miferable fcene; you, pitying, faw
To infant-weaknefs funk the warrior's arm;
Saw the deep-racking pang, the ghaftly form,
The lip pale-quivering, and the beamlefs eye
No more with ardour bright: you heard the groans
Of agonizing fhips, from fhore to fhore;
Heard, nightly plung'd amid the fullen waves,

The frequent corfe; while on each other fix'd,
In fad prefage, the blank affiftants feem'd,
Silent, to afk, whom Fate would next demand.

What need I mention thofe inclement fkies,
Where, frequent o'er the fickening city, Plague,
The fierceft child of NEMESIS divine,
Defcends? From *Ethiopia*'s poifoned woods,
From ftifled *Cairo*'s filth, and fetid fields
With locuft-armies putrefying * heap'd,
This great deftroyer fprung. Her awful rage
The brutes efcape: Man is her deftin'd prey,
Intemperate Man! and, o'er his guilty domes,
She draws a clofe incumbent cloud of death;
Uninterrupted by the living winds,
Forbid to blow a wholefome breeze; and ftain'd
With many a mixture by the fun, fuffus'd,
Of angry afpect. Princely wifdom, then,
Dejects his watchful eye; and from the hand
Of feeble juftice, ineffectual, drop
The fword and balance: mute the voice of joy,
And hufh'd the clamour of the bufy world.
Empty the ftreets, with uncouth verdure clad;
Into the worft of defarts fudden turn'd
The chearful haunt of Men: unlefs efcap'd
From the doom'd houfe, where matchlefs horror reigns,
Shut up by barbarous fear, the fmitten wretch,
With frenzy wild, breaks loofe; and, loud to heaven
Screaming, the dreadful policy arraigns,
Inhuman, and unwife. The fullen door,
Yet uninfected, on its cautious hinge
Fearing to turn, abhors fociety:

* Thefe are the caufes fuppofed to be the firft origin of the *Plague*, in Dr. MEAD's elegant book on that fubject.

Dependants, friends, relations, Love himfelf,
Savag'd by woe, forget the tender.tie,
The fweet engagement of the feeling heart.
But vain their felfifh care: the circling fky,
The wide enlivening air is full of fate;
And, ftruck by turns, in folitary pangs
They fall, unbleft, untended, and unmourn'd.
Thus o'er the proftrate city black Defpair
Extends her raven wing; while, to complete
The fcene of defolation, ftretch'd around,
The grim guards ftand, denying all retreat,
And give the flying wretch a better death.
     Much yet remains unfung: the rage intenfe
Of brazen-vaulted fkies, of iron fields,
Where drought and famine ftarve the blafted year:
Fir'd by the torch of noon to tenfold rage,
The infuriate hill that fhoots the pillar'd flame;
And, rous'd within the fubterranean world,
Th' expanding earthquake, that refiftlefs fhakes
Afpiring cities from their folid bafe,
And buries mountains in the flaming gulph.
But 'tis enough; return, my vagrant Mufe:
A nearer fcene of horror calls thee home.
     Behold, flow-fettling o'er the lurid grove
Unufual darknefs broods; and growing gains
The full poffeffion of the fky, furcharg'd
With wrathful vapour, from the fecret beds,
Where fleep the mineral generations, drawn.
Thence Nitre, Sulphur, and the fiery fpume
Of fat Bitumen, fteaming on the day,
With various-tinctur'd trains of latent flame,
Pollute the fky, and in yon baleful cloud,
A reddening gloom, a magazine of fate,
Ferment; till, by the touch ethereal rous'd,

The dafh of clouds, or irritating war
Of fighting winds, while all is calm below,
They furious fpring. A boding filence reigns,
Dread thro' the dun expanfe ; fave the dull found
That from the mountain, previous to the ftorm,
Rolls o'er the muttering earth, difturbs the flood,
And fhakes the foreft-leaf without a breath.
Prone, to the loweft vale, the aërial tribes
Defcend: the tempeft-loving raven fcarce ·
Dares wing the dubious dufk. In rueful gaze
The cattle ftand, and on the fcowling heavens
Caft a deploring eye; by Man forfook,
Who to the crowded cottage hies him faft,
Or feeks the fhelter of the downward cave.
    'Tis liftening fear, and dumb amazement all:
When to the ftartled eye the fudden glance
Appears far fouth, eruptive thro' the cloud;
And following flower, in explofion vaft,
The Thunder raifes his tremendous voice.
At firft, heard folemn o'er the verge of heaven,
The tempeft growls; but as it nearer comes,
And rolls its awful burden on the wind,
The lightnings flafh a larger curve, and more
The noife aftounds: till over head a fheet
Of livid flame difclofes wide; then fhuts,
And opens wider; fhuts and opens ftill
Expanfive, wrapping ether in a blaze.
Follows the loofen'd aggravated roar,
Enlarging, deepening, mingling; peal on peal
Crufh'd horrible, convulfing heaven and earth.
    Down comes a deluge of fonorous hail,
Or prone-defcending rain. Wide-rent, the clouds
Pour a whole flood; and yet, its flame unquench'd,
Th' unconquerable lightning ftruggles through,

Ragged and fierce, or in red whirling balls,
And fires the mountains with redoubled rage.
Black from the ſtroke, above, the ſmouldering pine
Stands a ſad ſhatter'd trunk; and, ſtretch'd below,
A lifeleſs groupe the blaſted cattle lie:
Here the ſoft flocks, with that ſame harmleſs look
They wore alive, and ruminating ſtill
In fancy's eye; and there the frowning bull,
And ox half-rais'd. Struck on the caſtled cliff,
The venerable tower and ſpiry fane
Reſign their aged pride. The gloomy woods
Start at the flaſh, and from their deep receſs,
Wide-flaming out, their trembling inmates ſhake.
Amid *Carnarvon*'s mountains rages loud
The repercuſſive roar: with mighty cruſh,
Into the flaſhing deep, from the rude rocks
Of *Penmanmaur* heap'd hideous to the ſky,
Tumble the ſmitten cliffs; and *Snowden*'s peak,
Diſſolving, inſtant yields his wintry load.
Far-ſeen, the heights of heathy *Cheviot* blaze,
And *Thulè* bellows thro' her utmoſt iſles.

  Guilt hears appall'd, with deeply troubled thought.
And yet not always on the guilty head
Deſcends the fated flaſh. Young CELADON
And his AMELIA were a matchleſs pair;
With equal virtue form'd, and equal grace,
The ſame, diſtinguiſh'd by their ſex alone:
Hers the mild luſtre of the blooming morn,
And his the radiance of the riſen day.
  They lov'd: but ſuch their guileleſs paſſion was,
As in the dawn of time inform'd the heart
Of innocence, and undiſſembling truth.
'Twas friendſhip heightened by the mutual wiſh,
Th' enchanting hope, and ſympathetic glow,

Beam'd from the mutual eye.   Devoting all
To love, each was to each a dearer felf;
Supremely happy in th' awakened power
Of giving joy.   Alone, amid the fhades,
Still in harmonious intercourfe they liv'd
The rural day, and talk'd the flowing heart,
Or figh'd and look'd unutterable things——
   So pafs'd their life, a clear united ftream,
By care unruffled; till, in evil hour,
The tempeft caught them on the tender walk,
Heedlefs how far, and where its mazes ftray'd,
While, with each other bleft, creative love
Still bade eternal *Eden* fmile around.
Prefaging inftant fate her bofom heav'd
Unwonted fighs, and ftealing oft a look
Of the big gloom on CELADON her eye
Fell tearful, wetting her difordered cheek.
In vain affuring love, and confidence
In HEAVEN, reprefs'd her fear; it grew, and fhook
Her frame near diffolution.   He perceiv'd
Th' unequal conflict, and as angels look
On dying faints, his eyes compaffion fhed,
With love illumin'd high.   " Fear not, he faid,
" Sweet innocence! thou ftranger to offence,
" And inward ftorm! HE, who yon fkies involves
" In frowns of darknefs, ever fmiles on thee
" With kind regard.   O'er thee the fecret fhaft
" That waftes at midnight, or th' undreaded hour
" Of noon, flies harmlefs: and that very voice,
" Which thunders terror thro' the guilty heart,
" With tongues of feraphs whifpers peace to thine.
" 'Tis fafety to be near thee fure, and thus
" To clafp perfection!"   From his void embrace,
Myfterious Heaven! that moment, to the ground,

A blackened corfe, was ftruck the beauteous maid.
But who can paint the lover, as he ftood,
Pierc'd by fevere amazement, hating life,
Speechlefs, and fix'd in all the death of woe!
So, faint refemblance! on the marble tomb,
The well-diffembled mourner ftooping ftands,
For ever filent, and for ever fad.

    As from the face of heaven the fhatter'd clouds
Tumultuous rove, th' interminable fky
Sublimer fwells, and o'er the world expands
A purer azure. Thro' the lightened air
A higher luftre and a clearer calm,
Diffufive, tremble; while, as if in fign
Of danger paft, a glittering robe of joy,
Set off abundant by the yellow ray,
Invefts the fields; and nature fmiles reviv'd.

    'Tis beauty all, and grateful fong around,
Join'd to the low of kine, and numerous bleat
Of flocks thick-nibbling thro' the clover'd vale.
And fhall the hymn be marr'd by thanklefs Man,
Moft-favour'd; who with voice articulate
Should lead the chorus of this lower world?
Shall he, fo foon forgetful of the hand
That hufh'd the thunder, and ferenes the fky,
Extinguifh'd feel that fpark the tempeft wak'd,
That fenfe of powers exceeding far his own,
Ere yet his feeble heart has loft its fears?

    Chear'd by the milder beam, the fprightly youth
Speeds to the well-known pool, whofe cryftal depth
A fandy bottom fhews. A while he ftands
Gazing th' inverted landfkip, half afraid
To meditate the blue profound below;
Then plunges headlong down the circling flood.
His ebon treffes, and his rofy cheek

Inftant emerge; and thro' the obedient wave,
At each fhort breathing by his lip repell'd,
With arms and legs according well, he makes,
As humour leads, an eafy-winding path;
While, from his polifh'd fides, a dewy light
Effufes on the pleas'd fpectators round.
   This is the pureft exercife of health,
The kind refrefher of the fummer heats;
Nor, when cold WINTER keens the brightening flood,
Would I weak-fhivering linger on the brink.
Thus life redoubles, and is oft preferv'd,
By the bold fwimmer, in the fwift illapfe
Of accident difaftrous. Hence the limbs
Knit into force; and the fame *Roman* arm,
That rofe victorious o'er the conquer'd earth,
Firft learn'd, while tender, to fubdue the wave.
Even, from the body's purity, the mind
Receives a fecret fympathetic aid.
   Clofe in the covert of an hazel copfe,
Where winded into pleafing folitudes
Runs out the rambling dale, young DAMON fat,
Penfive, and pierc'd with love's delightful pangs.
There to the ftream that down the diftant rocks
Hoarfe-murmuring fell, and plaintive breeze that play'd
Among the bending willows, falfely he
Of MUSIDORA's cruelty complain'd.
She felt his flame; but deep within her breaft,
In bafhful coynefs, or in maiden pride,
The foft return conceal'd; fave when it ftole
In fide-long glances from her downcaft eye,
Or from her fwelling foul in ftifled fighs.
Touch'd by the fcene, no ftranger to his vows,
He fram'd a melting lay, to try her heart;
And, if an infant paffion ftruggled there,

To call that paffion forth. Thrice happy fwain!
A lucky chance, that oft decides the fate
Of mighty monarchs, then decided thine.
For lo! conducted by the laughing Loves,
This cool retreat his MUSIDORA fought:
Warm in her cheek the fultry feafon glow'd;
And, rob'd in loofe array, fhe came to bathe
Her fervent limbs in the refrefhing ftream.
What fhall he do? In fweet confufion loft,
And dubious flutterings, he a while remain'd:
A pure ingenuous elegance of foul,
A delicate refinement, known to few,
Perplex'd his breaft, and urg'd him to retire:
But love forbade. Ye prudes in virtue, fay,
Say, ye fevereft, what would you have done?
Meantime, this fairer nymph than ever bleft
Arcadian ftream, with timid eye around
The banks furveying, ftripp'd her beauteous limbs,
To tafte the lucid coolnefs of the flood.
Ah then! not *Paris* on the piny top
Of *Ida* panted ftronger, when afide
The rival-goddeffes the veil divine
Caft unconfin'd, and gave him all their charms,
Than, DAMON, thou; as from the fnowy leg,
And flender foot th' inverted filk fhe drew;
As the foft touch diffolv'd the virgin zone;
And, thro' the parting robe, th' alternate breaft,
With youth wild-throbbing, on thy lawlefs gaze
In full luxuriance rofe. But, defperate youth,
How durft thou rifque the foul-diftracting view;
As from her naked limbs, of glowing white,
Harmonious fwell'd by Nature's fineft hand,
In folds loofe-floating fell the fainter lawn;
And fair-expos'd fhe ftood, fhrunk from herfelf,

With fancy blufhing, at the doubtful breeze
Alarm'd, and ftarting like the fearful fawn?
Then to the flood fhe rufh'd; the parted flood
Its lovely gueft with clofing waves receiv'd;
And every beauty foftening, every grace
Flufhing anew, a mellow luftre fhed:
As fhines the lily thro' the cryftal mild;
Or as the rofe amid the morning dew,
Frefh from *Aurora*'s hand, more fweetly glows.
While thus fhe wanton'd, now beneath the wave
But ill-conceal'd; and now with ftreaming locks,
That half-embrac'd her in a humid veil,
Rifing again, the latent DAMON drew
Such madning draughts of beauty to the foul,
As for a while o'erwhelm'd his raptur'd thought
With luxury too-daring. Check'd, at laft,
By love's refpectful modefty, he deem'd
The theft profane, if aught profane to love
Can e'er be deem'd; and, ftruggling from the fhade,
With headlong hurry fled: but firft thefe lines,
Trac'd by his ready pencil, on the bank
With trembling hand he threw. " Bathe on, my fair,
" Yet unbeheld fave by the facred eye
" Of faithful love: I go to guard thy haunt,
" To keep from thy recefs each vagrant foot,
" And each licentious eye." With wild furprife,
As if to marble ftruck, devoid of fenfe,
A ftupid moment motionlefs fhe ftood:
So ftands the ftatue * that enchants the world,
So bending tries to veil the matchlefs boaft,
The mingled beauties of exulting *Greece*.
Recovering, fwift fhe flew to find thofe robes

* The Venus of *Medici.*

Which blifsful *Eden* knew not; and, array'd
In carelefs hafte, th' alarming paper fnatch'd.
But, when her DAMON's well-known hand fhe faw,
Her terrors vanifh'd, and a fofter train
Of mixt emotions, hard to be defcrib'd,
Her fudden bofom feiz'd: fhame void of guilt,
The charming blufh of innocence, efteem
And admiration of her lover's flame,
By modefty exalted: even a fenfe
Of felf-approving beauty ftole acrofs
Her bufy thought.   At length, a tender calm
Hufh'd by degrees the tumult of her foul;
And on the fpreading beech, that o'er the ftream
Incumbent hung, fhe with the filvan pen
Of rural lovers this confeffion carv'd,
Which foon her DAMON kifs'd with weeping joy:
" Dear youth! fole judge of what thefe verfes mean,
" By fortune too much favour'd, but by love,
" Alas! not favour'd lefs, be ftill as now
" Difcreet: the time may come you need not fly."
   The fun has loft his rage: his downward orb
Shoots nothing now but animating warmth,
And vital luftre; that, with various ray,
Lights up the clouds, thofe beauteous robes of heaven,
Inceffant roll'd into romantic fhapes,
The dream of waking fancy! Broad below,
Cover'd with ripening fruits, and fwelling faft
Into the perfect year, the pregnant earth
And all her tribes rejoice.   Now the foft hour
Of walking comes: for him who lonely loves
To feek the diftant hills, and there converfe
With Nature; there to harmonize his heart,
And in pathetic fong to breathe around
The harmony to others.. Social friends,

Attun'd to happy unifon of foul;
To whofe exalting eye a fairer world,
Of which the vulgar never had a glimpfe,
Difplays its charms; whofe minds are richly fraught
With philofophic ftores, fuperior light;
And in whofe breaft, enthufiaftic, burns
Virtue, the fons of intereft deem romance;
Now call'd abroad enjoy the falling day:
Now to the verdant *Portico* of woods,
To Nature's vaft *Lyceum*, forth they walk;
By that kind *School* where no proud mafter reigns,
The full free converfe of the friendly heart,
Improving and improv'd.　Now from the world,
Sacred to fweet retirement, lovers fteal,
And pour their fouls in tranfport, which the SIRE
Of love approving hears, and *calls it good*.
Which way, AMANDA, fhall we bend our courfe?
The choice perplexes.　Wherefore fhould we chufe?
All is the fame with thee.　Say, fhall we wind
Along the ftreams? or walk the fmiling mead?
Or court the foreft-glades? or wander wild
Among the waving harvefts? or afcend,
While radiant Summer opens all its pride,
Thy hill, delightful *Shene* *?　Here let us fweep
The boundlefs landfkip: now the raptur'd eye,
Exulting fwift, to huge AUGUSTA fend,
Now to the *Sifter Hills* † that fkirt her plain,
To lofty *Harrow* now, and now to where
Majeftic *Windfor* lifts his princely brow.
In lovely contraft to this glorious view

* The old name of *Richmond*, fignifying in Saxon *Shining*, or *Splendor*.

† *Highgate* and *Hampftead*.

Calmly magnificent, then will we turn
To where the filver THAMES firft rural grows.
There let the feafted eye unwearied ftray:
Luxurious, there, rove thro' the pendant woods
That nodding hang o'er HARRINGTON's retreat;
And, ftooping thence to *Ham*'s embowering walks,
Beneath whofe fhades, in fpotlefs peace retir'd,
With HER the pleafing partner of his heart,
The worthy QUEENSB'RY yet laments his GAY,
And polifh'd CORNBURY wooes the willing Mufe,
Slow let us trace the matchlefs VALE OF THAMES;
Fair-winding up to where the Mufes haunt
In *Twit'nam's* bowers, and for their POPE implore
The healing GOD*; to royal *Hampton*'s pile,
To *Clermont*'s terrafs'd height, and *Efher*'s groves,
Where in the fweeteft folitude, embrac'd
By the foft windings of the filent *Mole*,
From courts and fenates PELHAM finds repofe.
Inchanting vale! beyond whate'er the Mufe
Has of *Achaia* or *Hefperia* fung!
O vale of blifs! O foftly-fwelling hills!
On which the *Power of Cultivation* lies,
And joys to fee the wonders of his toil.

Heavens! what a goodly profpect fpreads around,
Of hills, and dales, and woods, and lawns, and fpires,
And glittering towns, and gilded ftreams, till all
The ftretching landfkip into fmoke decays!
Happy BRITANNIA! where the QUEEN OF ARTS,
Infpiring vigour, LIBERTY abroad
Walks, unconfin'd, even to thy fartheft cotts,
And fcatters plenty with unfparing hand.

* In his laft ficknefs.

Rich is thy foil, and merciful thy clime;
Thy ftreams unfailing in the Summer's drought;
Unmatch'd thy guardian-oaks; thy valleys float
With golden waves: and on thy mountains flocks
Bleat numberlefs; while, roving round their fides,
Bellow the blackening herds in lufty droves.
Beneath, thy meadows glow, and rife unquell'd
Againft the mower's fcythe. On every hand
Thy villas fhine. Thy country teems with wealth;
And property affures it to the fwain,
Pleas'd, and unwearied, in his guarded toil.

Full are thy cities with the fons of art;
And trade and joy, in every bufy ftreet,
Mingling are heard: even Drudgery himfelf,
As at the car he fweats, or dufty hews
The palace-ftone, looks gay. Thy crowded ports,
Where rifing mafts an endlefs profpect yield,
With labour burn, and echo to the fhouts
Of hurried failor, as he hearty waves
His laft adieu, and loofening every fheet,
Refigns the fpreading veffel to the wind.

Bold, firm, and graceful, are thy generous youth,
By hardfhip finew'd, and by danger fir'd,
Scattering the nations where they go; and firft
Or on the lifted plain, or ftormy feas.
Mild are thy glories too, as o'er the plans
Of thriving peace thy thoughtful fires prefide;
In genius, and fubftantial learning, high;
For every virtue, every worth, renown'd;
Sincere, plain-hearted, hofpitable, kind;
Yet like the muftering thunder when provok'd,
The dread of tyrants, and the fole refource
Of thofe that under grim oppreffion groan,

G 3

Thy Sons of Glory many! Alfred thine,
In whom the fplendor of heroic war,
And more heroic peace, when govern'd well,
Combine; whofe hallowed name the virtues faint,
And *his own* Mufes love; the beft of *Kings!*
With him thy Edwards and thy Henrys fhine,
Names dear to Fame; the firft who deep imprefs'd
On haughty *Gaul* the terror of thy arms,
That awes her genius ftill.   In *Statefmen* thou,
And *Patriots*, fertile.   Thine a fteady More,
Who, with a generous tho' miftaken zeal,
Withftood a brutal tyrant's ufeful rage,
Like Cato firm, like Aristides juft,
Like rigid Cincinnatus nobly poor,
A dauntlefs foul erect, who fmil'd on death.
Frugal, and wife, a Walsingham is thine;
A Drake, who made thee miftrefs of the deep,
And bore thy name in thunder round the world.
Then flam'd thy fpirit high: but who can fpeak   *Elizabeth.*
The numerous worthies of the Maiden Reign?
In Raleigh mark their every glory mix'd;
Raleigh, the fcourge of *Spain!* whofe breaft with all
The fage, the patriot, and the hero burn'd.
Nor funk his vigour when a coward-reign
The warrior fettered, and at laft refign'd,
To glut the vengeance of a vanquifh'd foe.
Then, active ftill and unreftrain'd, his mind
Explor'd the vaft extent of ages paft,
And with his prifon-hours enrich'd the world;
Yet found no times, in all the long refearch,
So glorious, or fo bafe, as thofe he prov'd,
In which he conquer'd, and in which he bled.
Nor can the Mufe the gallant Sidney pafs,

The plume of war! with early laurels crown'd,
The Lover's myrtle, and the Poet's bay.
A HAMDEN too is thine, illuftrious land,
Wife, ftrenuous, firm, of unfubmitting foul,
Who ftem'd the torrent of a downward age
To flavery prone, and bade thee rife again,
In all thy native pomp of freedom bold.
Bright, at his call, thy Age of *Men* effulg'd,
Of Men on whom late time a kindling eye
Shall turn, and tyrants tremble while they read.
Bring every fweeteft flower, and let me ftrew
The grave where RUSSEL lies; whofe temper'd blood,
With calmeft chearfulnefs for thee refign'd,
Stain'd the fad annals of a giddy reign;
Aiming at lawlefs power, tho' meanly funk
In loofe inglorious luxury.   With him
His friend, the BRITISH CASSIUS *, fearlefs bled;
Of high determin'd fpirit, roughly brave,
By ancient learning to th' enlightened love
Of ancient freedom warm'd.   Fair thy renown
In awful *Sages* and in noble *Bards*;
Soon as the light of dawning Science fpread
Her orient ray, and wak'd the Mufes' fong.
Thine is a BACON; haplefs in his choice,
Unfit to ftand the civil ftorm of ftate,
And thro' the fmooth barbarity of courts,
With firm but pliant virtue, forward ftill
To urge his courfe: him for the ftudious fhade
Kind Nature form'd, deep, comprehenfive, clear,
Exact, and elegant; in one rich foul,
PLATO, the STAGYRITE, and TULLY join'd.
The great deliverer he! who from the gloom

* ALGERNON SIDNEY.

G 4

Of cloifter'd monks, and jargon-teaching fchools,
Led forth the true Philofophy, there long
Held in the magic chain of words and forms,
And definitions void: he led her forth,
Daughter of HEAVEN! that flow-afcending ftill,
Inveftigating fure the chain of things,
With radiant finger points to HEAVEN again.
The generous ASHLEY * thine, the friend of Man;
Who fcann'd his Nature with a brother's eye,
His weaknefs prompt to fhade, to raife his aim,
To touch the finer movements of the mind,
And with the *moral beauty* charm the heart.
Why need I name thy BOYLE, whofe pious fearch
Amid the dark receffes of his works,
The great CREATOR fought? And why thy LOCKE,
Who made the whole internal world his own?
Let NEWTON, *pure Intelligence,* whom GOD
To mortals lent, to trace his boundlefs works
From laws fublimely fimple, fpeak thy fame
In all philofophy. For lofty fenfe,
Creative fancy, and infpection keen
Thro' the deep windings of the human heart,
Is not wild SHAKESPEARE thine and Nature's boaft?
Is not each great, each amiable Mufe
Of claffic ages in thy MILTON met?
A genius univerfal as his theme;
Aftonifhing as Chaos, as the bloom
Of blowing Eden fair, as Heaven fublime.
Nor fhall my verfe that elder bard forget,
The gentle SPENSER, Fancy's pleafing fon;
Who, like a copious river, pour'd his fong
O'er all the mazes of enchanted ground:

* ANTONY ASHLEY COOPER, Earl of *Shaftefbury.*

Nor thee, his ancient mafter, laughing fage,
CHAUCER, whofe native manners-painting verfe,
Well-moraliz'd, fhines thro' the Gothic cloud
Of time and language o'er thy genius thrown.

 May my fong foften, as thy DAUGHTERS I,
BRITANNIA, hail; for beauty is their own,
The feeling heart, fimplicity of life,
And elegance, and tafte: the faultlefs form,
Shap'd by the hand of harmony; the cheek,
Where the live crimfon, thro' the native white
Soft-fhooting, o'er the face diffufes bloom,
And every namelefs grace; the parted lip,
Like the red rofe-bud moift with morning-dew,
Breathing delight; and, under flowing jet,
Or funny ringlets, or of circling brown,
The neck flight-fhaded, and the fwelling breaft;
The look refiftlefs, piercing to the foul,
And by the foul inform'd, when dreft in love
She fits high-fmiling in the confcious eye.

 Ifland of blifs! amid the fubject feas,
That thunder round thy rocky coafts, fet up,
At once the wonder, terror, and delight,
Of diftant nations; whofe remoteft fhores
Can foon be fhaken by thy naval arm;
Not to be fhook thyfelf, but all affaults
Baffling, as thy hoar cliffs the loud fea-wave.

 O THOU! by whofe almighty *Nod* the fcale
Of empire rifes, or alternate falls,
Send forth the faving VIRTUES round the land,
In bright patrol: white *Peace*, and focial *Love*;
The tender-looking *Charity*, intent
On gentle deeds, and fhedding tears thro' fmiles;
Undaunted *Truth*, and *Dignity* of mind;
Courage compos'd, and keen; found *Temperance,*

Healthful in heart and look; clear *Chaſtity*,
With bluſhes reddening as ſhe moves along,
Diſordered at the deep regard ſhe draws;
Rough *Induſtry*; *Activity* untir'd,
With copious life inform'd, and all awake:
While in the radiant front, ſuperior ſhines
That firſt paternal virtue, *Public Zeal*;
Who throws o'er all an equal wide ſurvey,
And, ever muſing on the common weal,
Still labours glorious with ſome great deſign.

   Low walks the ſun, and broadens by degrees,
Juſt o'er the verge of day. The ſhifting clouds
Aſſembled gay, a richly-gorgeous train,
In all their pomp attend his ſetting throne.
Air, earth, and ocean ſmile immenſe. And now,
As if his weary chariot ſought the bowers
Of *Amphitritè*, and her tending nymphs,
(So *Grecian* fable ſung) he dips his orb;
Now half-immers'd; and now a golden curve
Gives one bright glance, then total diſappears.

   For ever running an enchanted round,
Paſſes the day, deceitful, vain, and void;
As fleets the viſion o'er the formful brain,
This moment hurrying wild th' impaſſion'd ſoul,
The next in nothing loſt. 'Tis ſo to him,
The dreamer of this earth, an idle blank:
A ſight of horror to the cruel wretch,
Who all day long in ſordid pleaſure roll'd,
Himſelf an uſeleſs load, has ſquander'd vile,
Upon his ſcoundrel train, what might have chear'd
A drooping family of modeſt worth.
But to the generous ſtill-improving mind,
That gives the hopeleſs heart to ſing for joy,
Diffuſing kind beneficence around,

Boaftlefs, as now defcends the filent dew;
To him the long review of order'd life
Is inward rapture, only to be felt.

   Confefs'd from yonder flow-extinguifh'd clouds,
All ether foftening, fober *Evening* takes
Her wonted ftation in the middle air;
A thoufand *fhadows* at her beck. Firft *this*
She fends on earth; then *that* of deeper dye
Steals foft behind; and then a *deeper* ftill,
In circle following circle, gathers round,
To clofe the face of things. A frefher gale
Begins to wave the wood, and ftir the ftream,
Sweeping with fhadowy guft the fields of corn;
While the quail clamours for his running mate.
Wide o'er the thiftly lawn, as fwells the breeze,
A whitening fhower of vegetable down
Amufive floats. The kind impartial care
Of Nature nought difdains: thoughtful to feed
Her loweft fons, and clothe the coming year,
From field to field the feathered feeds fhe wings.

   His folded flock fecure, the fhepherd home
Hies, merry-hearted; and by turns relieves
The ruddy milk-maid of her brimming pail;
The beauty whom perhaps his witlefs heart,
Unknowing what the joy-mixt anguifh means,
Sincerely loves, by that beft language fhewn
Of cordial glances, and obliging deeds.
Onward they pafs, o'er many a panting height,
And valley funk, and unfrequented; where
At fall of eve the fairy people throng,
In various game, and revelry, to pafs
The fummer night, as village-ftories tell.
But far about they wander from the grave
Of him, whom his ungentle fortune urg'd

Againſt his own ſad breaſt to lift the hand
Of impious violence. The lonely tower
Is alſo ſhun'd; whoſe mournful chambers hold,
So night-ſtruck Fancy dreams, the yelling ghoſt.
    Among the crooked lanes, on every hedge,
The glow-worm lights his gem; and, thro' the dark,
A moving radiance twinkles. *Evening* yields
The world to *Night*; not in her winter-robe
Of maſſy Stygian woof, but looſe array'd
In mantle dun. A faint erroneous ray,
Glanc'd from th' imperfect ſurfaces of things,
Flings half an image on the ſtraining eye;
While wavering woods, and villages, and ſtreams,
And rocks, and mountain-tops, that long retain'd
Th' aſcending gleam, are all one ſwimming ſcene,
Uncertain if beheld. Sudden to heaven
Thence weary viſion turns; where, leading ſoft
The ſilent hours of love, with pureſt ray
Sweet *Venus* ſhines; and from her genial riſe,
When day-light ſickens till it ſprings afreſh,
Unrival'd reigns, the faireſt lamp of night.
As thus th' effulgence tremulous I drink,
With cheriſh'd gaze, the lambent lightnings ſhoot
Acroſs the ſky; or horizontal dart
In wondrous ſhapes: by fearful murmuring crowds
Portentous deem'd. Amid the radiant orbs,
That more than deck, that animate the ſky,
The life-infuſing ſuns of other worlds;
Lo! from the dread immenſity of ſpace
Returning, with accelerated courſe,
The ruſhing comet to the ſun deſcends;
And as he ſinks below the ſhading earth,
With awful train projected o'er the heavens,
The guilty nations tremble. But, above

Thofe fuperftitious horrors that enflave
The fond fequacious herd, to myftic faith
And blind amazement prone, the enlightened few,
Whofe godlike minds philofophy exalts,
The glorious ftranger hail. They feel a joy
Divinely great; they in their powers exult,
That wondrous force of thought, which mounting fpurns
This dufky fpot, 'and meafures all the fky;
While, from his far excurfion thro' the wilds
Of barren ether, faithful to his time,
They fee the blazing wonder rife anew,
In feeming terror clad, but kindly bent
To work the will of all-fuftaining LOVE:
From his huge vapoury train perhaps to fhake
Reviving moifture on the numerous orbs,
Thro' which his long ellipfis winds; perhaps
To lend new fuel to 'declining funs,
To light up worlds, and feed th' eternal fire.
    With thee, ferene PHILOSOPHY, with thee,
And thy bright garland, let me crown my fong!
Effufive fource of evidence, and truth!
A luftre fhedding o'er th' ennobled mind,
Stronger than fummer-noon; and pure as that,
Whofe mild vibrations footh the parted foul,
New to the dawning of celeftial day.
Hence thro' her nourifh'd powers, enlarg'd by thee,
She fprings aloft, with elevated pride,
Above the tangling mafs of low defires,
That bind the fluttering crowd; and, angel-wing'd,
The heights of fcience and of virtue gains,
Where all is calm and clear; with Nature round,
Or in the ftarry regions, or th' abyfs,
To Reafon's and to Fancy's eye difplay'd:
The *Firft* up-tracing, from the dreary void,

The chain of caufes and effects to HIM,
The world-producing ESSENCE, who alone
Poffeffes being; while the *Laft* receives
The whole magnificence of heaven and earth,
And every beauty, delicate or bold,
Obvious or more remote, with livelier fenfe,
Diffufive painted on the rapid mind.

    Tutor'd by thee, hence POETRY exalts
Her voice to ages; and informs the page
With mufic, image, fentiment, and thought,
Never to die! the treafure of mankind!
Their higheft honour, and their trueft joy!

    Without thee what were unenlightened Man?
A favage roaming thro' the woods and wilds,
In queft of prey; and with th' unfafhioned furr
Rough-clad; devoid of every finer art,
And elegance of life. Nor happinefs
Domeftic, mix'd of tendernefs and care,
Nor moral excellence, nor focial blifs,
Nor guardian law were his; nor various fkill
To turn the furrow, or to guide the tool
Mechanic; nor the heaven-conducted prow
Of navigation bold, that fearlefs braves
The burning line or dares the wintry pole;
Mother fevere of infinite delights!
Nothing, fave rapine, indolence, and guile,
And woes on woes, a ftill-revolving train!
Whofe horrid circle had made human life
Than non-exiftence worfe: but, taught by thee,
Ours are the plans of policy, and peace;
To live like brothers, and conjunctive all
Embellifh life. While thus laborious crowds
Ply the tough oar, PHILOSOPHY directs
The ruling helm; or like the liberal breath

Of potent Heaven, invifible, the fail
Swells out, and bears th' inferior world along.
  Nor to this evanefcent fpeck of earth
Poorly confin'd, the radiant tracts on high
Are her exalted range; intent to gaze
Creation thro'; and, from that full complex
Of never-ending wonders, to conceive
Of the SOLE BEING right, who *fpoke the Word,*
And Nature mov'd complete.   With inward view,
Thence on th' ideal kingdom fwift fhe turns
Her eye; and inftant, at her powerful glance,
Th' obedient phantoms vanifh or appear;
Compound, divi⬤, and into order fhift,
Each to his rank, from plain perception up
To the fair forms of Fancy's fleeting train:
To reafon then, deducing truth from truth;
And notion quite abftract; where firft begins
The world of fpirits, action all, and life
Unfettered, and unmixt.   But here the cloud,
So wills ETERNAL PROVIDENCE, fits deep.
Enough for us to know that this dark ftate,
In wayward paffions loft, and vain purfuits,
This Infancy of Being, cannot prove
The final Iffue of the works of GOD,
By boundlefs LOVE and perfect WISDOM form'd,
And ever rifing with the rifing mind.

Dodd del.   T. Cook sculp.

AUTUMN.

Published as the Act directs Jan.ʸᵈ 1ˢᵗ 1778 by Thoˢ Cadell, in the Strand.

UTUMN

Vol. I.   H

THE ARGUMENT.

The fubject propofed. Addreffed to Mr. Onslow; A profpect of the fields ready for harveft. Reflections in praife of induftry raifed by that view. Reaping. A tale relative to it. A harveft ftorm. Shooting and hunting, their barbarity. A ludicrous account of fox-hunting. A view of an orchard. Wall-fruit. A vineyard. A defcription of fogs, frequent in the latter part of *Autumn :* whence a digreffion, enquiring into the rife of fountains and rivers. Birds of feafon confidered, that now fhift their habitation. The prodigious number of them that cover the northern and weftern ifles of SCOT-LAND. Hence a view of the country. A profpect of the dif-coloured, fading woods. After a gentle dufky day, moon-light. Autumnal meteors. Morning: to which fucceeds a calm, pure, fun-fhiny day, fuch as ufually fhuts up the feafon. The harveft being gathered in, the country diffolved in joy. The whole con-cludes with a panegyric on a philofophical country life.

A U T U M N.

CROWN'D with the fickle and the wheaten fheaf,
    While AUTUMN, nodding o'er the yellow plain,
Comes jovial on; the *Doric* reed once more,
Well pleas'd, I tune. Whate'er the Wintry froft
Nitrous prepar'd; the various-bloffom'd Spring
Put in white promife forth; and Summer funs
Concofted ftrong, rufh boundlefs now to view,
Full, perfeft all, and fwell my glorious theme.
    ONSLOW! the Mufe, ambitious of thy name,
To grace, infpire, and dignify her fong,
Would from the *Public Voice* thy gentle ear
A while engage. Thy noble cares fhe knows,
The patriot virtues that diftend thy thought,
Spread on thy front, and in thy bofom glow;
While liftening fenates hang upon thy tongue,
Devolving thro' the maze of eloquence
A roll of periods, fweeter than her fong.
But fhe too pants for public virtue, fhe,
Tho' weak of power, yet ftrong in ardent will,
Whene'er her country rufhes on her heart,
Affumes a bolder note, and fondly tries
To mix the patriot's with the poet's flame.

When the bright *Virgin* gives the beauteous days,
And *Libra* weighs in equal fcales the year;
From heaven's high cope the fierce effulgence fhook
Of parting Summer, a ferener blue,
With golden light enlivened, wide invefts
The happy world. Attemper'd funs arife,
Sweet-beam'd, and fhedding oft thro' lucid clouds
A pleafing calm; while broad, and brown, below
Extenfive harvefts hang the heavy head.
Rich, filent, deep, they ftand; for not a gale
Rolls its light billows o'er the bending plain:
A calm of plenty! till the ruffled air
Falls from its poife, and gives the breeze to blow.
Rent is the fleecy mantle of the fky;
The clouds fly different; and the fudden fun
By fits effulgent gilds th' illumin'd field,
And black by fits the fhadows fweep along.
A gaily-checker'd heart-expanding view,
Far as the circling eye can fhoot around,
Unbounded toffing in a flood of corn.
    Thefe are thy bleffings, INDUSTRY! rough power!
Whom labour ftill attends, and fweat, and pain;
Yet the kind fource of every gentle art,
And all the foft civility of life:
Raifer of human kind! by Nature caft,
Naked, and helplefs, out amid the woods
And wilds, to rude inclement elements;
With various feeds of art deep in the mind
Implanted, and profufely pour'd around
Materials infinite; but idle all.
Still unexerted, in th' unconfcious breaft,
Slept the lethargic powers; corruption ftill,
Voracious, fwallowed what the liberal hand

Of bounty fcatter'd o'er the favage year:
And ftill the fad barbarian, roving, mix'd
With beafts of prey; or for his acorn-meal
Fought the fierce tufky boar; a fhivering wretch!
Aghaft, and comfortlefs, when the bleak north,
With Winter charg'd, let the mix'd tempeft fly,
Hail, rain, and fnow, and bitter-breathing froft:
Then to the fhelter of the hut he fled;
And the wild feafon, fordid, pin'd away.
For home he had not; home is the refort
Of love, of joy, of peace and plenty, where,
Supporting and fupported, polifh'd friends,
And dear relations mingle into blifs.
But this the rugged favage never felt,
Even defolate in crowds; and thus his days
Roll'd heavy, dark, and unenjoy'd along:
A wafte of time! till INDUSTRY approach'd,
And rous'd him from his miferable floth:
His faculties unfolded; pointed out,
Where lavifh Nature the directing hand
Of Art demanded; fhew'd him how to raife
His feeble force by the mechanic powers,
To dig the mineral from the vaulted earth,
On what to turn the piercing rage of fire,
On what the torrent, and the gather'd blaft;
Gave the tall ancient foreft to his ax;
Taught him to chip the wood, and hew the ftone,
Till by degrees the finifh'd fabric rofe;
Tore from his limbs the blood-polluted fur,
And wrapt them in the woolly veftment warm,
Or bright in gloffy filk, and flowing lawn;
With wholefome viands fill'd his table, pour'd
The generous glafs around, infpir'd to wake
The life-refining foul of decent wit:

Nor ſtopp'd at barren bare neceſſity;
But ſtill advancing bolder, led him on
To pomp, to pleaſure, elegance, and grace;
And, breathing high ambition thro' his ſoul,
Set ſcience, wiſdom, glory, in his view,
And bade him be the *Lord* of all below.

 Then gathering men their natural powers combin'd,
And form'd a *Public*; to the general good
Submitting, aiming, and conducting all.
For this the *Patriot-Council* met, the full,
The free, and fairly repreſented *Whole*;
For this they plann'd the holy guardian laws,
Diſtinguiſh'd orders, animated arts,
And with joint force *Oppreſſion* chaining, ſet
Imperial Juſtice at the helm; yet ſtill
To them accountable: nor ſlaviſh dream'd
That toiling millions muſt reſign their weal,
And all the honey of their ſearch, to ſuch
As for themſelves alone themſelves have rais'd.

 Hence every form of cultivated life
In order ſet, protected, and inſpir'd,
Into perfection wrought. Uniting all,
Society grew numerous, high, polite,
And happy. Nurſe of art! the city rear'd
In beauteous pride her tower-encircled head;
And, ſtretching ſtreet on ſtreet, by thouſands drew,
From twining woody haunts, or the tough yew
To bows ſtrong-ſtraining, her aſpiring ſons.

 Then COMMERCE brought into the public walk
The buſy merchant; the big warehouſe built;
Rais'd the ſtrong crane; choak'd up the loaded ſtreet
With foreign plenty; and thy ſtream, O THAMES,
Large, gentle, deep, majeſtic, king of floods!
Choſe for his grand reſort. On either hand,

Like a long wintry foreft, groves of mafts
Shot up their fpires; the bellying fheet between
Poffefs'd the breezy void; the footy hulk
Steer'd fluggifh on; the fplendid barge along
Row'd, regular, to harmony; around,
The boat, light-fkimming, ftretch'd its oary wings;
While deep the various voice of fervent toil
From bank to bank increas'd; whence ribb'd with oak,
To bear the BRITISH THUNDER, black, and bold,
The roaring veffel rufh'd into the main.
   Then too the pillar'd dome, magnific, heav'd
Its ample roof; and Luxury within
Pour'd out her glittering ftores: the canvas fmooth,
With glowing life protuberant, to the view
Embodied rofe; the ftatue feem'd to breathe,
And foften into flefh, beneath the touch
Of forming art, imagination-flufh'd.
   All is the gift of INDUSTRY; whate'er
Exalts, embellifhes, and renders life
Delightful. Penfive Winter chear'd by him
Sits at the focial fire, and happy hears
Th' excluded tempeft idly rave along;
His harden'd fingers deck the gaudy Spring;
Without him Summer were an arid wafte;
Nor to th' Autumnal months could thus tranfmit
Thofe full, mature, immeafurable ftores,
That, waving round, recall my wandering fong.
   Soon as the morning trembles o'er the fky,
And, unperceiv'd, unfolds the fpreading day;
Before the ripened field the reapers ftand,
In fair array; each by the lafs he loves,
To bear the rougher part, and mitigate
By namelefs gentle offices her toil.
At once they ftoop and fwell the lufty fheaves;
H 4

While thro' their chearful band the rural talk,
The rural fcandal, and the rural jeft,
Fly harmlefs, to deceive the tedious time,
And fteal unfelt the fultry hours away.
Behind the mafter walks, builds up the fhocks;
And, confcious, glancing oft on every fide
His fated eye, feels his heart heave with joy.
The gleaners fpread around, and here and there,
Spike after fpike, their fcanty harveft pick.
Be not too narrow, hufbandmen! but fling
From the full fheaf, with charitable ftealth,
The liberal handful. Think, oh grateful think!
How good the God of Harvest is to you;
Who pours abundance o'er your flowing fields;
While thefe unhappy partners of your kind
Wide-hover round you, like the fowls of heaven,
And afk their humble dole. The various turns
Of fortune ponder; that your fons may want
What now, with hard reluctance, faint, ye give.
    The lovely young Lavinia once had friends;
And Fortune fmil'd, deceitful, on her birth.
For, in her helplefs years depriv'd of all,
Of every ftay, fave Innocence and Heaven,
She, with her widow'd mother, feeble, old,
And poor, liv'd in a cottage, far retir'd
Among the windings of a woody vale;
By folitude and deep furrounding fhades,
But more by bafhful modefty, conceal'd.
Together thus they fhunn'd the cruel fcorn
Which virtue, funk to poverty, would meet
From giddy paffion and low-minded pride:
Almoft on Nature's common bounty fed;
Like the gay birds that fung them to repofe,
Content, and carelefs of to-morrow's fare.

Her form was freſher than the morning roſe,
When the dew wets its leaves; unſtain'd and pure,
As is the lily, or the mountain ſnow.
The modeſt virtues mingled in her eyes,
Still on the ground dejeċted, darting all
Their humid beams into the blooming flowers:
Or when the mournful tale her mother told,
Of what her faithleſs fortune promis'd once,
Thrill'd in her thought, they, like the dewy ſtar
Of evening, ſhone in tears. A native grace
Sat fair-proportion'd on her poliſh'd limbs,
Veil'd in a ſimple robe, their beſt attire,
Beyond the pomp of dreſs; for lovelineſs
Needs not the foreign aid of ornament,
But is when unadorn'd adorn'd the moſt.
Thoughtleſs of beauty, ſhe was beauty's ſelf,
Recluſe amid the cloſe-embowering woods.
As in the hollow breaſt of *Appenine*,
Beneath the ſhelter of encircling hills,
A myrtle riſes, far from human eye,
And breathes its balmy fragrance o'er the wild:
So flouriſh'd blooming, and unſeen by all,
The ſweet LAVINIA; till, at length, compell'd
By ſtrong Neceſſity's ſupreme command,
With ſmiling patience in her looks, ſhe went
To glean PALEMON's fields. The pride of ſwains
PALEMON was, the generous, and the rich;
Who led the rural life in all its joy
And elegance, ſuch as *Arcadian* ſong
Tranſmits from ancient uncorrupted times;
When tyrant cuſtom had not ſhackled Man,
But free to follow Nature was the mode.
He then, his fancy with autumnal ſcenes
Amuſing, chanc'd beſide his reaper-train

To walk, when poor Lavinia drew his eye;
Unconfcious of her power, and turning quick
With unaffected bluſhes from his gaze:
He faw her charming, but he faw not half
The charms her downcaſt modeſty conceal'd.
That very moment love and chaſte defire
Sprung in his boſom, to himſelf unknown;
For ſtill the world prevail'd, and its dread laugh,
Which ſcarce the firm phiļoſopher can ſcorn,
Should his heart own a gleaner in the field:
And thus in ſecret to his ſoul he ſigh'd.
   " What pity! that ſo delicate a form,
" By beauty kindled, where enlivening ſenſe
" And more than vulgar goodneſs ſeem to dwell,
" Should be devoted to the rude embrace
" Of ſome indecent clown! She looks, methinks,
" Of old Acasto's line; and to my mind
" Recalls that patron of my happy life,
" From whom my liberal fortune took its riſe;
" Now to the duſt gone down; his houſes, lands,
" And once fair-ſpreading family, diſſolv'd.
" 'Tis ſaid that in ſome lone obſcure retreat,
" Urg'd by remembrance ſad, and decent pride,
" Far from thoſe ſcenes which knew their better days,
" His aged widow and his daughter live,
" Whom yet my fruitleſs ſearch could never find.
" Romantic wiſh! would this the daughter were!"
   When, ſtrict enquiring, from herſelf he found
She was the ſame, the daughter of his friend,
Of bountiful Acasto; who can ſpeak
The mingled paſſions that ſurpriz'd his heart,
And thro' his nerves in ſhivering tranſport ran?
Then blaz'd his ſmother'd flame, avow'd, and bold:
And as he view'd her, ardent, o'er and o'er,

Love, gratitude, and pity wept at once.
Confus'd, and frightened at his fudden tears,
Her rifing beauties flufh'd a higher bloom,
As thus PALEMON, paffionate and juft,
Pour'd out the pious rapture of his foul.

   " And art thou then ACASTO's dear remains?
" She, whom my reftlefs gratitude has fought,
" So long in vain? O heavens! the very fame,
" The foftened image of my noble friend,
" Alive his every look, his every feature,
" More elegantly touch'd. Sweeter than Spring!
" Thou fole furviving bloffom from the root
" That nourifh'd up my fortune! Say, ah where,
" In what fequefter'd defart, haft thou drawn
" The kindeft afpect of delighted HEAVEN?
" Into fuch beauty fpread, and blown fo fair;
" Tho' poverty's cold wind, and crufhing rain,
" Beat keen, and heavy, on thy tender years?
" O let me now, into a richer foil,
" Tranfplant thee fafe! where vernal funs, and fhowers,
" Diffufe their warmeft, largeft influence;
" And of my garden be the pride, and joy!
" Ill it befits thee, oh it ill befits
" ACASTO's daughter, his whofe open ftores,
" Tho' vaft, were little to his ampler heart,
" The father of a country, thus to pick
" The very refufe of thofe harveft-fields,
" Which from his bounteous friendfhip I enjoy.
" Then throw that fhameful pittance from thy hand,
" But ill apply'd to fuch a rugged tafk;
" The fields, the mafter, all, my fair, are thine;
" If to the various bleffings which thy houfe
" Has on me lavifh'd, thou wilt add that blifs,
" That deareft blifs, the power of bleffing thee!"

Here ceas'd the youth: yet ftill his fpeaking eye
Exprefs'd the facred triumph of his foul,
With confcious virtue, gratitude, and love,
Above the vulgar joy divinely rais'd.
Nor waited he reply.   Won by the charm
Of goodnefs irrefiftible, and all
In fweet diforder loft, fhe blufh'd confent.
The news immediate to her mother brought,
While, pierc'd with anxious thought, fhe pin'd away
The lonely moments for LAVINIA's fate;
Amaz'd, and fcarce believing what fhe heard,
Joy feiz'd her wither'd veins, and one bright gleam
Of fetting life fhone on her evening-hours:
Not lefs enraptur'd than the happy pair;
Who flourifh'd long in tender blifs, and rear'd
A numerous offspring, lovely like themfelves,
And good, the grace of all the country round.
    Defeating oft the labours of the year,
The fultry fouth collects a potent blaft.
At firft, the groves are fcarcely feen to ftir
Their trembling tops; and a ftill murmur runs
Along the foft-inclining fields of corn.
But as the aërial tempeft fuller fwells,
And in one mighty ftream, invifible,
Immenfe, the whole excited atmofphere,
Impetuous rufhes o'er the founding world:
Strain'd to the root, the ftooping foreft pours
A ruftling fhower of yet untimely leaves.
High-beat, the circling mountains eddy in,
From the bare wild, the diffipated ftorm,
And fend it in a torrent down the vale.
Expos'd, and naked, to its utmoft rage,
Thro' all the fea of harveft rolling round,
The billowy plain floats wide; nor can evade,

Tho' pliant to the blaft, its feizing force;
Or whirl'd in air, or into vacant chaff
Shook wafte.   And fometimes too a burft of rain,
Swept from the black horizon, broad, defcends
In one continuous flood.   Still over head
The mingling tempeft weaves its gloom, and ftill
The deluge deepens; till the fields around
Lie funk, and flatted, in the fordid wave.
Sudden, the ditches fwell; the meadows fwim.
Red, from the hills, innumerable ftreams
Tumultuous roar; and high above its banks
The river lift; before whofe rufhing tide,
Herds, flocks, and harvefts, cottages, and fwains,
Roll mingled down; all that the winds had fpar'd
In one wild moment ruin'd; the big hopes,
And well-earn'd treafures of the painful year.
Fled. to fome eminence, the hufbandman
Helplefs beholds the miferable wreck
Driving along; his drowning ox at once
Defcending, with his labours fcatter'd round,
He fees; and inftant o'er his fhivering thought
Comes Winter unprovided, and a train
Of clamant children dear.   Ye mafters, then,
Be mindful of the rough laborious hand,
That finks you foft in elegance and eafe;
Be mindful of thofe limbs in ruffet clad,
Whofe toil to yours is warmth, and graceful pride;
And oh be mindful of that fparing board,
Which covers yours with luxury profufe,
Makes your glafs fparkle, and your fenfe rejoice!
Nor cruelly demand what the deep rains,
And all-involving winds have fwept away.
    Here the rude clamour of the fportfman's joy,
The gun faft-thundering, and the winded horn,

Would tempt the Mufe to fing the *rural Game*:
How, in his mid-career, the fpaniel ftruck,
Stiff, by the tainted gale, with open nofe,
Outftretch'd, and finely fenfible, *draws* full,
Fearful, and cautious, on the latent prey;
As in the fun the circling covey bafk
Their varied plumes, and watchful every way,
Thro' the rough ftubble turn the fecret eye.
Caught in the mefhy fnare, in vain they beat
Their idle wings, intangled more and more:
Nor on the furges of the boundlefs air,
Tho' borne triumphant, are they fafe; the gun,
Glanc'd juft, and fudden, from the fowler's eye
O'ertakes their founding pinions; and again,
Immediate, brings them from the towering wing,
Dead to the ground; or drives them wide-difpers'd,
Wounded, and wheeling various, down the wind.

    Thefe are not fubjects for the peaceful mufe,
Nor will fhe ftain with fuch her fpotlefs fong;
Then moft delighted, when fhe focial fees
The whole mix'd animal-creation round
Alive, and happy. 'Tis not joy to her,
This falfely-chearful barbarous game of death;
This rage of pleafure, which the reftlefs youth
Awakes, impatient, with the gleaming morn;
When beafts of prey retire, that all night long,
Urg'd by neceffity, had rang'd the dark,
As if their confcious ravage fhun'd the light,
Afham'd. Not fo the fteady tyrant Man,
Who with the thoughtlefs infolence of power
Inflam'd, beyond the moft infuriate wrath
Of the worft monfter that e'er roam'd the wafte,
For fport alone purfues the cruel chace,
Amid the beamings of the gentle days.

Upbraid, ye ravening tribes, our wanton rage,
For hunger kindles you, and lawlefs want;
But lavifh fed, in Nature's bounty roll'd,
To joy át anguifh, and delight in blood,
Is what your horrid bofoms never knew.

   Poor is the triumph o'er the timid hare!
Scar'd from the corn, and now to fome lone feat
Retir'd: the rufhy fen; the ragged furze,
Stretch'd o'er the ftony heath; the ftubble chapt;
The thiftly lawn; the thick entangled broom;
Of the fame friendly hue, the wither'd fern;
The fallow ground laid open to the fun,
Concoftive; and the nodding fandy bank,
Hung o'er the mazes of the mountain brook.
Vain is her beft precaution; tho' fhe fits
Conceal'd, with folding ears; unfleeping eyes,
By Nature rais'd to take the horizon in;
And head couch'd clofe betwixt her hairy feet,
In aft to fpring away. The fcented dew
Betrays her early labyrinth; and deep,
In fcattered fullen openings, far behind,
With every breeze fhe hears the coming ftorm.
But nearer, and more frequent, as it loads
The fighing gale, fhe fprings amaz'd, and all
The favage foul of game is up at once:
The pack full-opening, various; the fhrill horn
Refounded from the hills; the neighing fteed,
Wild for the chace; and the loud hunter's fhout;
O'er a weak, harmlefs, flying creature, all
Mix'd in mad tumult, and difcordant joy.

   The ftag too, fingled from the herd, where long
He rang'd the branching monarch of the fhades,
Before the tempeft drives. At firft, in fpeed
He, fprightly, puts his faith; and, rous'd by fear,

Gives all his fwift aërial foul to flight;
Againft the breeze he darts, that way the more
To leave the leffening murderous cry behind:
Deception fhort! tho' fleeter than the winds
Blown o'er the keen-air'd mountain by the north,
He burfts the thickets, glances thro' the glades,
And plunges deep into the wildeft wood;
If flow, yet fure, adhefive to the track
Hot-fteaming, up behind him come again
Th' inhuman rout, and from the fhady depth
Expel him, circling thro' his every fhift.
He fweeps the foreft oft; and fobbing fees
The glades, mild opening to the golden day;
Where, in kind conteft, with his butting friends
He wont to ftruggle, or his loves enjoy.
Oft in the full-defcending flood he tries
To lofe the fcent, and lave his burning fides:
Oft feeks the herd; the watchful herd, alarm'd,
With felfifh care avoid a brother's woe.
What fhall he do? His once fo vivid nerves,
So full of buoyant fpirit, now no more.
Infpire the courfe; but fainting breathlefs toil,
Sick, feizes on his heart: he ftands at bay;
And puts his laft weak refuge in defpair.
The big round tears run down his dappled face;
He groans in anguifh; while the growling pack,
Blood-happy, hang at his fair jutting cheft,
And mark his beauteous checker'd fides with gore.
    Of this enough.   But if the filvan youth,
Whofe fervent blood boils into violence,
Muft have the chace; behold, defpifing flight,
The rous'd-up lion, refolute, and flow,
Advancing full on the protended fpear,
And coward-band, that circling wheel aloof.

Slunk from the cavern, and the troubled wood,
See the grim wolf; on him his fhaggy foe
Vindictive fix, and let the ruffian die:
Or, growling horrid, as the brindled boar
Grins fell deftruction, to the monfter's heart
Let the dart lighten from the nervous arm.
　　Thefe BRITAIN knows not; give, ye BRITONS, then
Your fportive fury, pitylefs, to pour
Loofe on the nightly robber of the fold:
Him, from his craggy winding haunts unearth'd,
Let all the thunder of the chace purfue.
Throw the broad ditch behind you; o'er the hedge
High-bound, refiftlefs; nor the deep morafs
Refufe, but thro' the fhaking wildernefs
Pick your nice way; into the perilous flood
Bear fearlefs, of the raging inftinct full;
And as you ride the torrent, to the banks
Your triumph found fonorous, running round,
From rock to rock, in circling echos toft;
Then fcale the mountains to their woody tops;
Rufh down the dangerous fteep; and o'er the lawn,
In fancy fwallowing up the fpace between,
Pour all your fpeed into the rapid game.
For happy he! who tops the wheeling chace;
Has every maze evolv'd, and every guile
Difclos'd; who knows the merits of the pack;
Who faw the villain feiz'd, and dying hard,
Without complaint, tho' by an hundred mouths
Relentlefs torn: O glorious he, beyond
His daring peers! when the retreating horn
Calls them to ghoftly halls of grey renown,
With woodland honours grac'd; the fox's fur,
Depending decent from the roof; and fpread
Round the drear walls, with antick figures fierce,

The ſtag's large front: he then is loudeſt heard,
When the night ſtaggers with ſeverer toils,
With feats *Theſſalian* Centaurs never knew,
And their repeated wonders ſhake the dome.

   But firſt the fuel'd chimney blazes wide;
The tankards foam; and the ſtrong table groans
Beneath the ſmoking ſirloin, ſtretch'd immenſe
From ſide to ſide; in which, with deſperate knife,
They deep inciſion make, and talk the while
Of ENGLAND's glory, ne'er to be defaced
While hence they borrow vigour: or amain
Into the paſty plung'd, at intervals,
If ſtomach keen can intervals allow,
Relating all the glories of the chace.
Then ſated *Hunger* bids his brother *Thirſt*
Produce the mighty bowl; the mighty bowl,
Swell'd high with fiery juice, ſteams liberal round
A potent gale, delicious, as the breath
Of *Maia* to the love-ſick ſhepherdeſs,
On violets diffus'd, while ſoft ſhe hears
Her panting ſhepherd ſtealing to her arms.
Nor wanting is the brown October, drawn,
Mature and perfect, from his dark retreat
Of thirty years; and now his honeſt front
Flames in the light refulgent, not afraid
Even with the vineyard's beſt produce to vie.
To cheat the thirſty moments, whiſt a while
Walks his dull round, beneath a cloud of ſmoke,
Wreath'd, fragrant, from the pipe; or the quick dice,
In thunder leaping from the box, awake
The ſounding gammon: while romp-loving miſs
Is haul'd about, in gallantry robuſt.

   At laſt theſe puling idleneſſes laid
Aſide, frequent and full, the dry divan

Clofe in firm circle; and fet, ardent, in
For ferious drinking.   Nor evafion fly;
Nor fober fhift, is to the puking wretch.
Indulg'd apart; but earneft, brimming bowls
Lave every foul, the table floating round,
And pavement, faithlefs to the fuddled foot.
Thus as they fwim in mutual fwill, the talk,
Vociferous at once from twenty tongues,
Reels faft from theme to theme; from horfes, hounds,
To church or miftrefs, politics or ghoft,
In endlefs mazes, intricate, perplex'd.
Mean-time, with fudden interruption, loud,
Th' impatient catch burfts from the joyous heart;
That moment touch'd is every kindred foul;
And, opening in a full-mouth'd *Cry* of joy,
The laugh, the flap, the jocund curfe go round;
While, from their flumbers fhook, the kennel'd hounds
Mix in the mufic of the day again.
As when the tempeft that has vex'd the deep
The dark night long, with fainter murmurs falls:
So gradual finks their mirth.   Their feeble tongues
Unable to take up the cumbrous word,
Lie quite diffolv'd.   Before their maudlin eyes,
Seen dim, and blue, the double tapers dance,
Like the fun wading thro' the mifty fky.
Then fliding foft, they drop.   Confus'd above,
Glaffes and bottles, pipes and gazetteers,
As if the table even itfelf was drunk,
Lie a wet broken fcene; and wide, below,
Is heap'd the focial flaughter: where aftride
The *lubber Power* in filthy triumph fits,
Slumbrous, inclining ftill from fide to fide,
And fteeps them drench'd in potent fleep till morn.
Perhaps fome doctor, of tremendous paunch,

Awful and deep, a black abyſs of drink,
Out-lives them all; and from his bury'd flock
Retiring, full of rumination ſad,
Laments the weakneſs of theſe latter times.

But if the rougher ſex by this fierce ſport
Is hurried wild, let not ſuch horrid joy
E'er ſtain the boſom of the BRITISH FAIR.
Far be the ſpirit of the chace from them!
Uncomely courage, unbeſeeming ſkill;
To ſpring the fence, to rein the prancing ſteed;
The cap, the whip, the maſculine attire;
In which they roughen to the ſenſe, and all
The winning ſoftneſs of their ſex is loſt.
In them 'tis graceful to diſſolve at woe;
With every motion, every word, to wave
Quick o'er the kindling cheek the ready bluſh;
And from the ſmalleſt violence to ſhrink
Uñequal, then the lovelieſt in their fears;
And by this ſilent adulation, ſoft,
To their protection more engaging Man.
O may their eyes no miſerable ſight,
Save weeping lovers, ſee! a nobler game,
Thro' Love's enchanting wiles purſued, yet fled,
In chace ambiguous. May their tender limbs
Float in the looſe ſimplicity of dreſs!
And, faſhion'd all to harmony, alone
Know they to ſeize the captivated ſoul,
In rapture warbled from love-breathing lips;
To teach the lute to languiſh; with ſmooth ſtep,
Diſcloſing motion in its every charm,
To ſwim along, and ſwell the mazy dance;
To train the foliage o'er the ſnowy lawn;
To guide the pencil, turn the tuneful page;
To lend new flavour to the fruitful year,

And heighten Nature's dainties: in their race
To rear their graces into fecond life;
To give Society its higheft tafte;
Well-ordered Home Man's beft delight.to make;
And by fubmiffive wifdom, modeft fkill,
With every gentle care-eluding art,
To raife the virtues, animate the blifs,
And fweeten all the toils of human life:
This be the female dignity, and praife.

   Ye fwains now haften to the hazel bank;
Where, down yon dale, the wildly-winding brook
Falls hoarfe from fteep to fteep. In clofe array,
Fit for the thickets and the tangling fhrub,
Ye virgins come. For you their lateft fong
The woodlands raife; the cluftering nuts for you
The lover finds amid the fecret fhade;
And, where they burnifh on the topmoft bough,   .
With active vigour crufhes down the tree;
Or fhakes them ripe from the refigning hufk,
A gloffy fhower, and of an ardent brown,
As are the ringlets of MELINDA's hair: ˙
MELINDA! form'd with every grace complete,
Yet thefe neglecting, above beauty wife,
And far tranfcending fuch a vulgar praife.

  Hence from the bufy joy-refounding fields,
In chearful error, let us tread the maze
Of Autumn, unconfin'd; and tafte, reviv'd,
The breath of orchard big with bending fruit.
Obedient to the breeze and beating ray,
From the deep-loaded bough a mellow fhower
Inceffant melts away. The juicy pear
Lies, in a foft profufion, fcattered round.
A various fweetnefs fwells the gentle race;
By Nature's all-refining hand prepar'd;

Of temper'd fun, and water, earth, and air,
In ever-changing compofition mixt.
Such, falling frequent thro' the chiller night,
The fragrant ftores, the wide-projected heaps
Of apples, which the lufty-handed year,
Innumerous, o'er the blufhing orchard fhakes.
A various fpirit, frefh, delicious, keen,
Dwells in their gelid pores; and, active, points
The piercing cyder for the thirfty tongue:
Thy *native* theme, and boon infpirer too,
PHILLIPS, *Pomona's* bard, the fecond thou
Who nobly durft, in rhyme-unfetter'd verfe,
With BRITISH freedom fing the BRITISH fong:
How, from *Siberian* vats, high-fparkling wines
Foam in tranfparent floods; fome ftrong, to cheer
The wintry revels of the labouring hind;
And tafteful fome, to cool the fummer-hours.
    In this glad feafon, while his fweeteft beams
The fun fheds equal o'er the meekened day;
Oh lofe me in the green delightful walks
Of, DODINGTON, thy feat, ferene, and plain;
Where fimple Nature reigns; and every view,
Diffufive, fpreads the pure *Dorfetian* downs,
In boundlefs profpect; yonder fhagg'd with wood,
Here rich with harveft, and there white with flocks!
Mean-time the grandeur of thy lofty dome,
Far-fplendid, feizes on the ravifh'd eye.
New beauties rife with each revolving day;
New columns fwell; and ftill the frefh Spring finds
New plants to quicken, and new groves to green,
Full of thy genius all! the Mufes' feat:
Where in the fecret bower, and winding walk,
For virtuous YOUNG and thee they twine the bay.
Here wandering oft, fir'd with the reftlefs thirft

Of thy applaufe, I folitary court
Th' infpiring breeze: and meditate the book
Of Nature ever open; aiming thence,
Warm from the heart, to learn the moral fong.
Here, as I fteal along the funny wall,
Where Autumn bafks, with fruit empurpled deep,
My pleafing Theme continual prompts my thought:
Prefents the downy peach; the fhining plum;
The ruddy, fragrant nectarine; and dark,
Beneath his ample leaf, the lufcious fig.
The vine too here her curling tendrils fhoots;
Hangs out her clufters, glowing to the fouth;
And fcarcely wifhes for a warmer fky,

   Turn we a moment Fancy's rapid flight
To vigorous foils, and climes of fair extent;
Where, by the potent fun elated high,
The vineyard fwells refulgent on the day;
Spreads o'er the vale; or up the mountain climbs,
Profufe; and drinks amid the funny rocks,
From cliff to cliff encreas'd, the heightened blaze.
Low bend the weighty boughs. The clufters clear,
Half thro' the foliage feen, or ardent flame,
Or fhine tranfparent; while perfection breathes
White o'er the turgent film the living dew.
As thus they brighten with exalted juice,
Touch'd into flavour by the mingling ray;
The rural youth and virgins o'er the field,
Each fond for each to cull th' autumnal prime,
Exulting rove, and fpeak the vintage nigh.
Then comes the crufhing fwain; the country floats,
And foams unbounded with the mafhy flood;
That by degrees fermented, and refin'd,
Round the rais'd nations pours the cup of joy:
The claret fmooth, red as the lip we prefs

In fparkling fancy, while we drain the bowl;
The mellow-tafted burgundy; and quick,
As is the wit it gives, the gay champaign.
   Now, by the cool declining year condens'd,
Defcend the copious exhalations, check'd
As up the middle fky unfeen they ftole,
And roll the doubling fogs around the hill.
No more the mountain, horrid, vaft, fublime,
Who pours a fweep of rivers from his fides,
And high between contending kingdoms rears
The rocky long divifion, fills the view
With great variety; but in a night
Of gathering vapour, from the baffled fenfe
Sinks dark and dreary. Thence expanding far,
The huge dufk, gradual, fwallows up the plain:
Vanifh the woods; the dim-feen river feems
Sullen, and flow, to roll the mifty wave.
Even in the height of noon oppreft, the fun
Sheds weak, and blunt, his wide-refracted ray;
Whence glaring oft, with many a broadened orb,
He frights the nations. Indiftinct on earth,
Seen thro' the turbid air, beyond the life
Objects appear; and, wilder'd, o'er the wafte
The fhepherd ftalks gigantic. ' Till at laft
Wreath'd dun around, in deeper circles ftill
Succeffive clofing, fits the general fog
Unbounded o'er the world; and, mingling thick,
A formlefs grey confufion covers all.
As when of old (fo fung the HEBREW BARD)
Light, uncollected, thro' the chaos urg'd
Its infant way; nor Order yet had drawn
His lovely train from out the dubious gloom.
   Thefe roving mifts, that conftant now begin
To fmoke along the hilly country, thefe,

With weighty rains, and melted Alpine fnows,
The mountain-cifterns fill, thofe ample ftores
Of water, fcoop'd among the hollow rocks;
Whence gufh the ftreams, the ceafelefs fountains play,
And their unfailing wealth the rivers draw.
Some fages fay, that, where the numerous wave
For ever lafhes the refounding fhore,
Drill'd thro' the fandy ftratum, every way,
The waters with the fandy ftratum rife;
Amid whofe angles infinitely ftrain'd,
They joyful leave their jaggy falts behind,
And clear and fweeten, as they foak along.
Nor ftops the reftlefs fluid, mounting ftill,
Tho' oft amidft th' irriguous vale it fprings;
But to the mountain courted by the fand,
That leads it darkling on in faithful maze,
Far from the parent-main, it boils again
Frefh into day; and all the glittering hill
Is bright with fpouting rills. But hence this vain
Amufive dream! why fhould the waters love
To take fo far a journey to the hills,
When the fweet valleys offer to their toil
Inviting quiet, and a nearer bed?
Or if, by blind ambition led aftray,
They muft afpire; why fhould they fudden ftop
Among the broken mountain's rufhy dells,
And, ere they gain its higheft peak, defert
Th' attractive fand that charm'd their courfe fo long?
Befides, the hard agglomerating falts,
The fpoil of ages, would impervious choke
Their fecret channels; or, by flow degrees,
High as the hills protrude the fwelling vales:
Old Ocean too, fuck'd thro' the porous globe,

Had long ere now forfook his horrid bed,
And brought *Deucalion*'s watry times again.

Say then, where lurk the vaft eternal fprings,
.That, like CREATING NATURE, lie conceal'd
From mortal eye, yet with their lavifh ftores
Refrefh the globe, and all its joyous tribes?
O thou pervading *Genius*, given to Man,
To trace the fecrets of the dark abyfs,
O lay the mountains bare! and wide difplay
Their hidden ftrufture to th' aftonifh'd view!
Strip from the branching *Alps* their piny load;
The huge incumbrance of horrific woods
From *Afian Taurus*, from *Imaus* ftretch'd
Athwart the roving *Tartar*'s fullen bounds!
Give opening *Hemus* to my fearching eye,
And high *Olympus* pouring many a ftream!
O from the founding fummits of the north,
The *Dofrine Hills*, thro' *Scandinavia* roll'd
To fartheft *Lapland* and the frozen main;
From lofty *Caucafus*, far-feen by thofe
Who in the *Cafpian* and black *Euxine* toil;
From cold *Riphean Rocks*, which the wild *Rufs*
Believes the *ftony girdle* * of the world;
And all the dreadful mountains, wrapt in ftorm,
Whence wide *Siberia* draws her lonely floods;
O fweep th' eternal fnows! Hung o'er the deep,
That, ever works beneath his founding bafe,
Bid *Atlas*, propping heaven, as Poets feign,
His fubterranean wonders fpread! unveil

* The *Mufcovites* call the *Riphean* Mountains *Weliki Camenypoys*,
that is, *the great ftony Girdle:* becaufe they fuppofe them to encompafs
the whole earth.

The miny caverns, blazing on the day,
Of *Abyſſinia*'s cloud-compelling cliffs,
And of the bending *Mountains of the Moon* * !
O'ertopping all theſe giant-ſons of earth,
Let the dire *Andes*, from the radiant Line
Stretch'd to the ſtormy ſeas that thunder round
The ſouthern pole, their hideous deeps unfold!
Amazing ſcene! Behold! the glooms diſcloſe,
I ſee the rivers in their infant beds!
Deep, deep I hear them, lab'ring to get free!
I ſee the leaning ſtrata, artful rang'd;
The gaping fiſſures to receive the rains,
The melting ſnows, and ever-dripping fogs.
Strow'd bibulous above I ſee the ſands,
The pebbly gravel next, the layers then
Of mingled moulds, of more retentive earths,
The gutter'd rocks and mazy-running clefts;
That, while the ſtealing moiſture they tranſmit,
Retard its motion, and forbid its waſte.
Beneath th' inceſſant weeping of theſe drains,
I ſee the rocky ſiphons ſtretch'd immenſe,
The mighty reſervoirs, of hardened chalk,
Or ſtiff compacted clay, capacious form'd.
O'erflowing thence, the congregated ſtores,
The cryſtal treaſures of the liquid world,
Thro' the ſtirr'd ſands a bubbling paſſage burſt;
And welling out, around the middle ſteep,
Or from the bottoms of the boſom'd hills,
In pure effuſion flow. United, thus,
Th' exhaling ſun, the vapour-burden'd air,
The gelid mountains, that to rain condens'd

* A range of Mountains in *Africa*, that ſurround almoſt all *Mono-mopata*.

Thefe vapours in continual current draw,
And fend them, o'er the fair-divided earth,
In bounteous rivers to the deep again,
A focial commerce hold, and firm fupport
The full-adjufted harmony of things.

 When Autumn fcatters his departing gleams,
Warn'd of approaching Winter, gathered, play
The fwallow-people; and tofs'd wide around,
O'er the calm fky, in convolution fwift,
The feathered eddy floats: rejoicing once,
Ere to their wintry flumbers they retire;
In clufters clung, beneath the mouldring bank,
And where, unpierc'd by froft, the cavern fweats,
Or rather into warmer climes convey'd,
With other kindred birds of feafon, there
They twitter chearful, till the vernal months
Invite them welcome back: for, thronging, now
Innumerous wings are in commotion all.

 Where the *Rhine* lofes his majeftic force
In *Belgian* plains, won from the raging deep,
By diligence amazing, and the ftrong
Unconquerable hand of Liberty,
The ftork-affembly meets; for many a day,
Confulting deep, and various, ere they take
Their arduous voyage thro' the liquid fky.
And now their rout defign'd, their leaders chofe,
Their tribes adjufted, clean'd their vigorous wings;
And many a circle, many a fhort effay,
Wheel'd round and round, in congregation full
The figur'd flight afcends; and, riding high
The aërial billows, mixes with the clouds.

 Or where the *Northern* ocean, in vaft whirls,
Boils round the naked melancholy ifles
Of fartheft *Thule*, and the *Atlantic* furge

Pours in among the ftormy *Hebrides*;
Who can recount what tranfmigrations there
Are annual made? what nations come and go?
And how the living clouds on clouds arife?
Infinite wings! till all the plume-dark air,
And rude refounding fhore are one wild cry.

Here the plain harmlefs native his fmall flock,
And herd diminutive of many hues,
Tends on the little ifland's verdant fwell,
The fhepherd's fea-girt reign; or, to the rocks
Dire-clinging, gathers his ovarious food;
Or fweeps the fifhy fhore; or treafures up
The plumage, rifing full, to form the bed
Of luxury. And here a while the Mufe,
High hovering o'er the broad cerulean fcene,
Sees CALEDONIA, in romantic view:
Her airy mountains, from the waving main,
Invefted with a keen diffufive fky,
Breathing the foul acute; her forefts huge,
Incult, robuft, and tall, by Nature's hand
Planted of old; her azure lakes between,
Pour'd out extenfive, and of watry wealth
Full; winding deep, and green, her fertile vales;
With many a cool tranflucent brimming flood
Wafh'd lovely, from the *Tweed* (pure *parent ftream*,
Whofe paftoral banks firft heard my *Doric* reed,
With, filvan *Jed*, thy tributary brook)
To where the north-inflated tempeft foams
O'er *Orca*'s or *Betubium*'s higheft peak:
Nurfe of a people, in misfortune's fchool
Train'd up to hardy deeds; foon vifited
By *Learning*, when before the *Gothic* rage
She took her weftern flight. A manly race,
Of unfubmitting fpirit, wife, and brave;

Who ftill thro' bleeding ages ftruggled hard,
(As well unhappy WALLACE can atteft,
Great patriot hero! ill-requited chief!)
To hold a generous undiminifh'd ftate;
Too much in vain! Hence of unequal bounds
Impatient, and by tempting glory borne
O'er every land, for every land their life
Has flow'd profufe, their piercing genius plann'd,
And fwell'd the pomp of peace their faithful toil.
As from their own clear north, in radiant ftreams,
Bright over *Europe* burfts the *Boreal Morn.*

 Oh is there not fome patriot, in whofe power
That beft, that godlike Luxury is placed,
Of blefling thoufands, thoufands yet unborn,
Thro' late pofterity? fome, large of foul,
To chear dejected induftry? to give
A double harveft to the pining fwain?
And teach the labouring hand the fweets of toil?
How, by the fineft art, the native robe
To weave; how, white as hyperborean fnow,
To form the lucid lawn; with venturous oar
How to dafh wide the billow; nor look on,
Shamefully paffive, while *Batavian* fleets
Defraud us of the glittering finny fwarms,
That heave our friths, and crowd upon our fhores;
How all-enlivening trade to roufe, and wing
The profperous fail, from every growing port,
Uninjur'd, round the fea-encircled globe;
And thus, in foul united as in name,
Bid BRITAIN reign the miftrefs of the deep?

 Yes, there are fuch. And full on thee, ARGYLE,
Her hope, her ftay, her darling, and her boaft,
From her firft patriots and her heroes fprung,
Thy fond-imploring Country turns her eye;

In thee, with all a mother's triumph, fees
Her every virtue, every grace combin'd,
Her genius, wisdom, her engaging turn,
Her pride of honour, and her courage try'd,
Calm, and intrepid, in the very throat
Of fulphurous war, on *Tenier*'s dreadful field.
Nor lefs the palm of peace inwreathes thy brow:
For, powerful as thy fword, from thy rich tongue
Perfuafion flows, and wins the high debate;
While mix'd in thee combine the charm of youth,
The force of manhood, and the depth of age.
Thee, FORBES, too, whom every worth attends,
As truth fincere, as weeping friendfhip kind,
Thee, truly generous, and in filence great,
Thy country feels thro' her reviving arts,
Plann'd by thy wifdom, by thy foul inform'd;
And feldom has fhe known a friend like thee.

But fee the fading many-colour'd woods,
Shade deepening over fhade, the country round
Imbrown; a crowded umbrage, dufk, and dun,
Of every hue, from wan declining green
To footy dark.   Thefe now the lonefome Mufe,
Low-whifpering, lead into their leaf-ftrown walks,
And give the feafon in its lateft view.

Mean-time, light-fhadowing all, a fober calm
Fleeces unbounded ether: whofe leaft wave
Stands tremulous, uncertain where to turn
The gentle current: while illumin'd wide,
The dewy-fkirted clouds imbibe the fun,
And thro' their lucid veil his foftened force
Shed o'er the peaceful world.   Then is the time,
For thofe whom wifdom and whom Nature charm,
To fteal themfelves from the degenerate crowd,
And foar above this little fcene of things;

To tread low-thoughted vice beneath their feet;
To footh the throbbing paffions into peace;
And woo lone *Quiet* in her filent walks.
　Thus folitary, and in penfive guife,
Oft let me wander o'er the ruffet mead,
And thro' the faddened grove, where fcarce is heard
One dying ftrain to chear the woodman's toil.
Haply fome widowed fongfter pours his plaint,
Far, in faint warblings, thro' the tawny copfe.
While congregated thrufhes, linnets, larks,
And each wild throat, whofe artlefs ftrains fo late
Swell'd all the mufic of the fwarming fhades,
Robb'd of their tuneful fouls, now fhivering fit
On the dead tree, a dull defpondent flock;
With not a brightnefs waving o'er their plumes,
And nought fave chattering difcord in their note.
O let not, aim'd from fome inhuman eye,
The gun the mufic of the coming year
Deftroy; and harmlefs, unfufpecting harm,
Lay the weak tribes a miferable prey,
In mingled murder, fluttering on the ground!
　The pale defcending year, yet pleafing ftill, .
A gentler mood infpires; for now the leaf
Inceffant ruftles from the mournful grove;
Oft ftartling fuch as, ftudious, walk below,　·
And flowly circles thro' the waving air.
But fhould a quicker breeze amid the boughs
Sob, o'er the fky the leafy deluge ftreams;
Till chok'd, and matted with the dreary fhower,
The foreft-walks, at every rifing gale,
Roll wide the wither'd wafte, and whiftle bleak.
Fled is the blafted verdure of the fields;
And, fhrunk into their beds, the flowery race
Their funny robes refign. Even what remain'd

Of ftronger fruits falls from the naked tree;
And woods, fields, gardens, orchards, all around
The defolated profpect thrills the foul.

He comes! he comes! in every breeze the POWER
Of PHILOSOPHIC MELANCHOLY comes!
His near approach the fudden-ftarting tear,
The glowing cheek, the mild dejected air,
The foftened feature, and the beating heart,
Pierc'd deep with many a virtuous pang, declare.
O'er all the foul his facred influence breathes!
Inflames imagination; thro' the breaft
Infufes every tendernefs;.and far
Beyond dim earth exalts the fwelling thought.
Ten thoufand thoufand fleet ideas, fuch
As never mingled with the vulgar dream,
Crowd faft into the Mind's creative eye.
As faft the correfpondent paffions rife,
As varied, and as high: Devotion rais'd
To rapture, and divine aftonifhment;
The love of Nature unconfin'd, and, chief,
Of human race; the large ambitious wifh,
To make them bleft; the figh for fuffering worth
Loft in obfcurity; the noble fcorn
Of tyrant-pride; the fearlefs great refolve;
The wonder which the dying patriot draws,
Infpiring glory thro' remoteft time;
Th' awakened throb for virtue, and for fame;
The fympathies of love, and friendfhip dear;
With all the *focial Offspring of the heart.*

Oh bear me then to vaft embowering fhades,
To twilight groves, and vifionary vales;
To weeping grottoes, and prophetic glooms;
Where angel forms athwart the folemn dufk,

VOL. I.   K

Tremendous fweep, or feem to fweep along;
And voices more than human, thro' the void
Deep-founding, feize th' enthufiaftic ear!
   Or is this gloom too much? Then lead, ye powers,
That o'er the garden and the rural feat
Prefide, which fhining thro' the chearful land
In countlefs numbers bleft BRITANNIA fees;
O lead me to the wide-extended walks,
The fair majeftic paradife of STOWE*!
Not *Perfian Cyrus* on *Ionia*'s fhore
E'er faw fuch filvan fcenes; fuch various art
By genius fir'd, fuch ardent genius tam'd
By cool judicious art; that, in the ftrife,
All-beauteous Nature fears to be outdone.
And there, O PITT, thy country's early boaft,
There let me fit beneath the fheltered flopes,
Or in that *Temple*† where, in future times,
Thou well fhalt merit a diftinguifh'd name;
And, with thy converfe bleft, catch the laft fmiles
Of Autumn beaming o'er the yellow woods.
While there with thee th' inchanted round I walk,
The regulated wild, gay Fancy then
Will tread in thought the groves of *Attic Land*;
Will from thy ftandard tafte refine her own,
Correct her pencil to the pureft truth
Of Nature, or, the unimpaffion'd fhades
Forfaking, raife it to the human mind.
Or if hereafter fhe, with *jufter* hand,
Shall draw the tragic fcene, inftruct her thou,
To mark the varied movements of the heart,
What every decent character requires,

* The feat of the Lord Vifcount *Cobham*.
† The Temple of Virtue in *Stow-Gardens*.

And every paſſion ſpeaks: O thro' her ſtrain
Breathe thy pathetic eloquence! that moulds
Th' attentive ſenate, charms, perſuades, exalts,
Of honeſt zeal th' indignant lightning throws,
And ſhakes corruption on her venal throne.
While thus we talk, and thro' *Elyſian Vales*
Delighted rove, perhaps a ſigh eſcapes:
What pity, COBHAM, thou thy verdant files
Of ordered trees ſhouldſt here inglorious range,
Inſtead of ſquadrons flaming o'er the field,
And long embattled hoſts! when the proud foe,
The faithleſs vain diſturber of mankind,
Inſulting *Gaul*, has rous'd the world to war;
When keen, once more, within their bounds to preſs
Thoſe poliſh'd robbers, thoſe ambitious ſlaves,
The BRITISH YOUTH would hail thy wiſe command,
Thy temper'd ardor and thy veteran ſkill.

The weſtern ſun withdraws the ſhortened day;
And humid evening, gliding o'er the ſky,
In her chill progreſs, to the ground condens'd
The vapours throws. Where creeping waters ooze,
Where marſhes ſtagnate, and where rivers wind,
Cluſter the rolling fogs, and ſwim along
The duſky mantled lawn. Mean-while the moon
Full-orb'd, and breaking thro' the ſcatter'd clouds,
Shews her broad viſage in the crimſon'd eaſt.
Turn'd to the ſun direct, her ſpotted diſk,
Where mountains riſe, umbrageous dales deſcend,
And caverns deep, as optic tube deſcries,
A ſmaller earth, gives us his blaze again,
Void of its flame, and ſheds a ſofter day.
Now thro' the paſſing cloud ſhe ſeems to ſtoop,
Now up the pure cerulean rides ſublime.

K 2

Wide the pale deluge floats, and ftreaming mild
O'er the fky'd mountain to the fhadowy vale,
While rocks and floods reflect the quivering gleam,
The whole air whitens with a boundlefs tide
Of filver radiance, trembling round the world.
   But when half blotted from the fky her light,
Fainting, permits the ftarry fires to burn
With keener luftre thro' the depth of heaven;
Or near extinct her deadened orb appears,
And fcarce appears, of fickly beamlefs white;
Oft in this feafon, filent from the north
A blaze of meteors fhoots: enfweeping firft
The lower fkies, they all at once converge
High to the crown of heaven, and all at once
Relapfing quick as quickly reafcend,
And mix, and thwart, extinguifh, and renew,
All ether courfing in a maze of light.
   From look to look, contagious thro' the crowd,
The panic runs, and into wondrous fhapes
Th' appearance throws: armies in meet array,
Throng'd with aërial fpears, and fteeds of fire;
Till the long lines of full-extended war
In bleeding fight commixt, the fanguine flood
Rolls a broad flaughter o'er the plains of heaven.
As thus they fcan the vifionary fcene,
On all fides fwells the fuperftitious din,
Incontinent; and bufy frenzy talks
Of blood and battle; cities overturn'd,
And late at night in fwallowing earthquake funk,
Or hideous wrapt in fierce afcending flame;
Of fallow famine, inundation, ftorm;
Of peftilence, and every great diftrefs;
Empires fubvers'd, when ruling fate has ftruck

The unalterable hour: even Nature's felf
Is deem'd to totter on the brink of time.
Not fo the Man of philofophic eye,
And infpect fage; the waving brightnefs he
Curious furveys, inquifitive to know
The caufes, and materials, yet unfix'd,
Of this appearance beautiful and new.
    Now black, and deep, the night begins to fall,
A fhade immenfe.   Sunk in the quenching gloom,
Magnificent and vaft, are heaven and earth.
Order confounded lies; all beauty void;
Diftinction loft; and gay variety
One univerfal blot: fuch the fair power
Of light, to kindle and create the whole.
Drear is the ftate of the benighted wretch,
Who then, bewilder'd, wanders thro' the dark,
Full of pale fancies, and chimeras huge;
Nor vifited by one directive ray,
From cottage ftreaming, or from airy hall.
Perhaps impatient as he ftumbles on,
Struck from the root of flimy rufhes, blue,
The wild-fire fcatters round, or gathered trails
A length of flame deceitful o'er the mofs:
Whither decoy'd by the fantaftic blaze,
Now loft and now renew'd, he finks abforpt,
Rider and horfe, amid the miry gulph:
While ftill, from day to day, his pining wife,
And plaintive children his return await,
In wild conjecture loft.   At other times,
Sent by the *better Genius* of the night,
Innoxious, gleaming on the horfe's mane,
The meteor fits; and fhews the narrow path,

That winding leads thro' pits of death, or elfe
Inftructs him how to take the dangerous ford.

 The lengthened night elaps'd, the morning fhines
Serene, in all her dewy beauty bright,
Unfolding fair the laft autumnal day.
And now the mounting fun difpels the fog;
The rigid hoar-froft melts before his beam;
And hung on every fpray, on every blade
Of grafs, the myriad dew-drops twinkle round.

 Ah fee where robb'd, and murder'd, in that pit
Lies the ftill-heaving hive! at evening fnatch'd,
Beneath the cloud of guilt-concealing night,
And fix'd o'er fulphur: while, not dreaming ill,
The happy people, in their waxen cells,
Sat tending public cares, and planning fchemes
Of temperance, for Winter poor; rejoiced
To mark, full-flowing round, their copious ftores.
Sudden the dark oppreffive fteam afcends;
And, us'd to milder fcents, the tender race,
By thoufands, tumble from their honeyed domes,
Convolv'd, and agonizing in the duft.
And was it then for this you roam'd the Spring,
Intent from flower to flower? for this you toil'd
Ceafelefs the burning Summer-heats away?
For this in Autumn fearch'd the blooming wafte,
Nor loft one funny gleam? for this fad fate?
O Man! tyrannic lord! how long, how long,
Shall proftrate Nature groan beneath your rage,
Awaiting renovation? When obliged,
Muft you deftroy? Of their ambrofial food
Can you not borrow; and, in juft return,
Afford them fhelter from the wintry winds;

Or, as the sharp year pinches, with their own
Again regale them on some smiling day?
See where the stony bottom of their town
Looks desolate, and wild; with here and there
A helpless number, who the ruin'd state
Survive, lamenting weak, cast out to death.
Thus a proud city, populous and rich,
Full of the works of peace, and high in joy,
At theatre or feast, or sunk in sleep,
(As late, *Palermo*, was thy fate) is seiz'd
By some dread earthquake, and convulsive hurl'd
Sheer from the black foundation, stench-involv'd,
Into a gulph of blue sulphureous flame.

   Hence every harsher sight! for now the day,
O'er heaven and earth diffus'd, grows warm, and high,
Infinite splendor! wide investing all.
How still the breeze! save what the filmy threads
Of dew evaporate brushes from the plain.
How clear the cloudless sky! how deeply ting'd
With a peculiar blue! the ethereal arch
How swell'd immense! amid whose azure thron'd
The radiant sun how gay! how calm below
The gilded earth! the harvest-treasures all
Now gather'd in, beyond the rage of storms,
Sure to the swain; the circling fence shut up;
And instant Winter's utmost rage defy'd.
While, loose to festive joy, the country round
Laughs with the loud sincerity of mirth,
Shook to the wind their cares. The toil-strung youth,
By the quick sense of music taught alone,
Leaps wildly graceful in the lively dance.
Her every charm abroad, the village-toast,
Young, buxom, warm, in native beauty rich,

Darts not unmeaning looks; and, where her eye
Points an approving fmile, with double force,
The cudgel rattles, and the wreftler twines.
Age too fhines out; and, garrulous, recounts
The feats of youth. Thus they rejoice; nor think
That, with to-morrow's fun, their annual toil
Begins again the never-ceafing round.

    Oh knew he but his happinefs, of Men
The happieft he! who far from public rage,
Deep in the vale, with a *choice Few* retir'd,
Drinks the pure pleafures of the RURAL LIFE.
What tho' the dome be wanting, whofe proud gate,
Each morning, vomits out the fneaking crowd
Of flatterers falfe, and in their turn abus'd?
Vile intercoufe! What tho' the glittering robe,
Of every hue reflected light can give,
Or floating loofe, or ftiff with mazy gold,
The pride and gaze of fools! opprefs him not?
What tho', from utmoft land and fea purvey'd,
For him each rarer tributary life
Bleeds not, and his infatiate table heaps
With luxury, and death? What tho' his bowl
Flames not with coftly juice; nor funk in beds,
Oft of gay care, he toffes out the night,
Or melts the thoughtlefs hours in idle ftate?
What tho' he knows not thofe fantaftic joys,
That ftill amufe the wanton, ftill deceive;
A face of pleafure, but a heart of pain;
Their hollow moments undelighted all?
Sure peace is his; a folid life, eftranged
To difappointment, and fallacious hope:
Rich in content, in Nature's bounty rich,
In herbs and fruits; whatever greens the Spring,

When heaven defcends in fhowers; or bends the bough
When Summer reddens, and when Autumn beams;
Or in the wintry glebe whatever lies
Conceal'd, and fattens with the richeft fap:
Thefe are not wanting; nor the milky drove,
Luxuriant, fpread o'er all the lowing vale;
Nor bleating mountains; nor the chide of ftreams,
And hum of bees, inviting fleep fincere
Into the guiltlefs breaft, beneath the fhade,
Or thrown at large amid the fragrant hay;
Nor ought befides of profpect, grove, or fong,
Dim grottoes, gleaming lakes, and fountain clear.
Here too dwells fimple truth; plain innocence;
Unfullied beauty; found unbroken youth,
Patient of labour, with a little pleas'd;
Health ever blooming; unambitious toil;
Calm contemplation, and poetic eafe.
    Let others brave the flood in queft of gain,
And beat, for joylefs months, the gloomy wave.
Let fuch as deem it glory to deftroy,
Rufh into blood, the fack of cities feek;
Unpierc'd, exulting in the widow's wail,
The virgin's fhriek, and infant's trembling cry.
Let fome, far diftant from their native foil,
Urg'd or by want or hardened avarice,
Find other lands beneath another fun.
Let *this* thro' cities work his eager way,
By legal outrage and eftablifh'd guile,
The focial fenfe extinct; and *that* ferment
Mad into tumult the feditious herd,
Or melt them down to flavery. Let *thefe*
Infnare the wretched in the toils of law,
Fomenting difcord, and perplexing right,

An iron race! and *thoſe* of fairer front,
But equal inhumanity, in courts,
Deluſive pomp, and dark cabals, delight;
Wreathe the deep bow, diffuſe the lying ſmile,
And tread the weary labyrinth of ſtate.
While he, from all the ſtormy paſſions free
That reſtleſs Men involve, hears, and but hears,
At diſtance ſafe, the human tempeſt roar,
Wrapt cloſe in conſcious peace. The fall of kings,
The rage of nations, and the cruſh of ſtates,
Move not the Man, who, from the world eſcap'd,
In ſtill retreats, and flowery ſolitudes,
To Nature's voice attends, from month to month,
And day to day, thro' the revolving year;
Admiring, ſees her in her every ſhape;
Feels all her ſweet emotions at his heart;
Takes what ſhe liberal gives, nor thinks of more.
He, when young Spring protrudes the burſting gems,
Marks the firſt bud, and ſucks the healthful gale
Into his freſhened ſoul; her genial hours
He full enjoys; and not a beauty blows,
And not an opening bloſſom breathes in vain.
In Summer he, beneath the living ſhade,
Such as o'er frigid *Tempe* wont to wave,
Or *Hemus* cool, reads what the Muſe, of theſe
Perhaps, has in immortal numbers ſung;
Or what ſhe dictates writes; and oft, an eye
Shot round, rejoices in the vigorous year.
When Autumn's yellow luſtre gilds the world,
And tempts the ſickled ſwain into the field,
Seiz'd by the general joy, his heart diſtends
With gentle throes; and thro' the tepid gleams
Deep muſing, then he *beſt* exerts his ſong.

Even Winter wild to him is full of blifs.
The mighty tempeft, and the hoary wafte,
Abrupt, and deep, ftretch'd o'er the buried earth,
Awake to folemn thought.   At night the fkies,
Difclos'd, and kindled, by refining froft,
Pour every luftre on th' exalted eye.
A friend, a book the ftealing hours fecure,
And mark them down for wifdom.   With fwift wing,
O'er land and fea imagination roams;
Or truth, divinely breaking on his mind,
Elates his being, and unfolds his powers;
Or in his breaft heroic virtue burns.
The touch of kindred too and love he feels;
The modeft eye, whofe beams on his alone
Ecftatic fhine; the little ftrong embrace
Of prattling children, twin'd around his neck,
And emulous to pleafe him, calling forth
The fond parental foul.   Nor purpofe gay,
Amufement, dance, or fong, he fternly fcorns;
For happinefs and true philofophy
Are of the focial ftill, and fmiling kind.
This is the life which thofe who fret in guilt,
And guilty cities, never knew; the life,
Led by primeval ages, uncorrupt,
When angels dwelt, and God himfelf, with Man!
   Oh Nature! all-fufficient! over all!
Inrich me with the knowledge of thy works!
Snatch me to heaven; thy rolling wonders there,
World beyond world, in infinite extent,
Profufely fcattered o'er the blue immenfe,
Shew me; their motions, periods, and their laws,
Give me to fcan; thro' the difclofing deep
Light my blind way; the mineral *ftrata* there;

Thruſt, blooming, thence the vegetable world;
O'er that the riſing ſyſtem, more complex,
Of animals; and higher ſtill, the mind,
The varied ſcene of quick-compounded thought,
And where the mixing paſſions endleſs ſhift;
Theſe ever open to my raviſh'd eye;
A ſearch, the flight of time can ne'er exhauſt!
But if to that unequal; if the blood,
In ſluggiſh ſtreams about my heart, forbid
That *beſt* ambition; under cloſing ſhades,
Inglorious, lay me by the lowly brook,
And whiſper to my dreams. From THEE begin,
Dwell all on THEE, with THEE conclude my ſong;
And.let me never never ſtray from THEE!

Dodd del.   T. Cook sculp

WINTER.

Published as the Act directs Jan.ʳ 1ˢᵗ 1778, by Thoˢ. Cadell, in the Strand.

THE ARGUMENT.

The fubject propofed. Addrefs to the Earl of WILMINGTON. Firft approach of Winter. According to the natural courfe of the feafon, various ftorms defcribed. Rain. Wind. Snow. The driving of the fnows: a man perifhing among them; whence reflections on the wants and miferies of human life. The wolves defcending from the *Alps* and *Apennines.* A winter-evening defcribed: as fpent by philofophers; by the country people; in the city. Froft. A view of Winter within the *polar Circle.* A thaw. The whole concluding with moral reflections on a future ftate.

W I N T E R.

SEE, WINTER comes, to rule the varied year,
Sullen and fad, with all his rifing train;
Vapours, and *Clouds*, and *Storms*. Be thefe my theme,
Thefe! that exalt the foul to folemn thought,
And heavenly mufing. Welcome, kindred glooms
Congenial horrors, hail! with frequent foot,
Pleas'd have I, in my chearful morn of life,
When nurs'd by carelefs folitude I liv'd,
And fung of Nature with unceafing joy,
Pleas'd have I wander'd thro' your rough domain;
Trod the pure virgin-fnows, myfelf as pure;
Heard the winds roar, and the big torrent burft;
Or feen the deep-fermenting tempeft brew'd,
In the grim evening fky. Thus pafs'd the time,
Till thro' the lucid chambers of the fouth
Look'd out the joyous SPRING, look'd out, and fmil'd.

　　To thee, the patron of *her firft* effay,
The Mufe, O WILMINGTON! renews her fong.
Since has fhe rounded the revolving year:
Skim'd the gay Spring; on eagle-pinions borne,
Attempted thro' the Summer-blaze to rife;
Then fwept o'er Autumn with the fhadowy gale;
And now among the wintry clouds again,

Roll'd in the doubling ſtorm, ſhe tries to ſoar;
To ſwell her note with all the ruſhing winds;
To ſuit her ſounding cadence to the floods;
As is her theme, her numbers wildly great:
Thrice happy! could ſhe fill thy judging ear
With bold deſcription, and with manly thought.
Nor art thou ſkill'd in awful ſchemes alone,
And how to make a mighty people thrive:
But equal goodneſs, ſound integrity,
A firm unſhaken uncorrupted ſoul
Amid a ſliding age, and burning ſtrong,
Not vainly blazing for thy country's weal,
A ſteady ſpirit regularly free;
Theſe, each exalting each, the ſtateſman light
Into the patriot; theſe, the public hope
And eye to thee converting, bid the Muſe
Record what envy dares not flattery call.
　　Now when the chearleſs empire of the ſky
To *Capricorn* the *Centaur Archer* yields,
And fierce *Aquarius*, ſtains th' inverted year;
Hung o'er the fartheſt verge of heaven, the ſun
Scarce ſpreads thro' ether the dejected day.
Faint are his gleams, and ineffectual ſhoot
His ſtruggling rays, in horizontal lines,
Thro' the thick air; as cloth'd in cloudy ſtorm,
Weak, wan, and broad, he ſkirts the ſouthern ſky;
And, ſoon-deſcending, to the long dark night,
Wide-ſhading all, the proſtrate world reſigns.
Nor is the night unwiſh'd; while vital heat,
Light, life, and joy, the dubious day forſake.
Mean-time, in ſable cincture, ſhadows vaſt,
Deep-ting'd and damp, and congregated clouds,
And all the vapoury turbulence of heaven,
Involve the face of things.　Thus Winter falls,

A heavy gloom oppreffive o'er the world,
Thro' Nature fhedding influence malign,
And roufes up the feeds of dark difeafe.
The foul of Man dies in him, loathing life,
And black with more than melancholy views.
The cattle droop; and o'er the furrowed land,
Frefh from the plough, the dun-difcoloured flocks,
Untended fpreading, crop the wholefome root.
Along the woods, along the moorifh fens,
Sighs the fad *Genius* of the coming ftorm;
And up among the loofe disjointed cliffs,
And fractur'd mountains wild, the brawling brook
And cave, prefageful, fend a hollow moan,
Refounding long in liftening Fancy's ear.
　　Then comes the father of the tempeft forth,
Wrapt in black glooms. Firft joylefs rains obfcure
Drive thro' the mingling fkies with vapour foul;
Dafh on the mountain's brow, and fhake the woods,
That grumbling wave below. The unfightly plain
Lies a brown deluge; as the low-bent clouds
Pour flood on flood, yet unexhaufted ftill
Combine, and deepening into night fhut up
The day's fair face. The wanderers of heaven,
Each to his home, retire; fave thofe that love
To take their paftime in the troubled air,
Or fkimming flutter round the dimply pool.
The cattle from the untafted fields return,
And afk, with meaning lowe, their wonted ftalls,
Or ruminate in the contiguous fhade.
Thither the houfhold feathery people crowd,
The crefted cock, with all his female train,
Penfive, and dripping; while the cottage-hind
Hangs o'er th' enlivening blaze, and taleful there
Recounts his fimple frolic: much he talks,

And much he laughs, nor recks the ftorm that blows
Without, and rattles on his humble roof.

Wide o'er the brim, with many a torrent fwell'd,
And the mix'd ruin of its banks o'erfpread,
At laft the rous'd-up river pours along:
Refiftlefs, roaring, dreadful, down it comes,
From the rude mountain, and the moffy wild,
Tumbling thro' rocks abrupt, and founding far;
Then o'er the fanded valley floating fpreads,
Calm, fluggifh, filent; till again, conftrain'd
Between two meeting hills, it burfts away,
Where rocks and woods o'erhang the turbid ftream;
There gathering triple force, rapid, and deep,
It boils, and wheels, and foams, and thunders through.

NATURE! great parent! whofe unceafing hand
Rolls round the Seafons of the changeful year,
How mighty, how majeftic, are thy works!
With what a pleafing dread they fwell the foul!
That fees aftonifh'd! and aftonifh'd fings!
Ye too, ye winds! that now begin to blow,
With boifterous fweep, I raife my voice to you.
Where are your ftores, ye powerful beings! fay,
Where your aërial magazines referv'd,
To fwell the brooding terrors of the ftorm?
In what far-diftant region of the fky,
Hufh'd in deep filence, fleep ye when 'tis calm?

When from the pallid fky the fun defcends,
With many a fpot, that o'er his glaring orb
Uncertain wanders, ftain'd; red fiery ftreaks
Begin to flufh around.   The reeling clouds
Stagger with dizzy poife, as doubting yet
Which mafter to obey: while rifing flow,
Blank, in the leaden-colour'd eaft, the moon
Wears a wan circle round her blunted horns.

Seen thro' the turbid fluctuating air,
The ftars obtufe emit a fhivered ray;
Or frequent feem to fhoot athwart the gloom,
And long behind them trail the whitening blaze.
Snatch'd in fhort eddies, plays the wither'd leaf;
And on the flood the dancing feather floats.
With broadened noftrils to the fky up-turn'd,
The confcious heifer fnuffs the ftormy gale.
Even as the matron, at her nightly tafk,
With penfive labour draws the flaxen thread,
The wafted taper and the crackling flame
Foretell the blaft. But chief the plumy race,
The tenants of the fky, its changes fpeak.
Retiring from the downs, where all day long
They pick'd their fcanty fare, a blackening train
Of clamorous rooks thick-urge their weary flight,
And feek the clofing fhelter of the grove;
Affiduous, in his bower, the wailing owl
Plies his fad fong. The cormorant on high
Wheels from the deep, and fcreams along the land.
Loud fhrieks the foaring hern; and with wild wing
The circling fea-fowl cleave the flaky clouds.
Ocean, unequal prefs'd, with broken tide
And blind commotion heaves; while from the fhore,
Eat into caverns by the reftlefs wave,
And foreft-ruftling mountains, comes a voice,
That folemn founding bids the world prepare.
Then iffues forth the ftorm with fudden burft,
And hurls the whole precipitated air,
Down, in a torrent. On the paffive main
Defcends th' ethereal force, and with ftrong guft
Turns from its bottom the difcolour'd deep.
Thro' the black night that fits immenfe around,

Lafh'd into foam, the fierce conflicting brine
Seems o'er a thoufand raging waves to burn:
Mean-time the mountain-billows, to the clouds
In dreadful tumult fwell'd, furge above furge,
Burft into chaos with tremendous roar,
And anchor'd navies from their ftations drive,
Wild as the winds acrofs the howling wafte
Of mighty waters: now th' inflated wave
Straining they fcale, and now impetuous fhoot
Into the fecret chambers of the deep,
The wintry *Baltic* thundering o'er their head.
Emerging thence again, before the breath
Of full-exerted heaven they wing their courfe,
And dart on diftant coafts; if fome fharp rock,
Or fhoal infidious break not their career,
And in loofe fragments fling them floating round.
    Nor lefs at land the loofened tempeft reigns.
The mountain thunders; and its fturdy fons
Stoop to the bottom of the rocks they fhade.
Lone on the midnight fteep, and all aghaft,
The dark way-faring ftranger breathlefs toils,
And, often falling, climbs againft the blaft.
Low waves the rooted foreft, vex'd, and fheds
What of its tarnifh'd honours yet remain;
Dafh'd down, and fcatter'd, by the tearing wind's
Affiduous fury, its gigantic limbs.
Thus ftruggling thro' the diffipated grove,
The whirling tempeft raves along the plain;
And on the cottage thatch'd, or lordly roof,
Keen-faftening, fhakes them to the folid bafe.
Sleep frighted flies; and round the rocking dome,
For entrance eager, howls the favage blaft.
Then too, they fay, thro' all the burden'd air,

Long groans are heard, fhrill founds, and diftant fighs,
That, uttered by the Demon of the night,
Warn the devoted wretch of woe and death.

Huge uproar lords it wide. The clouds commix'd
With ftars fwift gliding fweep along the fky.
All nature reels. Till Nature's KING, who oft
Amid tempeftuous darknefs dwells alone,
And on the wings of the careering wind
Walks dreadfully ferene, commands a calm;
Then ftrait air, fea, and earth, are hufh'd at once.

As yet 'tis midnight deep. The weary clouds,
Slow-meeting, mingle into folid gloom.
Now, while the drowfy world lies loft in fleep,
Let me affociate with the ferious *Night*,
And *Contemplation* her fedate compeer;
Let me fhake off th' intrufive cares of day,
And lay the meddling fenfes all afide.

Where now, ye lying vanities of life!
Ye ever-tempting ever-cheating train!
Where are you now? and what is your amount?
Vexation, difappointment, and remorfe.
Sad, fickening thought! and yet deluded Man,
A fcene of crude difjointed vifions paft,
And broken flumbers, rifes ftill refolv'd,
With new-flufh'd hopes, to run the giddy round.

FATHER of light and life! thou GOOD SUPREME!
O teach me what is good! teach me THYSELF!
Save me from folly, vanity, and vice,
From every low purfuit! and feed my foul
With knowledge, confcious peace, and virtue pure;
Sacred, fubftantial, never-fading blifs!

The keener tempefts rife: and fuming dun
From all the livid eaft, or piercing north,
Thick clouds afcend; in whofe capacious womb

A vapoury deluge lies, to fnow congeal'd.
Heavy they roll their fleecy world along;
And the fky faddens with the gathered ftorm.
Thro' the hufh'd air the whitening fhower defcends,
At firft thin wavering, till at laft the flakes
Fall broad, and wide, and faft, dimming the day,
With a continual flow. The cherifh'd fields
Put on their winter-robe of pureft white.
'Tis brightnefs all; fave where the new fnow melts
Along the mazy current. Low, the woods
Bow their hoar head; and, ere the languid fun
Faint from the weft emits his evening ray,
Earth's univerfal face, deep hid, and chill,
Is one wild dazzling wafte, that buries wide
The works of Man. Drooping, the labourer-ox
Stands cover'd o'er with fnow, and then demands
The fruit of all his toil. The fowls of heaven,
Tam'd by the cruel feafon, crowd around
The winnowing ftore, and claim the little boon
Which PROVIDENCE affigns them. One alone,
The red-breaft, facred to the houfhold gods,
Wifely regardful of th' embroiling fky,
In joylefs fields, and thorny thickets, leaves
His fhivering mates, and pays to trufted Man
His annual vifit. Half-afraid, he firft
Againft the window beats; then, brifk, alights
On the warm hearth; then, hopping o'er the floor,
Eyes all the fmiling family afkance,
And pecks, and ftarts, and wonders where he is:
Till more familiar grown, the table-crumbs
Attract his flender feet. The foodlefs wilds
Pour forth their brown inhabitants. The hare,
Tho' timorous of heart, and hard befet
By death in various forms, dark fnares, and dogs,

And more unpitying Men, the garden feeks,
Urg'd on by fearlefs want.   The bleating kind
Eye the bleak heaven, and next the gliftening earth,
With looks of dumb defpair; then, fad difpers'd,
Dig for the withered herb thro' heaps of fnow.

   Now, fhepherds, to your helplefs charge be kind,
Baffle the raging year, and fill their penns
With food at will; lodge them below the ftorm,
And watch them ftrict: for from the bellowing eaft,
In this dire feafon, oft the whirlwind's wing
Sweeps up the burden of whole wintry plains
At one wide waft, and o'er the haplefs flocks,
Hid in the hollow of two neighbouring hills,
The billowy tempeft whelms; till, upward urg'd,
The valley to a fhining mountain fwells,
Tipt with a wreath high-curling in the fky.

   As thus the fnows arife; and foul, and fierce,
All Winter drives along the darkened air;
In his own loofe-revolving fields, the fwain
Difafter'd ftands; fees other hills afcend,
Of unknown joylefs brow; and other fcenes,
Of horrid profpect, fhag the tracklefs plain:
Nor finds the river, nor the foreft, hid
Beneath the formlefs wild; but wanders on
From hill to dale, ftill more and more aftray;
Impatient flouncing thro' the drifted heaps,
Stung with the thoughts of home; the thoughts of home
Rufh on his nerves, and call their vigour forth
In many a vain attempt.   How finks his foul!
What black defpair, what horror fills his heart!
When for the dufky fpot, which fancy feign'd
His tufted cottage rifing thro' the fnow,
He meets the roughnefs of the middle wafte,
Far from the track, and bleft abode of Man;

While round him night refiftlefs clofes faft,
And every tempeft, howling o'er his head,
Renders the favage wildernefs more wild.
Then throng the bufy fhapes into his mind,
Of cover'd pits, unfathomably deep,
A dire defcent! beyond the power of froft;
Of faithlefs bogs; of precipices huge,
Smooth'd up with fnow; and, what is land, unknown;
What water, of the ftill unfrozen fpring,
In the loofe marfh or folitary lake,   .
Where the frefh fountain from the bottom boils.
Thefe check his fearful fteps; and down he finks
Beneath the fhelter of the fhapelefs drift,
Thinking o'er all the bitternefs of death,
Mix'd with the tender anguifh Nature fhoots
Thro' the wrung bofom of the dying Man,
His wife, his children, and his friends unfeen.
In vain for him th' officious wife prepares
The fire fair-blazing, and the veftment warm;
In vain his little children, peeping out
Into the mingling ftorm, demand their fire,
With tears of artlefs innocence. Alas!
Nor wife, nor children, more fhall he behold,
Nor friends, nor facred home. On every nerve
The deadly Winter feizes; fhuts up fenfe;
And, o'er his inmoft vitals creeping cold,
Lays him along the fnows, a ftiffened corfe,
Stretch'd out, and bleaching in the northern blaft.
    Ah little think the gay licentious proud,
Whom pleafure, power, and affluence furround;
They, who their thoughtlefs hours in giddy mirth,
And wanton, often cruel, riot wafte;
Ah little think they, while they dance along,
How many feel, this very moment, death

And all the fad variety of pain.
How many fink in the devouring flood,
Or more devouring flame. How many bleed,
By fhameful variance betwixt Man and Man.
How many pine in want, and dungeon glooms;
Shut from the common air, and common ufe
Of their own limbs. How many drink the cup
Of baleful grief, or eat the bitter bread
Of fery. Sore pierc'd by wintry winds,
How many fhrink into the fordid hut
Of cheerlefs poverty. How many fhake
With all the fiercer tortures of the mind,
Unbounded paffion, madnefs, guilt, remorfe;
Whence tumbled headlong from the height of life,
They furnifh matter for the tragic Mufe.
Even in the vale, where wifdom loves to dwell,
With friendfhip, peace, and contemplation join'd,
How many, rack'd with honeft paffions, droop
In deep retir'd diftrefs. How many ftand
Around the death-bed of their deareft friends,
And point the parting anguifh. Thought fond Man
Of thefe, and all the thoufand namelefs ills,
That one inceffant ftruggle render life,
One fcene of toil, of fuffering, and of fate,
Vice in his high career would ftand appall'd,
And heedlefs rambling Impulfe learn to think;
The confcious heart of Charity would warm,
And her wide wifh Benevolence dilate;
The focial tear would rife, the focial figh;
And into clear perfection, gradual blifs,
Refining ftill, the focial paffions work.
    And here can I forget the generous band*,
Who, touch'd with human woe, redreffive fearch'd

* The Jail Committee, in the year 1729.

Into the horrors of the gloomy jail?
Unpitied, and unheard, where mifery moans;
Where ficknefs pines; where thirft and hunger burn,
And poor misfortune feels the lafh of vice.
While in the land of liberty, the land
Whofe every ftreet and public meeting glow.
With open freedom, little tyrants rag'd;
Snatch'd the lean morfel from the ftarving mouth;
Tore from cold wintry limbs the tatter'd weed;
Even robb'd them of the laft of comforts, fleep;
The free-born BRITON to the dungeon chain'd,
Or, as the luft of cruelty prevail'd,
At pleafure mark'd him with inglorious ftripes;
And crufh'd out lives, by fecret barbarous ways,
That for their country would have toil'd, or bled
O great defign! if executed well,
With patient care, and wifdom-temper'd zeal.
Ye fons of mercy! yet refume the fearch;
Drag forth the legal monfters into light,
Wrench from their hands oppreffion's iron rod,
And bid the cruel feel the pains they give.
Much ftill untouch'd remains; in this rank age,
Much is the patriot's weeding hand requir'd.
The toils of law, (what dark infidious Men
Have cumbrous added to perplex the truth,
And lengthen fimple juftice into trade)
How glorious were the day! that faw thefe broke,
And every Man within the reach of right.
  By wintry famine rous'd, from all the tract
Of horrid mountains which the fhining *Alps*,
And wavy *Appenine*, and *Pyrenees*,
Branch out ftupendous into diftant lands;
Cruel as death, and hungry as the grave!
Burning for blood! bony, and ghaunt, and grim!

Aſſembling wolves in raging troops deſcend;
And, pouring o'er the country, bear along,
Keen as the north-wind ſweeps the gloſſy ſnow.
All is their prize. They faſten on the ſteed,
Preſs him to earth, and pierce his mighty heart.
Nor can the bull his awful front defend,
Or ſhake the murdering ſavages away.
Rapacious, at the mother's throat they fly,
And tear the ſcreaming infant from her breaſt.
The godlike face of Man avails him nought.
Even beauty, force divine! at whoſe bright glance
The generous lion ſtands in ſoftened gaze,
Here bleeds, a hapleſs undiſtinguiſh'd prey.
But if, appriz'd of the ſevere attack,
The country be ſhut up, lur'd by the ſcent,
On church-yards drear (inhuman to relate!).
The diſappointed prowlers fall, and dig
The ſhrouded body from the grave; o'er which,
Mix'd with foul ſhades, and frighted ghoſts, they howl.
    Among thoſe hilly regions, where embrac'd
In peaceful vales the happy *Griſons* dwell;
Oft, ruſhing ſudden from the loaded cliffs,
Mountains of ſnow their gathering terrors roll.
From ſteep to ſteep, loud-thundering down they come,
A wintry waſte in dire commotion all;
And herds, and flocks, and travellers, and ſwains,
And ſometimes whole brigades of marching troops,
Or hamlets ſleeping in the dead of night,
Are deep beneath the ſmothering ruin whelm'd.
    Now, all amid the rigours of the year,
In the wild depth of Winter, while without
The ceaſeleſs winds blow ice, be my retreat,
Between the groaning foreſt and the ſhore
Beat by the boundleſs multitude of waves,

A rural, ſhelter'd, ſolitary ſcene;
Where ruddy fire and beaming tapers join,
To cheer the gloom.   There ſtudious let me ſit,
And hold high converſe with the MIGHTY DEAD;
Sages of ancient time, as gods rever'd,
As gods beneficent, who bleſt mankind
With arts, with arms, and humaniz'd a world.
Rous'd at th' inſpiring thought, I throw aſide
The long-liv'd volume; and, deep-muſing, hail
The ſacred ſhades, that ſlowly-riſing paſs
Before my wondering eyes.   Firſt SOCRATES,
Who, firmly good in a corrupted ſtate,
Againſt the rage of tyrants *ſingle* ſtood,
Invincible! calm Reaſon's holy law,
That *Voice* of GOD within th' attentive mind,
Obeying, fearleſs, or in life, or death:
Great moral teacher! *Wiſeſt of Mankind!*
SOLON the next, who built his common-weal
On equity's wide baſe; by *tender laws*
A lively people curbing, yet undamp'd
Preſerving ſtill that quick peculiar fire,
Whence in the laurel'd field of finer arts,
And of bold freedom, they unequal'd ſhone,
The pride of ſmiling GREECE, and human-kind.
LYCURGUS then, who bow'd beneath the force
Of ſtricteſt diſcipline, *ſeverely wiſe*,
All human paſſions.   Following him, I ſee,
As at *Thermopylæ* he glorious fell,
The firm DEVOTED CHIEF *, who prov'd by deeds
The hardeſt leſſon which the *other* taught.
Then ARISTIDES lifts his honeſt front;
Spotleſs of heart, to whom th' unflattering voice

* LEONIDAS.

Of freedom gave the noblest name of *Juft*;
In pure majeftic poverty rever'd;
Who, even his glory to his country's weal
Submitting, fwell'd a haughty *Rival*'s * fame.
Rear'd by his care, of fofter ray appears
CIMON fweet-foul'd; whofe genius, rifing ftrong,
Shook off the load of young debauch; abroad
The fcourge of *Perfian* pride, at home the friend
Of every worth and every fplendid art;
Modeft, and fimple, in the pomp of wealth.
Then the laft worthies of declining GREECE,
Late call'd to glory, in *unequal* times,
Penfive, appear. The fair *Corinthian* boaft,
TIMOLEON, happy temper! mild, and firm,
Who wept the *Brother* while the *Tyrant* bled.
And, equal to the beft, the THEBAN PAIR†,
Whofe virtues, in heroic concord join'd,
Their country rais'd to freedom, empire, fame.
He too, with whom *Athenian* honour funk,
And left a mafs of fordid lees behind,
PHOCION the *Good*; in public life fevere,
To virtue ftill inexorably firm;
But when, beneath his low illuftrious roof,
Sweet peace and happy wifdom fmooth'd his brow,
Not friendfhip fofter was, nor love more kind.
And he, the *laft* of old LYCURGUS' fons,
The generous victim to that vain attempt,
To fave a rotten State, AGIS, who faw
Even SPARTA's felf to fervile avarice funk.
The two *Achaian* heroes clofe the train.
ARATUS, who a while relum'd the foul

* THEMISTOCLES.
† PELOPIDAS and EPAMINONDAS.

Of fondly lingering liberty in GREECE:
And he her darling as her lateſt hope,
The *gallant* PHILOPOEMEN; who to arms
Turn'd the luxurious pomp he could not cure;
Or toiling in his farm, a ſimple ſwain;
Or, bold and ſkilful, thundering in the field.
 Of rougher front, a mighty people come!
A race of heroes! in thoſe virtuous times
Which knew no ſtain, ſave that with partial flame
Their *deareſt* country they *too fondly* lov'd:
Her *better Founder* firſt, the light of ROME,
NUMA, who ſoften'd her rapacious ſons:
SERVIUS the *King*, who laid the ſolid baſe
On which o'er earth the *vaſt republic* ſpread.
Then the great confuls venerable riſe.
The PUBLIC FATHER * who the *Private* quell'd,
As on the dread tribunal ſternly ſad.
He, whom his thankleſs country *could not* loſe,
CAMILLUS, only vengeful to her foes.
FABRICIUS, ſcorner of all-conquering gold;
And CINCINNATUS, awful from the plough.
Thy WILLING VICTIM †, *Carthage*, burſting looſe
From all that pleading Nature could oppoſe,
From a whole city's tears, by rigid faith
Imperious call'd, and honour's dire command.
SCIPIO, the *gentle chief*, humanely brave,
Who ſoon the race of ſpotleſs glory ran,
And, warm in youth, to the *Poetic ſhade*
With *Friendſhip* and *Philoſophy* retir'd.
TULLY, whoſe powerful eloquence a while
Reſtrain'd the rapid fate of ruſhing ROME.
Unconquer'd CATO, virtuous in *extreme*.

  * MARCUS JUNIUS. BRUTUS.   † REGULUS.

And thou, unhappy Brutus, kind of heart,
Whofe fteady arm, by awful virtue urg'd,
Lifted the *Roman fteel* againft thy *Friend.*
Thoufands befides the tribute of a verfe
Demand; 'but who can count the ftars of heaven?
Who fing their influence on this lower world?

 Behold, who yonder comes! in fober ftate,
Fair, mild, and ftrong, as is a vernal fun:
'Tis *Phœbus'* felf, or elfe the *Mantuan Swain!*
Great Homer too appears, of daring wing,
Parent of fong! and *equal* by his fide,
The British Muse; join'd hand in hand they walk,
Darkling, full up the middle fteep to fame.
Nor abfent are thofe fhades, whofe fkilful touch
Pathetic drew th' impaffion'd heart, and charm'd
Tranfported *Athens* with the moral scene:
Nor thofe who, tuneful, wak'd th' enchanting lyre.

 Firft of your kind! fociety divine!
Still vifit thus my nights, for you referv'd,
And mount my foaring foul to thoughts like yours.
Silence, thou lonely power! the door be thine;
See on the hallowed hour that none intrude,
Save a few chofen friends, who fometimes deign
To blefs my humble roof, with fenfe refin'd,
Learning digefted well, exalted faith,
Unftudy'd wit, and humour ever gay.
Or from the Mufes' hill will Pope defcend,
To raife the facred hour, to bid it fmile,
And with the focial fpirit warm the heart:
For tho' not fweeter his own Homer fings,
Yet is his life the more endearing fong.

 Where art thou, Hammond? thou the darling pride,
The friend and lover of the tuneful throng!
Ah why, dear youth, in all the blooming prime

Of vernal genius, where difclofing faft
Each active worth, each manly virtue lay,
Why wert thou ravifh'd from our hope fo foon?
What now avails that noble thirft of fame,
Which ftung thy fervent breaft? that treafur'd ftore
Of knowledge, early gain'd? that eager zeal
To ferve thy country, glowing in the band
Of YOUTHFUL PATRIOTS, who fuftain her name?
What now, alas! that life-diffufing charm
Of fprightly wit? that rapture for the Mufe,
That heart of friendfhip, and that foul of joy,
Which bade with fofteft light thy virtue fmile?
Ah! only fhew'd, to check our fond purfuits,
And teach our humbled hopes that life is vain!
    Thus in fome deep retirement would I pafs
The winter-glooms, with friends of pliant foul,
Or blithe, or folemn, as the theme infpir'd:
With them would fearch, if Nature's boundlefs frame
Was call'd, late-rifing from the void of night,
Or fprung *eternal* from th' ETERNAL MIND;
Its life, its laws, its progrefs, and its end.
Hence larger profpects of the beauteous whole
Would, gradual, open on our opening minds;
And each diffufive harmony unite
In full perfection to th' aftonifh'd eye.
Then would we try to fcan the *moral World*,
Which, tho' to us it feems embroil'd, moves on
In higher order; fitted, and impell'd,
By WISDOM's fineft hand, and iffuing all
In *general Good.* The fage hiftoric Mufe
Should next conduct us thro' the deeps of time:
Shew us how empire grew, declin'd, and fell,
In fcatter'd ftates; what makes the nations fmile,
Improves their foil, and gives them double funs;

And why they pine beneath the brighteſt ſkies,
In Nature's richeſt lap. As thus we talk'd,
Our hearts would burn within us, would inhale
That portion of divinity, that ray
Of pureſt heaven, which lights the public ſoul
Of patriots, and of heroes. But if doom'd,
In powerleſs humble fortune, to repreſs
Theſe ardent riſings of the kindling ſoul;
Then, even ſuperior to ambition, we
Would learn the private virtues; how to glide
Thro' ſhades and plains, along the ſmootheſt ſtream
Of rural life: or ſnatch'd away by hope,
Thro' the dim ſpaces of futurity,
With earneſt eye anticipate thoſe ſcenes
Of happineſs, and wonder; where the mind,
In endleſs growth and infinite aſcent,
Riſes from ſtate to ſtate, and world to world.
But when with theſe the ſerious thought is foil'd,
We, ſhifting for relief, would play the ſhapes
Of frolic fancy; and inceſſant form
Thoſe rapid pictures, that aſſembled train
Of fleet ideas, never join'd before.
Whence lively *Wit* excites to gay ſurprize;
Or folly-painting *Humour*, grave himſelf,
Calls Laughter forth, deep-ſhaking every nerve.

　　Mean-time the village rouſes up the fire;
While well atteſted, and as well believ'd,
Heard ſolemn, goes the goblin-ſtory round;
Till ſuperſtitious horror creeps o'er all.
Or, frequent in the ſounding hall, they wake
The rural gambol. Ruſtic mirth goes round;
The ſimple joke that takes the ſhepherd's heart,
Eaſily pleas'd; the long loud laugh, ſincere;

Vol. I.　　　　　　M

The kifs, fnatch'd hafty from the fide-long maid,
On purpofe guardlefs, or pretending fleep:
The leap, the flap, the haul; and, fhook to notes
Of native mufic, the refpondent dance.
Thus jocund fleets with them the winter-night.
The city fwarms intenfe. The public haunt,
Full of each theme, and warm with mixt difcourfe,
Hums indiftinct. The fons of riot flow
Down the loofe ftream of falfe inchanted joy,
To fwift deftruction. On the rankled foul
The gaming fury falls; and in one gulph
Of total ruin, honour, virtue, peace,
Friends, families, and fortune, headlong fink.
Up-fprings the dance along the lighted dome,
Mix'd, and evolv'd, a thoufand fprightly ways.
The glittering court effufes every pomp;
The circle deepens: beam'd from gaudy robes,
Tapers, and fparkling gems, and radiant eyes,
A foft effulgence o'er the palace waves:
While, a gay infect in *his* fummer-fhine,
The fop, light-fluttering, fpreads his mealy wings.

Dread o'er the fcene, the ghoft of HAMLET ftalks;
OTHELLO rages; poor MONIMIA mourns;
And BELVIDERA pours her foul in love.
Terror alarms the breaft; the comely tear
Steals o'er the cheek: or elfe the COMIC MUSE
Holds to the world a picture of itfelf,
And raifes fly the fair impartial laugh.
Sometimes fhe lifts her ftrain, and paints the fcenes
Of beauteous life; whate'er can deck mankind,
Or charm the heart, in generous BEVIL* fhew'd.

* A character in the CONSCIOUS LOVERS, written by Sir RICHARD
STEELE.

O Thou, whose wisdom, solid yet refin'd,
Whose patriot-virtues, and consummate skill
To touch the finer springs that move the world,
Join'd to whate'er the *Graces* can bestow,
And all *Apollo*'s animating fire,
Give thee, with pleasing dignity, to shine
At once the guardian, ornament, and joy,
Of polish'd life; permit the *Rural Muse*,
O CHESTERFIELD, to grace with thee her song!
Ere to the shades again she humbly flies,
Indulge her fond ambition, in thy train,
(For every Muse has in thy train a place)
To mark thy various full-accomplish'd mind:
To mark that spirit, which, with *British scorn*,
Rejects th' allurements of corrupted power;
That elegant politeness, which excels,
Even in the judgment of presumptuous *France*,
The boasted manners of her shining court;
/That wit, the vivid energy of sense,
The truth of Nature, which, with *Attic* point,
And kind well-temper'd satire, smoothly keen,
Steals thro' the soul, and without pain corrects.
Or, rising thence with yet a brighter flame,
O let me hail thee on some glorious day,
When to the listening senate, ardent, crowd
BRITANNIA's sons to hear her pleaded cause.
Then drest by thee, more amiably fair,
Truth the soft robe of mild persuasion wears:
Thou to assenting reason giv'st again
Her own enlightened thoughts; call'd from the heart,
Th' obedient passions on thy voice attend;
And even reluctant party feels a while
Thy gracious power: as thro' the varied maze

Of eloquence, now fmooth, now quick, now ftrong,
Profound and clear, you roll the copious flood.

To thy lov'd haunt return, my happy Mufe:
For now, behold, the joyous winter-days,
Frofty, fucceed; and thro' the blue ferene,
For fight too fine, th' ethereal nitre flies;
Killing infectious damps, and the fpent air
Storing afrefh with elemental life.
Clofe crowds the fhining atmofphere; and binds
Our ftrengthened bodies in its cold embrace,
Conftringent; feeds, and animates our blood;
Refines our fpirits, thro' the new-ftrung nerves,
In fwifter fallies darting to the brain;
Where fits the foul, intenfe, collected, cool,
Bright as the fkies, and as the feafon keen.
All Nature feels the renovating force
Of Winter, only to the thoughtlefs eye
In ruin feen. The froft-concocted glebe
Draws in abundant vegetable foul,
And gathers vigour for the coming year.
A ftronger glow fits on the lively cheek
Of ruddy fire: and luculent along
The purer rivers flow; their fullen deeps,
Tranfparent, open to the fhepherd's gaze,
And murmur hoarfer at the fixing froft.

What art thou, froft? and whence are thy keen ftores
Deriv'd, thou fecret all-invading power,
Whom even th' illufive fluid cannot fly?
Is not thy potent energy, unfeen,
Myriads of little falts, or hook'd, or fhap'd
Like double wedges, and diffus'd immenfe
Thro' water, earth, and ether? Hence at eve,
Steam'd eager from the red horizon round,

With the fierce rage of Winter deep fuffus'd,
An icy gale, oft fhifting, o'er the pool
Breathes a blue film, and in its mid career
Arrefts the bickering ftream. The loofened ice,
Let down the flood, and half diffolv'd by day,
Ruftles no more; but to the fedgy bank
Faft grows, or gathers round the pointed ftone,
A cryftal pavement, by the breath of heaven
Cemented firm; till, feiz'd from fhore to fhore,
The whole imprifon'd river growls below.
Loud rings the frozen earth, and hard reflects
A double noife; while, at his evening watch,
The village-dog deters the nightly thief;
The heifer lows; the diftant water-fall
Swells in the breeze; and, with the hafty tread
Of traveller, the hollow-founding plain
Shakes from afar. The full ethereal round,
Infinite worlds difclofing to the view,
Shines out intenfely keen; and, all one cope
Of ftarry glitter, glows from pole to pole.
From pole to pole the rigid influence falls,
Thro' the ftill night, inceffant, heavy, ftrong,
And feizes Nature faft. It freezes on;
Till morn, late-rifing o'er the drooping world,
Lifts her pale eye unjoyous. Then appears
The various labour of the filent night:
Prone from the dripping eave, and dumb cafcade,
Whofe idle torrents only feem to roar,
The pendant icicle; the froft-work fair,
Where tranfient hues, and fancy'd figures rife;
Wide-fpouted o'er the hill, the frozen brook,
A livid tract, cold-gleaming on the morn;
The foreft bent beneath the plumy wave;

And by the froſt refin'd the whiter ſnow,
Incruſted hard, and ſounding to the tread
Of early ſhepherd, as he penſive ſeeks
His pining flock, or from the mountain top,
Pleas'd with the ſlippery ſurface, ſwift deſcends.

　　On blithſome frolics bent, the youthful ſwains,
While every work of Man is laid at reſt,
Fond o'er the river crowd, in various ſport
And revelry diſſolv'd; where mixing glad,
Happieſt of all the train! the raptur'd boy
Laſhes the whirling top. Or, where the *Rhine*
Branch'd out in many a long canal extends,
From every province ſwarming, void of care,
Batavia ruſhes forth; and as they ſweep,
On ſounding ſkates, a thouſand different ways,
In circling poiſe, ſwift as the winds, along,
The *then gay* land is maddened all to joy.
Nor leſs the northern courts, wide o'er the ſnow,
Pour a new pomp. Eager, on rapid ſleds,
Their vigorous youth in bold contention wheel
The long-reſounding courſe. Mean-time, to raiſe
The manly ſtrife, with highly blooming charms,
Fluſh'd by the ſeaſon, *Scandinavia*'s dames,
Or *Ruſſia*'s buxom daughters, glow around.

　　Pure, quick, and ſportful, is the wholeſome day;
But ſoon elaps'd. The horizontal ſun,
Broad o'er the ſouth, hangs at his utmoſt noon:
And, ineffeⅽtual, ſtrikes the gelid cliff:
His azure gloſs the mountain ſtill maintains,
Nor feels the feeble touch. Perhaps the vale
Relents a while to the refleⅽted ray;
Or from the foreſt falls the cluſter'd ſnow,
Myriads of gems, that in the waving gleam

Gay-twinkle as they fcatter. Thick around
Thunders the fport of thofe, who with the gun,
And dog impatient bounding at the fhot,
Worfe than the feafon, defolate the fields;
And, adding to the ruins of the year,
Diftrefs the footed or the feathered game.

But what is this? Our infant Winter finks,
Divefted of his grandeur, fhould our eye
Aftonifh'd fhoot into the *Frigid Zone*;
Where, for relentlefs months, continual night
Holds o'er the glittering wafte her ftarry reign.

There, thro' the prifon of unbounded wilds,
Barr'd by the hand of Nature from efcape,
Wide-roams the *Ruffian* exile. Nought around
Strikes his fad eye, but defarts loft in fnow;
And heavy-loaded groves; and folid floods,
That ftretch, athwart the folitary vaft,
Their icy horrors to the frozen main;
And chearlefs towns far-diftant, never blefs'd,
Save when its annual courfe the caravan
Bends to the golden coaft of rich *Cathay* *,
With news of human-kind. Yet there life glows;
Yet cherifh'd there, beneath the fhining wafte,
The furry nations harbour: tipt with jet,
Fair ermines, fpotlefs as the fnows they prefs;
Sables, of gloffy black; and dark-embrown'd,
Or beauteous freakt with many a mingled hue,
Thoufands befides, the coftly pride of courts.
There, warm together prefs'd, the trooping deer
Sleep on the new-fallen fnows; and, fcarce his head
Rais'd o'er the happy wreath, the branching elk

* The old name for *China*.

Lies flumbering fullen in the white abyfs.
The ruthlefs hunter wants nor dogs nor toils,
Nor with the dread of founding bows he drives
The fearful flying race; with ponderous clubs,
As weak againft the mountain heaps they pufh
Their beating breaft in vain, and piteous bray,
He lays them quivering on th' enfanguin'd fnows,
And with loud fhouts rejoicing bears them home.
There thro' the piny foreft half-abforpt,
Rough tenant of thefe fhades, the fhapelefs bear,
With dangling ice all horrid, ftalks forlorn;
Slow-pac'd, and fourer as the ftorms increafe,
He makes his bed beneath th' inclement drift,
And, with ftern patience, fcorning weak complaint,
Hardens his heart againft affailing want.

 Wide o'er the fpacious regions of the north,
That fee *Boötes* urge his tardy wain,
A boifterous race, by frofty *Caurus* * pierc'd,
Who little pleafure know and fear no pain,
Prolific fwarm. They once relum'd the flame
Of loft mankind in polifh'd flavery funk,
Drove martial horde on horde†, with dreadful fweep
Refiftlefs rufhing o'er th' enfeebled fouth,
And gave the vanquifh'd world another form.
Not fuch the fons of *Lapland:* wifely they
Defpife th' infenfate barbarous trade of war;
They afk no more than fimple Nature gives,
They love their mountains and enjoy their ftorms.
No falfe defires, no pride-created wants,
Difturb the peaceful current of their time;

 * The North-weft Wind.
 † The wandering *Scythian Clans.*

And thro' the reftlefs ever-tortur'd maze
Of pleafure, or ambition, bid it rage.
/ Their rein-deer form their riches. Thefe their tents,
Their robes, their beds, and all their homely wealth
Supply, their wholefome fare, and chearful cups.
Obfequious at their call, the docile tribe
Yield to the fled their necks, and whirl them fwift
O'er hill and dale, heap'd into one expanfe
Of marbled fnow, as far as eye can fweep
With a blue cruft of ice unbounded glaz'd.
By dancing meteors then, that ceafelefs fhake
A waving blaze refracted o'er the heavens,
And vivid moons, and ftars that keener play
With double luftre from the gloffy wafte,
Even in the depth of *Polar Night*, they find
A wondrous day: enough to light the chafe,
Or guide their daring fteps to *Finland*-fairs.
Wifh'd Spring returns; and from the hazy fouth,
While dim Aurora flowly moves before,
The welcome fun, juft verging up at firft,
By fmall degrees extends the fwelling curve;
Till feen at laft for gay rejoicing months,
Still round and round, his fpiral courfe he winds,
And as he nearly dips his flaming orb,
Wheels up again, and re-afcends the fky.
In that glad feafon, from the lakes and floods,
Where pure *Niemi*'s* fairy mountains rife,

---

* *M. de Maupertuis*, in his book on *the Figure of the Earth*, after
having defcribed the beautiful Lake and Mountain of *Niemi* in *Lapland*,
fays, " From this height we had opportunity feveral times to fee
" thofe vapours rife from the Lake which the people of the country
" call *Haltios*, and which they deem to be the guardian Spirits of the
" Mountains. We had been frighted with ftories of Bears that haunt-
" ed this place, but faw none. It feemed rather a place of refort for
" *Fairies* and *Genii*, than Bears."

And fring'd with rofes *Tenglio* * rolls his ftream,
They draw the copious fry.   With thefe, at eve,
They chearful-loaded to their tents repair;
Where, all day long in ufeful cares employ'd,
Their kind unblemifh'd wives the fire prepare.
Thrice happy race! by poverty fecur'd
From legal plunder and rapacious power:
In whom fell intereft never yet has fown
The feeds of vice: whofe fpotlefs fwains ne'er knew
Injurious deed, nor, blafted by the breath
Of faithlefs love, their blooming daughters woe.

Still preffing on, beyond *Tornéa*'s lake,
And *Hecla* flaming thro' a wafte of fnow,
And fartheft *Greenland*, to the pole itfelf,
Where, failing gradual, life at length goes out,
The Mufe expands her folitary flight;
And, hovering o'er the wild ftupendous fcene,
Beholds new feas beneath another fky †.
Thron'd in his palace of cerulean ice,
Here WINTER holds his unrejoicing court;
And thro' his airy hall the loud mifrule
Of driving tempeft is for ever heard:
Here the grim tyrant meditates his wrath;
Here arms his winds with all-fubduing froft;
Moulds his fierce hail, and treafures up his fnows,
With which he now opprefles half the globe.

Thence winding eaftward to the *Tartar*'s coaft
She fweeps the howling margin of the main;
Where undiffolving, from the firft of time,
Snows fwell on fnows amazing to the fky;

* The fame Author obferves: " I was furprized to fee upon the
" banks of this river (the *Tenglio*) rofes of as lively a red as any that
" are in our gardens."

† The other Hemifphere.

And icy mountains high on mountains pil'd,
Seem to the fhivering failor from afar,
Shapelefs and white, an atmofphere of clouds.
Projected huge, and horrid, o'er the furge,
Alps frown on Alps; or rufhing hideous down,
As if old Chaos was again return'd,
Wide-rend the deep, and fhake the folid pole.
Ocean itfelf no longer can refift
The binding fury; but, in all its rage
Of tempeft taken by the boundlefs froft,
Is many a fathom to the bottom chain'd,
And bid to roar no more: a bleak expanfe,
Shagg'd o'er with wavy rocks, chearlefs, and void
Of every life, that from the dreary months
Flies confcious fouthward. Miferable they!
Who, here entangled in the gathering ice,
Take their laft look of the defcending fun;
While, full of death, and fierce with tenfold froft,
The long long night, incumbent o'er their heads,
Falls horrible. Such was the BRITON's* fate,
As with *firft* prow, (what have not BRITONS dar'd!)
He for the paffage fought, attempted fince
So much in vain, and feeming to be fhut
By jealous Nature with eternal bars.
In thefe fell regions, in *Arzina* caught,
And to the ftony deep his idle fhip
Immediate feal'd, he with his haplefs crew,
Each full exerted at his feveral tafk,
Froze into ftatues; to the cordage glued
The failor, and the pilot to the helm.

---

* Sir HUGH WILLOUGHBY, fent by QUEEN ELIZABETH to
difcover the North-eaft Paffage.

Hard by thefe fhores, where fcarce his freezing ftream
Rolls the wild *Oby*, live the laft of Men;
And half enlivened by the diftant fun,
That rears and ripens Man, as well as plants,
Here human Nature wears its rudeft form.
Deep from the piercing feafon funk in caves,
Here by dull fires, and with unjoyous cheer,
They wafte the tedious gloom. Immers'd in furs,
Doze the grofs race. Nor fprightly jeft, nor fong,
Nor tendernefs they know; nor aught of life,
Beyond the kindred bears that ftalk without.
Till morn at length, her rofes drooping all,
Sheds a long twilight brightening o'er their fields,
And calls the quivered favage to the chace.
    What cannot active government perform,
New-moulding Man? Wide-ftretching from thefe fhores,
A people favage from remoteft time,
A huge neglected empire ONE VAST MIND,
By HEAVEN infpir'd, from Gothic darknefs call'd.
Immortal PETER! firft of monarchs! He
His ftubborn country tam'd, her rocks, her fens,
Her floods, her feas, her ill-fubmitting fons;
And while the fierce *Barbarian* he fubdu'd,
To more exalted foul he rais'd the *Man*.
Ye fhades of ancient heroes, ye who toil'd
Thro' long fucceffive ages to build up
A labouring plan of ftate, behold at once
The wonder done! behold the matchlefs prince!
Who left his native throne, where reign'd till then
A mighty fhadow of unreal power;
Who greatly fpurn'd the flothful pomp of courts;
And roaming every land, in every port
His fceptre laid afide, with glorious hand

Unwearied plying the mechanic tool,
Gather'd the feeds of trade, of useful arts,
Of civil wifdom, and of martial fkill.
Charg'd with the ftores of *Europe* home he goes!
Then cities rife amid th' illumin'd wafte;
O'er joylefs defarts fmiles the rural reign;
Far-diftant flood to flood is focial join'd;
Th' aftonifh'd *Euxine* hears the *Baltic* roar;
Proud navies ride on feas that never foam'd
With daring keel before; and armies ftretch
Each way their dazzling files, repreffing here
The frantic *Alexander* of the north,
And awing there ftern *Othman*'s fhrinking fons.
Sloth flies the land, and *Ignorance*, and *Vice*,
Of old difhonour proud: it glows around,
Taught by the ROYAL HAND that rous'd the whole,
One fcene of arts, of arms, of rifing trade:
For what his wifdom plann'd, and power enforc'd,
More potent ftill, his great *example* fhew'd.

   Muttering, the winds at eve, with blunted point,
Blow hollow-bluftering from the fouth.   Subdu'd,
The froft refolves into a trickling thaw.
Spotted the mountains fhine; loofe fleet defcends,
And floods the country round.   The rivers fwell,
Of bonds impatient.   Sudden from the hills,
· O'er rocks and woods, in broad brown cataracts,
A thoufand fnow-fed torrents fhoot at once;
And, where they rufh, the wide-refounding plain
Is left one flimy wafte.   Thofe fullen feas,
That wafh'd th' ungenial pole, will reft no more
Beneath the fhackles of the mighty north;
But, roufing all their waves, refiftlefs heave.

And hark! the lengthening roar continuous runs
Athwart the rifted deep: at once it burfts,
And piles a thoufand mountains to the clouds.
Ill fares the bark with trembling wretches charg'd,
That, toft amid the floating fragments, moors
Beneath the fhelter of an icy ifle,
While night o'erwhelms the fea, and horror looks
More horrible.   Can human force endure
Th' affembled mifchiefs that befiege them round?
Heart-gnawing hunger, fainting wearinefs,
The roar of winds and waves, the crufh of ice,
Now ceafing, now renew'd with louder rage,
And in dire echoes bellowing round the main.
More to embroil the deep, Leviathan
And his unwieldy train, in dreadful fport,
Tempeft the loofened brine, while thro' the gloom,
Far, from the bleak inhofpitable fhore,
Loading the winds, is heard the hungry howl
Of famifh'd monfters, there awaiting wrecks.
Yet PROVIDENCE, that *ever-waking* eye,
Looks down with pity on the feeble toil
Of mortals loft to hope, and lights them fafe,
Thro' all this dreary labyrinth of fate.

     'Tis done! dread WINTER fpreads his lateft glooms,
And reigns tremendous o'er the conquer'd year.
How dead the vegetable kingdom lies!
How dumb the tuneful! Horror wide extends
His defolate domain.   Behold, fond Man!
See here thy pictur'd life; pafs fome few years,
Thy flowering Spring, thy Summer's ardent ftrength,
Thy fober Autumn fading into age,
And pale concluding Winter comes at laft,

And fhuts the fcene. Ah! whither now are fled,
Thofe dreams of greatnefs? thofe unfolid hopes
Of happinefs? thofe longings after fame?
Thofe reftlefs cares? thofe bufy buftling days?
Thofe gay-fpent, feftive nights? thofe veering thoughts
Loft between good and ill, that fhar'd thy life?
All now are vanifh'd! VIRTUE fole-furvives,
Immortal never-failing friend of Man,
His guide to happinefs on high. And fee!
'Tis come, the glorious morn! the fecond birth
Of heaven, and earth! awakening Nature hears
The *new-creating word*, and ftarts to life,
In every heightened form, from pain and death
For ever free. *The great eternal fcheme,*
Involving all, and in a *perfect whole*
Uniting, as the profpect wider fpreads,
To reafon's eye refin'd clears up apace.
Ye vainly wife! ye blind prefumptuous! now,
Confounded in the duft, adore that POWER,
And WISDOM oft arraign'd: fee now the caufe,
Why unaffuming worth in fecret liv'd,
And dy'd, neglected: why the good Man's fhare
In life was gall and bitternefs of foul:
Why the lone widow and her orphans pin'd
In ftarving folitude; while luxury,
In palaces, lay ftraining her low thought,
To form unreal wants: why heaven-born Truth,
And Moderation fair, wore the red marks
Of Superftition's fcourge: why licens'd Pain,
That cruel fpoiler, that embofom'd foe,
Imbitter'd all our blifs. Ye good diftreft!
Ye noble few! who here unbending ftand

Beneath life's preffure, yet bear up a while,
And what your bounded view, which only faw
A little part, deem'd Evil, is no more:
The ftorms of Wintry Time will quickly pafs,
And one unbounded Spring encircle all.

A

H Y M N.

THESE, as they change, ALMIGHTY FATHER, thefe
Are but the *varied* GOD. The rolling year
Is full of THEE. Forth in the pleafing Spring
THY beauty walks, THY tendernefs and love.
Wide flufh the fields; the foftening air is balm;
Echo the mountains round; the foreft fmiles;
And every fenfe, and every heart is joy.
Then comes THY glory in the Summer-months,
With light and heat refulgent. Then THY fun
Shoots full perfection thro' the fwelling year:
And oft THY voice in dreadful thunder fpeaks;
And oft at dawn, deep noon, or falling eve,
By brooks and groves, in hollow-whifpering gales.
THY bounty fhines in Autumn unconfin'd,
And fpreads a common feaft for all that lives.
In Winter awful THOU! with clouds and ftorms
Around THEE thrown, tempeft o'er tempeft roll'd,
Majeftic darknefs! on the whirlwind's wing,
Riding fublime, THOU bidft the world adore,
And humbleft Nature with THY northern blaft.

Myfterious round! what fkill, what force divine,
Deep felt, in thefe appear! a fimple train,
Yet fo delightful mix'd with fuch kind art,
Such beauty and beneficence combin'd;

Shade, unperceiv'd, so softening into shade;
And all so forming an harmonious whole;
That, as they still succeed, they ravish still.
But wandering oft, with brute unconscious gaze,
Man marks not THEE, marks not the mighty hand,
That, ever-busy, wheels the silent spheres;
Works in the secret deep; shoots, steaming, thence
The fair profusion that o'erspreads the Spring:
Flings from the sun direct the flaming day;
Feeds every creature; hurls the tempest forth;
And, as on earth this grateful change revolves,
With transport touches all the springs of life.

 NATURE, attend! join every living soul,
Beneath the spacious temple of the sky, .
In adoration join; and, ardent, raise
One general song! To HIM, ye vocal gales,
Breathe soft, whose SPIRIT in your freshness breathes:
Oh talk of HIM in solitary glooms!
Where, o'er the rock, the scarcely waving pine
Fills the brown shade with a religious awe.
And ye, whose bolder note is heard afar,
Who shake th' astonish'd world, lift high to heaven
Th' impetuous song, and say from whom you rage.
His praise, ye brooks, attune, ye trembling rills;
And let me catch it as I muse along.
Ye headlong torrents, rapid, and profound;
Ye softer floods, that lead the humid maze
Along the vale; and thou, majestic main,
A secret world of wonders in thyself,
Sound His stupendous praise; whose greater voice
Or bids you roar, or bids your roarings fall.
Soft-roll your incense, herbs, and fruits, and flowers,
In mingled clouds to HIM; whose sun exalts,
Whose breath perfumes you, and whose pencil paints.

Ye forefts bend, ye harvefts wave, to HIM;
Breathe your ftill fong into the reaper's heart,
As home he goes beneath the joyous moon.
Ye that keep watch in heaven, as earth afleep
Unconfcious lies, effufe your mildeft beams,
Ye conftellations, while your angels ftrike,
Amid the fpangled fky, the filver lyre.
Great fource of day! beft image here below
Of thy Creator, ever pouring wide,
From world to world, the vital ocean round,
On Nature write with every beam His praife.
The thunder rolls: be hufh'd the proftrate world;
While cloud to cloud returns the folemn hymn.
Bleat out afrefh, ye hills: ye mofly rocks,
Retain the found: the broad refponfive lowe,
Ye valleys, raife; for the GREAT SHEPHERD reigns;
And his *unfuffering* kingdom yet will come.
Ye woodlands all, awake: a boundlefs fong
Burft from the groves! and when the reftlefs day,
Expiring, lays the warbling world afleep,
Sweeteft of birds! fweet Philomela, charm
The liftening fhades, and teach the night His praife.
Ye chief, for whom the whole creation fmiles,
At once the head, the heart, and tongue of all,
Crown the great hymn! in fwarming cities vaft,
Affembled men, to the deep organ join
The long-refounding voice, oft-breaking clear,
At folemn paufes, through the fwelling bafe;
And, as each mingling flame increafes each,
In one united ardor rife to heaven.
Or if you rather chufe the rural fhade,
And find a fane in every facred grove;
There let the fhepherd's flute, the virgin's lay,
The prompting feraph, and the poet's lyre,

Still ſing the GOD OF SEASONS, as they roll.
For me, when I forget the darling theme,
Whether the bloſſom blows, the ſummer-ray
Ruſſets the plain, *inſpiring* Autumn gleams;
Or Winter riſes in the blackening eaſt;
Be my tongue mute, my fancy paint no more,
And, dead to joy, forget my heart to beat!

    Should fate command me to the fartheſt verge
Of the green earth, to diſtant barbarous climes,
Rivers unknown to ſong; where firſt the ſun
Gilds *Indian* mountains, or his ſetting beam
Flames on th' *Atlantic* iſles; 'tis nought to me:
Since GOD is ever preſent, ever felt,
In the void waſte as in the city full;
And where HE vital breathes there muſt be joy.
When even at laſt the ſolemn hour ſhall come,
And wing my myſtic flight to future worlds,
I chearful will obey; there, with new powers,
Will riſing wonders ſing: I cannot go
Where UNIVERSAL LOVE not ſmiles around,
Suſtaining all yon orbs, and all their ſons;
From *ſeeming Evil* ſtill educing *Good*,
And *Better* thence again, and *Better* ſtill,
In infinite progreſſion. But I loſe
Myſelf in HIM, in LIGHT INEFFABLE;
Come then, expreſſive ſilence, muſe HIS praiſe.

THE

CASTLE

OF

INDOLENCE.

AN ALLEGORICAL POEM.

N 3

EXPLANATION

OF THE

OBSOLETE WORDS ufed in this POEM.

ARchimage—*the chief or greateft of magicians, or enchanters.*
Apaid—*paid.*
Appal—*affright.*
Atween—*between.*
Ay—*always.*

Bale—*forrow, trouble, misfortune.*
Benempt—*named.*
Blazon—*painting, difplaying.*
Breme—*cold, raw.*

Carol—*to fing fongs of joy.*
Caucus—*the north-eaft wind.*
Certes—*certainly.*

Dan—*a word prefixed to names.*
Deftly—*fkilfully.*
Depainted—*painted.*
Drowfy-head—*drowfinefs.*

Eath—*eafy.*
Eftfoons—*immediately, often, afterwards.*
Eke—*alfo.*

Fays—*fairies.*

N 4

Gear *or* Geer—*furniture, equipage, drefs.*
Glaive—*fword.* (Fr.)
Glee—*joy, pleafure.*

Han—*have.*
Hight—*named, called*; and fometimes it is ufed
for *is called.* See Stanza vii.

Idlefs—*Idlenefs.*
Imp—*Child, or offspring; from the* Saxon *impan,
to graft or plant.*

Keft—*for caft.*

Lad—*for led.*
Lea—*a piece of land, or meadow.*
Libbard—*leopard.*
Lig—*to lie.*
Lithe—*loofe, lax.*
Lofel—*a loofe idle fellow.*
Louting—*bowing, bending.*

Mell—*mingle.*
Moe—*more.*
Moil—*to labour.*
Mote—*might.*
Muchel *or* Mochel—*much, great.*

Nathlefs—*neverthelefs.*
Ne—*nor.*
Needments—*neceffaries.*
Nourfling—*a child that is nurfed.*
Noyance—*harm.*

Perdie (Fr. *par Dieu*)—*an old oath.*
Prankt—*coloured, adorned gayly.*
Prick'd thro' the foreft—*rode thro' the foreft.*

Sear—*dry, burnt up.*
Sheen—*bright, fhining.*
Sicker—*fure, furely.*
Smackt—*favoured.*
Soot—*fweet, or fweetly.*
Sooth—*true, or truth.*

Stound—*misfortune, pang.*
Sweltry—*sultry, consuming with heat.*
Swink—*to labour.*

Thrall—*slave.*
Transmew'd—*transformed.*

Vild—*vile.*
Unkempt (Lat. *incomptus*)—*unadorned.*

Ween—*to think, be of opinion.*
Weet—*to know; to weet, to wit.*
Whilom—*ere-while, formerly.*
Wight—*man.*
Wis, *for* Wist—*to know, think, understand.*
Wonne (a Noun)—*Dwelling.*
Wroke—*wreakt.*

> N. B. *The letter* Y *is frequently placed in the beginning of a word, by* Spenser, *to lengthen it a syllable, and* en *at the end of a word, for the same reason, as* withouten, casten, *&c.*

Yborn—*born*
Yblent, *or* blent—*blended, mingled.*
Yclad—*clad.*
Ycleped—*called, named.*
Yfere—*together.*
Ymolten—*melted.*
Yode *(preter tense of* yede)—*went.*

ADVERTISEMENT.

T HIS poem being writ in the manner of *Spenſer*, the obſolete words, and a ſimplicity of diction in ſome of the lines, which borders on the ludicrous, were neceſſary to make the imitation more perfect. And the ſtyle of that admirable poet, as well as the meaſure in which he wrote, are, as it were, appropriated by Cuſtom to all allegorical Poems writ in our language; juſt as in *French* the ſtyle of *Marot*, who lived under *Francis* I. has been uſed in tales, and familiar epiſtles, by the politeſt writers of the age of *Louis* XIV.

THE

CASTLE

OF

INDOLENCE.

The caſtle hight of indolence,
And its falſe luxury;
Where for a little time, alas!
We liv'd right jollily.

I.

O Mortal man, who liveſt here by toil,
   Do not complain of this thy hard eſtate;
That like an emmet thou muſt ever moil,
Is a ſad ſentence of an ancient date;
And, certes, there is for it reaſon great;
For, tho' ſometimes it makes thee weep and wail,
And curſe thy ſtar, and early drudge and late,
Withouten that would come an heavier bale,
Looſe life, unruly paſſions, and diſeaſes pale.

II.

In lówly dale, faſt by a river's ſide,
With woody hill o'er hill encompaſs'd round,
A moſt enchanting wizard did abide,
Than whom a fiend more fell is no where found.
It was, I ween, a lovelý ſpot of ground;
And there a feaſon atween *June* and *May*,
Half prankt with ſpring, with ſummer half im-
    brown'd,
A liſtleſs climate made, where, ſooth to ſay,
No living wight could work, ne cared even for play.

III.

Was nought around but images of reſt :
Sleep-ſoothing groves, and quiet lawns between;
And flowery beds that ſlumbrous influence keſt,
From poppies breath'd; and beds of pleaſant green,
Where never yet was creeping creature ſeen.
Mean time unnumber'd glittering ſtreamlets play'd,
And hurled every-where their waters ſheen;
That, as they bicker'd through the ſunny glade,
Though reſtleſs ſtill themſelves, a lulling murmur made.

IV.

Join'd to the prattle of the purling rills,
Were heard the lowing herds along the vale,
And flocks loud-bleating from the diſtant hills,
And vacant ſhepherds piping in the dale :
And now and then ſweet Philomel would wail,
Or ſtock-doves plain amid the foreſt deep,
That drowſy ruſtled to the ſighing gale;
And ſtill a coil the graſhopper did keep;
Yet all theſe ſounds yblent inclined all to ſleep.

V.

Full in the paffage of the vale above,
A. fable, filent, folemn foreft ftood;
Where nought but fhadowy forms was feen to move,
As *Idlefs* fancy'd in her dreaming mood:
And up the hills, on either fide, a wood
Of blackening pines, ay waving to and fro,
Sent forth a fleepy horror thro' the blood;
And where this valley winded out, below,
The murmuring main was heard, and fcarcely heard
   to flow.

VI.

A pleafing land of drowfy-head it was,
Of dreams that wave before the half-fhut eye;
And of gay caftles in the clouds that pafs,
For ever flufhing round a fummer-fky:
There eke the foft delights, that witchingly
Inftil a wanton fweetnefs through the breaft,
And the calm pleafures always hover'd nigh;
But whate'er fmack'd of noyance, or unreft,
Was far far off expell'd from this delicious neft.

VII.

The landfkip fuch, infpiring perfect eafe,
Where INDOLENCE (for fo the wizard hight)
Clofe-hid his caftle mid embowering trees,
That half-fhut out the beams of Phœbus bright,
And made a kind of checker'd day and night;
Mean while, unceafing at the maffy gate,
Beneath a fpacious palm, the wicked wight
Was plac'd; and to his lute, of cruel fate,
And labour harfh, complain'd, lamenting man's eftate.

VIII.

Thither continual pilgrims crowded ftill,
From all the roads of earth that pafs there by:
For, as they chaunc'd to breathe on neighbouring hill,
The frefhnefs of this valley fmote their eye,
And drew them ever and anon more nigh;
Till cluftering round th' enchanter falfe they hung,
Ymolten with his fyren melody;
While o'er th' enfeebling lute his hand he flung,
And to the trembling chords thefe tempting verfes fung:

IX.

" Behold! ye pilgrims of this earth, behold!
" See all but man with unearn'd pleafure gay:
" See her bright robes the butterfly unfold,
" Broke from her wintry tomb in prime of *May!*
" What youthful bride can equal her array?
" Who can with her for eafy pleafure vie?
" From mead to mead with gentle wing to ftray,
" From flower to flower on balmy gales to fly,
" Is all fhe has to do beneath the radiant fky.

X.

" Behold the merry minftrels of the morn,
" The fwarming fongfters of the carelefs grove,
" Ten thoufand throats! that, from the flowering
        thorn,
" Hymn their good God, and carol fweet of love,
" Such grateful kindly raptures them emove:
" They neither plough nor fow; ne, fit for flail,
" E'er to the barn the nodden fheaves they drove;
" Yet theirs each harveft dancing in the gale,
" Whatever crowns the hill, or fmiles along the vale.

XI.

" Outcaft of Nature, man! the wretched thrall
" Of bitter-dropping fweat, of fweltry pain,
" Of cares that eat away thy heart with gall,
' " And of the vices, an inhuman train,
" That all proceed from favage thirft of gain:
" For when hard-hearted *Intereft* firft began
" To poifon earth, *Aftræa* left the plain;
" Guile, violence, and murder feiz'd on man,
" And, for foft milky ftreams, with blood the rivers ran.

XII.

" Come, ye, who ftill the cumbrous load of life
" Pufh hard up hill; but as the fartheft fteep
" You truft to gain, and put an end to ftrife,
" Down thunders back the ftone with mighty fweep,
" And hurls your labours to the valley deep,
" For-ever vain: come, and, withouten fee,
" I in oblivion will your forrows fteep,
" Your cares, your toils, will fteep you in a fea
" Of full delight: O come, ye weary wights, to me!

XIII.

" With me, you need not rife at early dawn,
" To pafs the joylefs day in various ftounds:
" Or, louting low, on upftart fortune fawn,
" And fell fair honour for fome paltry pounds;
" Or through the city take your dirty rounds,
" To cheat, and dun, and lye, and vifit pay,
" Now flattering bafe, now giving fecret wounds;
" Or proul in courts of law for human prey,
" In venal fenate thieve, or rob on broad highway.

XIV.

" No cocks, with me, to ruftic labour call,
" From village on to village founding clear :
" To tardy fwain no fhrill-voic'd matrons fquall ;
" No dogs, no babes, no wives, to ftun your ear ;
" No hammers thump ; no horrid blackfmith fear,
" Ne noify tradefman your fweet flumbers ftart,
" With founds that are a mifery to hear :
" But all is calm, as would delight the heart
" Of *Sybarite* of old, all nature, and all art.

XV.

" Here nought but candour reigns, indulgent eafe,
" Good-natur'd lounging, fauntering up and down :
" They who are pleas'd themfelves muft always
        pleafe ;
" On others' ways they never fquint a frown,
" Nor heed what haps in hamlet or in town :
" Thus, from the fource of tender indolence,
" With milky blood the heart is overflown,
" Is footh'd and fweeten'd by the focial fenfe ;
" For intereft, envy, pride, and ftrife are banifh'd hence.

XVI.

" What, what is virtue, but repofe of mind,
" A pure ethereal calm, that knows no ftorm ;
" Above the reach of wild ambition's wind,
" Above thofe paffions that this world deform,
" And torture man, a proud malignant worm ?
" But here, inftead, foft gales of paffion play,
" And gently ftir the heart, thereby to form
" A quicker fenfe of joy ; as breezes ftray
" Acrofs th' enliven'd fkies, and make them ftill more
        gay.

XVII.

" The beft of men have ever lov'd repofe:
" They hate to mingle in the filthy fray;
" Where the foul fours, and gradual rancour grows,
" Imbitter'd more from peevifh day to day.
" Even thofe whom Fame has lent her faireft ray,
" The moft renown'd of worthy wights of yore,
" From a bafe world at laft have ftol'n away:
" So Scipio, to the foft *Cumæan* fhore
" Retiring, tafted Joy he never knew before.

XVIII.

" But if a little exercife you chufe,
" Some zeft for eafe, 'tis not forbidden here.
" Amid the groves you may indulge the mufe,
" Or tend the blooms, and deck the vernal year;
" Or foftly ftealing, with your watry gear,
" Along the brooks, the crimfon fpotted fry
" You may delude: the whilft, amus'd, you hear
" Now the hoarfe ftream, and now the Zephir's figh,
" Attuned to the birds, and woodland melody.

XIX.

" O grievous folly! to heap up eftate,
" Lofing the days you fee beneath the fun;
" When, fudden, comes blind unrelenting fate,
" And gives th' untafted portion you have won,
" With ruthlefs toil, and many a wretch undone,
" To thofe who mock you gone to *Pluto*'s reign,
" There with fad ghofts to pine, and fhadows dun:
" But fure it is of vanities moft vain,
" To toil for what you here untoiling may obtain."

XX.

He ceas'd. But ftill their trembling ears retain'd
The deep vibrations of his witching fong;
That, by a kind of magic power, conftrain'd
To enter in, pell-mell, the liftening throng.
Heaps pour'd on heaps, and yet they flipt along,
In filent eafe: as when beneath the beam
Of fummer-moons, the diftant woods among,
Or by fome flood all filver'd with the gleam,
The foft-embodied Fays through airy portal ftream:

XXI.

By the fmooth demon fo it order'd was,
And here his baneful bounty firft began:
Though fome there were who would not further pafs,
And his alluring baits fufpected han.
The wife diftruft the too fair-fpoken man.
Yet through the gate they caft a wifhful eye:
Not to move on, perdie, is all they can;
For do their very beft they cannot fly,
But often each way look, and often forely figh.

XXII.

When this the watchful wicked wizard faw,
With fudden fpring he leap'd upon them ftrait;
And foon as touch'd by his unhallow'd paw,
They found themfelves within the curfed gate;
Full hard to be repafs'd, like that of fate.
Not ftronger were of old the giant-crew,
Who fought to pull high *Jove* from regal ftate;
Though feeble wretch he feem'd, of fallow hue:
Certes, who bides his grafp, will that encounter rue.

XXIII.

For whomſoe'er the villain takes in hand,
Their joints unknit, their ſinews melt apace;
As lithe they grow as any willow-wand,
And of their vaniſh'd force remains no trace:
So when a maiden fair, of modeſt grace,
In all her buxom blooming *May* of charms,
Is ſeized in ſome loſel's hot embrace,
She waxeth very weakly as ſhe warms,
Then ſighing yields her up to love's delicious harms.

XXIV.

Wak'd by the crowd, ſlow from his bench aroſe
A comely full-ſpread porter, ſwoln with ſleep:
His calm, broad, thoughtleſs aſpect breath'd repoſe;
And in ſweet torpor he was plunged deep,
Ne could himſelf from ceaſeleſs yawning keep;
While o'er his eyes the drowſy liquor ran,
Through which his half-wak'd ſoul would faintly peep.
Then taking his black ſtaff he call'd his man,
And rous'd himſelf as much as rouſe himſelf he can.

XXV.

The lad leap'd lightly at his maſter's call.
He was, to weet, a little roguiſh page,
Save ſleep and play who minded nought at all,
Like moſt the untaught ſtriplings of his age.
This boy he kept each band to diſengage,
Garters and buckles, taſk for him unfit,
But ill-becoming his grave perſonage,
And which his portly paunch would not permit,
So this ſame limber page to all performed it.

O 2

XXVI.

Mean time the mafter-porter wide difplay'd
Great ftore of caps, of flippers, and of gowns;
Wherewith he thofe who enter'd in, array'd
Loofe, as the breeze that plays along the downs,
And waves the fummer-woods when evening frowns.
O fair undrefs, beft drefs! it checks no vein,
But every flowing limb in pleafure drowns,
And heightens eafe with grace. This done, right fain,
Sir porter fat him down, and turn'd to fleep again.

XXVII.

Thus eafy rob'd, they to the fountain fped,
That in the middle of the court up-threw
A ftream, high-fpouting from its liquid bed,
And falling back again in drizzly dew:
There each deep draughts, as deep he thirfted, drew.
It was a fountain of *Nepenthe* rare:
Whence, as Dan HOMER fings, huge pleafaunce grew,
And fweet oblivion of vile earthly care;
Fair gladfome waking thoughts, and joyous dreams
            more fair.

XXVIII.

This rite perform'd, all inly pleas'd and ftill,
Withouten tromp, was proclamation made.
  " Ye fons of INDOLENCE, do what you will;
  " And wander where you lift, thro' hall or glade!
  " Be no man's pleafure for another ftaid;
  " Let each as likes him beft his hours employ,
  " And curft be he who minds his neighbour's trade!
  " Here dwells kind eafe and unreproving joy:
" He little merits blifs who others can annoy."

XXIX.

Strait of thefe endlefs numbers, fwarming round,
As thick as idle motes in funny ray,
Not one eftfoons in view was to be found,
But every man ftroll'd off his own glad way,
Wide o'er this ample court's blank area,
With all the lodges that thereto pertain'd,
No living creature could be feen to ftray;
While folitude, and perfect filence reign'd:
So that to think you dreamt you almoft was conftrain'd.

XXX.

As when a fhepherd of the *Hebrid-Ifles* *,
Plac'd far amid the melancholy main,
(Whether it be lone fancy him beguiles;
Or that aërial beings fometimes deign
To ftand embodied, to our fenfes plain)
Sees on the naked hill, or valley low,
The whilft in ocean *Phœbus* dips his wain,
A vaft affembly moving to and fro:
Then all at once in air diffolves the wondrous fhow.

XXXI.

Ye gods of quiet, and of fleep profound!
Whofe fóft dominion o'er this caftle fways,
And all the widely-filent places round,
Forgive me, if my trembling pen difplays
What never yet was fung in mortal lays.
But how fhall I attempt fuch arduous ftring,
I who have fpent my nights and nightly days,
In this foul-deadening place, loofe-loitering?
Ah! how fhall I for this uprear my moulted wing?

* Thofe iflands on the weftern coaft of *Scotland* called the *Hebrides*.

O 3

XXXII.

Come on, my mufe, nor ftoop to low defpair,
Thou imp of *Jove*, touch'd by celeftial fire!
Thou yet fhalt fing of war, and actions fair,
Which the bold fons of *Britain* will infpire;
Of ancient bards thou yet fhalt fweep the lyre;
Thou yet fhalt tread in tragic pall the ftage,
Paint love's enchanting woes, the heroe's ire,
The fage's calm, the patriot's noble rage,
Dafhing corruption down through every worthlefs age.

XXXIII.

The doors, that knew no fhrill alarming bell,
Ne curfed knocker ply'd by villain's hand,
Self-open'd into halls, where, who can tell
What elegance and grandeur wide expand
The pride of *Turkey* and of *Perfia* land?
Soft quilts on quilts, on carpets carpets fpread,
And couches ftretch'd around in feemly band;
And endlefs pillows rife to prop the head;
So that each fpacious room was one full-fwelling bed.

XXXIV.

And every where huge cover'd tables ftood,
With wines high-flavour'd and rich viands crown'd;
Whatever fprightly juice or tafteful food
On the green bofom of this earth are found,
And all old ocean genders in his round:
Some hand unfeen thefe filently difplay'd,
Even undemanded by a fign or found;
You need but wifh; and, inftantly obey'd,
Fair rang'd the difhes rofe, and thick the glaffes play'd.

XXXV.

Here freedom reign'd, without the leaft alloy;
Nor goffip's tale, nor ancient maiden's gall,
Nor faintly fpleen durft murmur at our joy,
And with envenom'd tongue our pleafures pall.
For why? there was but one great rule for all;
To wit, that each fhould work his own defire,
And eat, drink, ftudy, fleep, as it may fall,
Or melt the time in love, or wake the lyre,
And carol what, unbid, the mufes might infpire.

XXXVI.

The rooms with coftly tapeftry were hung,
Where was inwoven many a gentle tale;
Such as of old the rural poets fung,
Or of *Arcadian* or *Sicilian* vale:
Reclining lovers, in the lonely dale,
Pour'd forth at large the fweetly-tortur'd heart;
Or, fighing tender paffion, fwell'd the gale,
And taught charm'd echo to refound their fmart;
While flocks, woods, ftreams, around, repofe and peace
    impart.

XXXVII.

Thofe pleas'd the moft, where, by a cunning hand,
Depainted was the patriarchal age;
What time Dan *Abraham* left the *Chaldee* land,
And paftur'd on from verdant ftage to ftage,
Where fields and fountains frefh could beft engage.
Toil was not then. Of nothing took they heed,
But with wild beafts the filvan war to wage,
And o'er vaft plains their herds and flocks to feed:
Bleft fons of Nature they! true golden age indeed!

XXXVIII.

Sometimes the pencil, in cool airy halls,
Bade the gay bloom of vernal landſkips riſe,
Or autumn's varied ſhades imbrown the walls:
Now the black tempeſt ſtrikes the aſtoniſh'd eyes;
Now down the ſteep the flaſhing torrent flies;
The trembling ſun now plays o'er ocean blue,
And now rude mountains frown amid the ſkies;
Whate'er *Lorrain* light-touch'd with ſoftening hue,
Or ſavage *Roſa* daſh'd, or learned *Pouſſin* drew.

XXXIX.

Each found too here to languiſhment inclin'd,
Lull'd the weak boſom, and induced eaſe.
Aërial muſic in the warbling wind,
At diſtance riſing oft, by ſmall degrees,
Nearer and nearer came, till o'er the trees
It hung, and breath'd ſuch ſoul-diſſolving airs,
As did, alas! with ſoft perdition pleaſe:
Entangled deep in its enchanting ſnares,
The liſtening heart forgot all duties and all cares.

XL.

A certain muſic, never known before,
Here lull'd the penſive melancholy mind;
Full eaſily obtain'd. Behoves no more,
But ſidelong, to the gently-waving wind,
To lay the well-tun'd inſtrument reclin'd;
From which, with airy flying fingers light,
Beyond each mortal touch the moſt refin'd,
The god of winds drew ſounds of deep delight:
Whence, with juſt cauſe, *The harp of Æolus** it hight.

---

* This is not an imagination of the author; there being in faƈt ſuch
an inſtrument, called *Æolus's harp*, which, when placed againſt a little
ruſhing or current of air, produces the effeƈt here deſcribed.

XLI.

Ah me! what hand can touch the ſtring ſo fine?
Who up the lofty Diapaſan roll
Such ſweet, ſuch ſad, ſuch ſolemn airs divine,
Then let them down again into the ſoul?
Now riſing love they fann'd; now pleaſing dole
They breath'd, in tender muſings, thro' the heart;
And now a graver ſacred ſtrain they ſtole,
As when ſeraphic hands an hymn impart:
Wild-warbling Nature all, above the reach of Art!

XLII.

Such the gay ſplendor, the luxurious ſtate,
Of *Caliphs* old, who on the *Tygris'* ſhore,
In mighty *Bagdat*, populous and great,
Held their bright court, where was of ladies ſtore;
And verſe, love, muſic ſtill the garland wore:
When ſleep was coy, the bard.*, in waiting there,
Chear'd the lone midnight with the Muſe's lore;
Compoſing muſic bade his dreams be fair,
And muſic lent new gladneſs to the morning air.

XLIII.

Near the pavilions where we ſlept, ſtill ran
Soft-tinkling ſtreams, and daſhing waters fell,
And ſobbing breezes ſigh'd, and oft began
(So work'd the wizard) wintry ſtorms to ſwell,
As heaven and earth they would together mell:
At doors and windows, threatening, ſeem'd to call
The demons of the tempeſt, growling fell,
Yet the leaſt entrance found they none at all;
Whence ſweeter grew our ſleep, ſecure in maſſy hall.

* The *Arabian Caliphs* had poets among the officers of their cou
whoſe office it was to do what is here mentioned.

XLIV.

And hither *Morpheus* fent his kindeft dreams,
Raifing a world of gayer tinct and grace;
O'er which were fhadowy caft elyfian gleams,
That play'd, in waving lights, from place to place,
And fhed a rofeate fmile on Nature's face.
Not *Titian's* pencil e'er could fo array,
So fleece with clouds the pure etherial fpace;
Ne could it e'er fuch melting forms difplay,
As loofe on flowery beds all languifhingly lay.

XLV.

, fair illufions! artful phantoms, no!
y Mufe will not attempt your fairy-land:
She has no colours that like you can glow:
To catch your vivid fcenes too grofs her hand.
But fure it is, was ne'er a fubtler band
Than thefe fame guileful angel-feeming fprights,,
Who thus in dreams, voluptuous, foft, and bland,
Pour'd all th' *Arabian Heaven* upon our nights,
And blefs'd them oft befides with more refin'd delights.

XLVI.

They were in footh a moft enchanting train,
Even feigning virtue; fkilful to unite
With evil good, and ftrew with pleafure pain.
But for thofe fiends, whom blood and broils delight;
Who hurl the wretch, as if to hell outright,
Down down black gulphs, where fullen waters fleep,
Or hol   m clambering all the fearful night
On be   cliffs, or pent in ruins deep;
ey, t   e time fhould ferve, were bid far hence
　　　to keep.

XLVII.

Ye guardian fpirits, to whom man is dear,
From thefe foul demons fhield the midnight gloom:
Angels of fancy and of love, be near,
And o'er the blank of fleep diffufe a bloom:
Evoke the facred fhades of *Greece* and *Rome*,
And let them virtue with a look impart:
But chief, a while O! lend us from the tomb
Thofe long-loft friends for whom in love we fmart,
And fill with pious awe and joy-mixt woe the heart.

XLVIII.

Or are you fportive——Bid the morn of youth
Rife to new light, and beam afrefh the days
Of innocence, fimplicity, and truth;
To cares eftrang'd, and manhood's thorny ways.
What tranfport, to retrace our boyifh plays,
Our eafy blifs, when each thing joy fupply'd;
The woods, the mountains, and the warbling maze
Of the wild brooks!—But, fondly wandering wide,
My Mufe, refume the tafk that yet doth thee abide.

XLIX.

One great amufement of our houfehold was,
In a huge cryftal magic globe to fpy,
Still as you turn'd it, all things that do pafs
Upon this ant-hill earth; where conftantly
Of idly-bufy men the reftlefs fry
Run buftling to and fro with foolifh hafte,
In fearch of pleafures vain that from them fly,
Or which obtain'd the caitiffs dare not tafte:
When nothing is enjoy'd, can there be greater wafte?

L.

Of vanity the mirror This was call'd.
Here you a muckworm of the town might fee,
At his dull defk, amid his legers ftall'd,
Eat up with carking care and penurie;
Moft like to carcafe parch'd on gallow-tree.
A penny faved is a penny got:
Firm to this fcoundrel maxim keepeth he,
Ne of its rigour will he bate a jot,
Till it has quench'd his fire, and banifhed his pot.

LI.

Strait from the filth of this low grub, behold!
Comes fluttering forth a gaudy fpendthrift heir,
All gloffy gay, enamel'd all with gold,
The filly tenant of the fummer-air,
In folly loft, of nothing takes he care;
Pimps, lawyers, ftewards, harlots, flatterers vile,
And thieving tradefmen him among them fhare:
His father's ghoft from limbo-lake, the while,
Sees this, which more damnation doth upon him pile.

LII.

This globe pourtray'd the race of learned men,
Still at their books, and turning o'er the page,
Backwards and forwards: oft they fnatch the pen,
As if infpir'd, and in a *Thefpian* rage;
Then write, and blot, as would your ruth engage.
Why, Authors, all this fcrawl and fcribbling fore?
To lofe the prefent, gain the future age,
Praifed to be when you can hear no more,
And much enrich'd with fame when ufelefs worldly ftore.

LIII.

Then would a fplendid city rife to view,
With carts, and cars, and coaches roaring all:
Wide pour'd abroad behold the giddy crew;
See how they dafh along from wall to wall!
At every door, hark how they thundering call!
Good lord! what can this giddy rout excite?
Why, on each other with fell tooth to fall;
A neighbour's fortune, fame, or peace, to blight,
And make new tirefome parties for the coming night.

LIV.

The puzzling fons of party next appear'd,
In dark cabals and nightly juntos met;
And now they whifper'd clofe, now fhrugging rear'd
Th' important fhoulder; then, as if to get
New light, their twinkling eyes were inward fet.
No fooner *Lucifer** recalls affairs,
Than forth they various rufh in mighty fret;
When lo! pufh'd up to power, and crown'd their cares,
In comes another fett, and kicketh them down ftairs.

LV.

But what moft fhew'd the vanity of life,
Was to behold the nations all on fire,
In cruel broils engag'd, and deadly ftrife:
Moft chriftian kings, inflam'd by black defire,
With honourable ruffians in their hire,
Caufe war to rage, and blood around to pour:
Of this fad work when each begins to tire,
They fit them down juft where they were before,
Till for new fcenes of woe peace fhall their force reftore.

* The morning-ftar.

LVI.

To number up the thoufands dwelling here,
An ufelefs were, and eke an endlefs tafk;
From kings, and thofe who at the helm appear,
To gipfies brown in fummer-glades who bafk.
Yea many a man perdie I could unmafk,
Whofe defk and table make a folemn fhow,
With tape-ty'd trafh, and fuits of fools that afk
For place or penfion laid in decent row;
But thefe I paffen by, with namelefs numbers moe.

LVII.

Of all the gentle tenants of the place,
  There was a man of fpecial grave remark:
A certain tender gloom o'erfpread his face,
Penfive, not fad, in thought involv'd not dark,
Sweet As foot this man could fing as morning-lark,
  And teach the noblest morals of the heart:
  But thefe his talents were yburied ftark;
Of the fine ftores he nothing would impart,
Which or boon Nature gave, or nature-painting Art.

LVIII.

To noontide fhades incontinent he ran,
Where purls the brook with fleep-inviting found;
Or when Dan *Sol* to flope his wheels began,
Amid the broom he bafk'd him on the ground,
Where the wild thyme and camomile are found:
There would he linger, till the lateft ray
Of light fat trembling on the welkin's bound;
  Then homeward thro' the twilight fhadows ftray,
Sauntering and flow.   So had he paffed many a day.

LIX.

Yet not in thoughtlefs flumber were they paft:
For oft the heavenly fire, that lay conceal'd
Beneath the fleeping embers, mounted faft,
And all its native light anew reveal'd:
Oft as he travers'd the cerulean field,
And markt the clouds that drove before the wind,
Ten thoufand glorious fyftems would he build,
Ten thoufand great ideas fill'd his mind;
But with the clouds they fled, and left no trace behind.

LX.

With him was fometimes join'd, in filent walk,
(Profoundly filent, for they never fpoke)
One fhyer ftill, who quite detefted talk:
Oft, ftung by fpleen, at once away he broke,
To groves of pine, and broad o'erfhading oak;
There, inly thrill'd, he wander'd all alone,
And on himfelf his penfive fury wroke,
Ne ever utter'd word, fave when firft fhone·
The glittering ftar of eve—" Thank Heaven! the day
is done."

LXI.

Here lurk'd a wretch, who had not crept abroad
For forty years, ne face of mortal feen;
In chamber brooding like a loathly toad:
And fure his linen was not very clean.
Through fecret loop-holes, that had practis'd been
Near to his bed, his dinner vile he took;
Unkempt, and rough, of fqualid face and mein,
Our caftle's fhame! whence, from his filthy nook,
We drove the villain out for fitter lair to look.

LXII.

One day there chaunc'd into thefe halls to rove
A joyous youth, who took you at firft fight;
Him the wild wave of pleafure hither drove,
Before the fprightly tempeft toffing light:
Certes, he was a moft engaging wight,
Of focial glee, and wit humane though keen,
Turning the night to day and day to night:
For him the merry bells had rung, I ween,
If in this nook of quiet bells had ever been.

LXIII.

But not even pleafure to excefs is good:
What moft elates then finks the foul as low:
When fpring-tide joy pours in with copious flood,
The higher ftill th' exulting billows flow,
The farther back again they flagging go,
And leave us groveling on the dreary fhore:
Taught by this fon of joy, we found it fo;
Who, whilft he ftaid, kept in a gay uproar
Our madden'd caftle all, th' abode of fleep no more.

LXIV.

As when in prime of *June* a burnifh'd fly,
Sprung from the meads, o'er which he fweeps along,
Chear'd by the breathing bloom and vital fky,
Tunes up amid thefe airy halls his fong,
Soothing at firft the gay repofing throng:
And oft he fips their bowl; or nearly drown'd,
He, thence recovering, drives their beds among,
And fcares their tender fleep, with trump profound;
Then out again he flies, to wing his mazy round.

LXV.

Another gueſt there was, of fenſe refin'd,
Who felt each worth, for every worth he had;
Serene yet warm, humane yet firm his mind,
As little touch'd as any man's with bad:
Him through their inmoſt walks the muſes lad,
To him the ſacred love of Nature lent,
And ſometimes would he make our valley glad;
Whenas we found he would not here be pent,
To him the better ſort this friendly meſſage ſent:

LXVI.

" Come, dwell with us! true ſon of virtue, come!
" But if, alas! we cannot thee perſuade
" To lie content beneath our peaceful dome,
" Ne ever more to quit our quiet glade;
" Yet when at laſt thy toils but ill apaid
" Shall dead thy fire, and damp its heavenly ſpark,
" Thou wilt be glad to ſeek the rural ſhade,
" There to indulge the muſe, and nature mark:
" We then a lodge for thee will rear in HAGLEY-PARK."

LXVII.

Here whilom ligg'd th' ESOPUS* of the age;
But call'd by Fame, in ſoul ypricked deep,
A noble pride reſtor'd him to the ſtage,
And rous'd him like a gyant from his ſleep.
Even from his ſlumbers we advantage reap:
With double force th' enliven'd ſcene he wakes,
Yet quits not Nature's bounds. He knows to keep
Each due decorum: now the heart he ſhakes,
And now with well-urg'd ſenſe th' enlighten'd judgment
takes.

* Mr. Quin.

LXVIII.

A bard here dwelt, more fat than bard befeems;
* Who, void of envy, guile, and luft of gain,
On virtue ftill, and Nature's pleafing themes,
Pour'd forth his unpremeditated ftrain:
The world forfaking with a calm difdain,
Here laugh'd he carelefs in his eafy feat;
Here quaff'd encircled with the joyous train,
Oft moralizing fage: his ditty fweet
He loathed much to write, ne cared to repeat.

LXIX.

Full oft by holy feet our ground was trod,
Of clerks good plenty here you mote efpy.
A little, round, fat, oily man of God,
Was one I chiefly mark'd among the fry:
He had a roguifh twinkle in his eye,
And fhone all glittering with ungodly dew,
If a tight damfel chaunc'd to trippen by;
Which when obferv'd, he fhrunk into his mew,
And ftrait would recolleĉt his piety anew.

LXX.

Nor be forgot a tribe, who minded nought
(Old inmates of the place) but ftate-affairs:
They look'd, perdie, as if they deeply thought;
And on their brow fat every nation's cares.
The world by them is parcel'd out in fhares,
When in the *Hall of Smoak* they congrefs hold,
And the fage berry fun-burnt *Mocha* bears
Has clear'd their inward eye: then, fmoak-enroll'd,
Their oracles break forth myfterious as of old.

* The following lines of this ftanza were writ by a friend of the author.

LXXI.

Here languid beauty kept her pale-fac'd court:
Bevies of dainty dames, of high degree,
From every quarter hither made resort;
Where, from gross mortal care and business free,
They lay, pour'd out in ease and luxury.
Or should they a vain shew of work assume,
Alas! and well-a-day! what can it be?
To knot, to twist, to range the vernal bloom;
But far is cast the distaff, spinning-wheel, and loom.

LXXII.

Their only labour was to kill the time;
And labour dire it is, and weary woe.
They sit, they loll, turn o'er some idle rhyme;
Then, rising sudden, to the glass they go,
Or saunter forth, with tottering step and slow:
This soon too rude an exercise they find;
Strait on the couch their limbs again they throw,
Where hours on hours they sighing lie reclin'd,
And court the vapoury god soft-breathing in the wind.

LXXIII.

Now must I mark the villainy we found,
But ah! too late, as shall eftsoons be shewn.
A place here was, deep, dreary, under ground;
Where still our inmates, when unpleasing grown,
Diseas'd, and loathsome, privily were thrown.
Far from the light of heaven, they languish'd there,
Unpity'd uttering many a bitter groan;
For of these wretches taken was no care:
Fierce fiends, and hags of hell, their only nurses were.

P 2

LXXIV.

Alas! the change! from fcenes of joy and reft,
To this dark den, where ficknefs tofs'd alway.
Here *Lethargy*, with deadly fleep oppreft,
Stretch'd on his back, a mighty lubbard, lay,
Heaving his fides, and fnored night and day;
To ftir him from his traunce it was not eath,
And his half-open'd eyne he fhut ftraitway:
He led, I wot, the fofteft way to death,
And taught withouten pain and ftrife to yield the breath.

LXXV.

Of limbs enormous, but withal unfound,
Soft-fwoln and pale, here lay the *Hydropfy*:
Unwieldy man; with belly monftrous round,
For ever fed with watery fupply;
For ftill he drank, and yet he ftill was dry.
And moping here did *Hypochondria* fit,
Mother of fpleen, in robes of various dye,
Who vexed was full oft with ugly fit;
And fome her frantic deem'd, and fome her deem'd a wit.

LXXVI.

A lady proud fhe was, of ancient blood,
Yet oft her fear her pride made crouchen low:
She felt, or fancy'd in her fluttering mood,
All the difeafes which the fpittles know,
And fought all phyfic which the fhops beftow,
And ftill new leaches and new drugs would try,
Her humour ever wavering to and fro;
For fometimes fhe would laugh, and fometimes cry,
Then fudden waxed wroth, and all fhe knew not why.

LXXVII.

Faſt by her ſide a liſtleſs maiden pin'd,
With aching head, and ſqueamiſh heart-burnings;
Pale, bloated, cold, ſhe ſeem'd to hate mankind,
Yet lov'd in ſecret all forbidden things.
And here the *Tertian* ſhakes his chilling wings;
The ſleepleſs *Gout* here counts the crowing cocks,
A wolf now gnaws him, now a ſerpent ſtings;
Whilſt *Apoplexy* cramm'd Intemperance knocks
Down to the ground at once, as butcher felleth ox.

P 3

CANTO II.

The knight of arts and induſtry,
And his atchievements fair;
That, by his caſtle's overthrow,
Secur'd, and crowned were.

I.

ESCAP'D the caſtle of the fire of ſin,
Ah! where ſhall I ſo ſweet a dwelling find?
For all around, without, and all within,
Nothing ſave what delightful was and kind,
Of goodneſs ſavouring and a tender mind,
E'er roſe to view.   But now another ſtrain,
Of doleful note, alas! remains behind:
I now muſt ſing of pleaſure turn'd to pain,
And of the falſe enchanter INDOLENCE complain.

II.

Is there no patron to protect the muſe,
And fence for her *Parnaſſus'* barren ſoil?
To every labour its reward accrues,
And they are ſure of bread who ſwink and moil;
But a fell tribe *th' Aonian hive* deſpoil,
As ruthleſs waſps oft rob the painful bee:
Thus while the laws not guard that nobleſt toil,
Ne for the muſes other meed decree,
They praiſed are alone, and ſtarve right merrily.

III.

I care not, Fortune, what you me deny:
You cannot rob me of free Nature's grace;
You cannot fhut the windows of the fky,
Thro' which *Aurora* fhews her brightening face;
You cannot bar my conftant feet to trace
The woods and lawns, by living ftream, at eve:
Let health my nerves and finer fibres brace,
And I their toys to the *great Children* leave:
Of fancy, reafon, virtue, nought can me bereave.

IV.

Come then, my mufe, and raife a bolder fong;
Come, lig no more upon the bed of floth,
Dragging the lazy languid line along,
Fond to begin, but ftill to finifh loth,
Thy half-writ fcrolls all eaten by the moth:
Arife, and fing that generous imp of fame,
Who with the fons of foftnefs nobly wroth,
To fweep away this human lumber came,
Or in a chofen few to roufe the flumbering flame.

V.

In *Fairy-land* there liv'd a knight of old,
Of feature ftern, *Selvaggio* well yclep'd,
A rough unpolifh'd man, robuft and bold,
But wondrous poor: he neither fow'd nor reap'd,
Ne ftores in fummer for cold winter heap'd;
In hunting all his days away he wore;
Now fcorch'd by *June*, now in *November* fteep'd,
Now pinch'd by biting *January* fore,
He ftill in woods purfu'd the libbard and the boar.

P 4

VI.

As he one morning, long before the dawn,
Prick'd through the foreſt to diſlodge his prey,
Deep in the winding boſom of a lawn,
With wood wild-fring'd, he mark'd a taper's ray,
That from the beating rain, and wintry fray,
Did to a lonely cott his ſteps decoy;
There, up to earn the needments of the day,
He found dame *Poverty*, nor fair nor coy:
Her he compreſs'd, and fill'd her with a luſty boy.

VII.

Amid the green-wood ſhade this boy was bred,
And grew at laſt a knight of muchel fame,
Of active mind and vigorous luſtyhed,
THE KNIGHT OF ARTS AND INDUSTRY by name.
Earth was his bed, the boughs his roof did frame;
He knew no beverage but the flowing ſtream;
His taſteful well-earn'd food the ſilvan game,
Or the brown fruit with which the wood-lands teem:
The ſame to him glad ſummer, or the winter breme.

VIII.

So paſs'd his youthly morning, void of care,
Wild as the colts that thro' the commons run:
For him no tender parents troubled were,
He of the foreſt ſeem'd to be the ſon,
And certes had been utterly undone;
But that *Minerva* pity of him took,
With all the gods that love the rural wonne,
That teach to tame the ſoil and rule the crook;
Ne did the ſacred nine diſdain a gentle look.

IX.

Of fertile genius him they nurtur'd well,
In every fcience, and in every art,
By which mankind the thoughtlefs brutes excel,
That can or ufe, or joy, or grace impart,
Difclofing all the powers of head and heart:
Ne were the goodly exercifes fpar'd,
That brace the nerves, or make the limbs alert,
And mix elaftic force with firmnefs hard:
Was never knight on ground mote be with him com-
    par'd.

X.

Sometimes, with early morn, he mounted gay
The hunter-fteed, exulting o'er the dale,
And drew the rofeat breath of orient day;
Sometimes, retiring to the fecret vale,
Yclad in fteel, and bright with burnifh'd mail,
He ftrain'd the bow, or tofs'd the founding fpear,
Or darting on the goal outftripp'd the gale,
Or wheel'd the chariot in its mid-career,
Or ftrenuous wreftled hard with many a tough compeer.

XI.

At other times he pry'd through Nature's ftore,
Whate'er fhe in th' etherial round contains,
What'er fhe hides beneath her verdant floor,
The vegetable and the mineral reigns;
Or elfe he fcann'd the Globe, thofe fmall domains,
Where reftlefs mortals fuch a turmoil keep,
Its feas, its floods, its mountains, and its plains;
But more he fearch'd the mind, and rous'd from fleep
Thofe moral feeds whence we heroic actions reap.

XII.

Nor would he fcorn to ftoop from high purfuits
Of heavenly truth, and practife what fhe taught.
Vain is the tree of knowledge without fruits.
Sometimes in hand the fpade or plough he caught,
Forth-calling all with which boon earth is fraught;
Sometimes he ply'd the ftrong mechanic tool,
Or rear'd the fabric from the fineft draught;
And oft he put himfelf to *Neptune*'s fchool,
Fighting with winds and waves on the vext ocean pool.

XIII.

To folace then thefe rougher toils, he try'd
To touch the kindling canvafs into life;
With Nature his creating pencil vy'd,
With Nature joyous at the mimic ftrife:
Or, to fuch fhapes as grac'd *Pygmalion*'s wife
He hew'd the marble; or, with varied fire,
He rous'd the trumpet and the martial fife,
Or bade the lute fweet tendernefs infpire,
Or verfes fram'd that well might wake *Apollo*'s lyre.

XIV.

Accomplifh'd thus he from the woods iffu'd,
Full of great aims, and bent on bold emprize;
The work, which long he in his breaft had brew'd,
Now to perform he ardent did devife;
To wit, a barbarous world to civilize.
Earth was till then a boundlefs foreft wild;
Nought to be feen but favage wood, and fkies;
No cities nourifh'd arts, no culture fmil'd,
No government, no laws, no gentle manners mild.

XV.

A rugged wight, the worſt of brutes, was man;
On his own wretched kind he, ruthleſs, prey'd:
The ſtrongeſt ſtill the weakeſt over-ran;
In every country mighty robbers ſway'd,
And guile and ruffian force were all their trade,
Life was a ſcene of rapine, want, and woe;
Which this brave knight, in noble anger, made
To ſwear, he would the raſcal rout o'erthrow,
For, by the powers divine, it ſhould no more be ſo!

XVI.

It would exceed the purport of my ſong,
To ſay how this *beſt Sun*, from orient climes
Came beaming life and beauty all along,
Before him chaſing indolence and crimes.
Still as he paſs'd, the nations he ſublimes,
And calls forth arts and virtues with his ray:
Then *Egypt*, *Greece*, and *Rome*, their golden times,
Succeſſive, had; but now in ruins grey
They lie, to ſlaviſh ſloth and tyranny a prey.

XVII.

To crown his toils, Sɪʀ Iɴᴅᴜsᴛʀʏ then ſpread.
The ſwelling ſail, and made for Bʀɪᴛᴀɪɴ's coaſt.
A ſylvan life till then the natives led,
In the brown ſhades and green-wood foreſt loſt,
All careleſs rambling where it lik'd them moſt:
Their wealth the wild-deer bouncing thro' the glade;
They lodg'd at large, and liv'd at Nature's coſt;
Save ſpear, and bow, withouten other aid;
Yet not the *Roman* ſteel their naked breaſt diſmay'd.

XVIII.

He lik'd the foil, he lik'd the clement fkies,
He lik'd the verdant hills and flowery plains
Be this my great, my chofen ifle, (he cries)
This, whilft my labours LIBERTY fuftains,
This·queen of ocean all affault difdains.
Nor lik'd he lefs the genius of the land,
To freedom apt and perfevering pains,
Mild to obey, and generous to command,
Temper'd by forming HEAVEN with kindeft firmeft hand.

XIX.

Here, by degrees, his mafter-work arofe,
Whatever arts and induftry can frame:
Whatever finifh'd agriculture knows,
Fair queen of arts! from heaven itfelf who came,
When *Eden* flourifh'd in unfpotted fame:
And ftill with her fweet innocence we find,
And tender peace, and joys without a name,
That, while they ravifh, tranquillize the mind:
Nature and Art at once, delight and ufe combin'd.

XX.

Then towns he quicken'd by mechanic arts,
And bade the fervent city glow with toil;
Bade focial Commerce raife renowned marts,
Join land to land, and marry foil to foil,
Unite the poles, and without bloody fpoil
Bring home of either *Ind* the gorgeous ftores;
Or, fhould defpotic rage the world embroil,
Bade tyrants tremble on remoteft fhores,
While o'er th' encircling deep *Britannia*'s thunder roars.

XXI.

The drooping mufes then he weftward call'd,
From the fam'd city * by *Propontic* fea,
What time the *Turk* th' enfeebled *Grecian* thrall'd;
Thence from their cloifter'd walks he fet them free,
And brought them to another *Caftalie*,
Where *Ifis* many a famous nourfling breeds;
Or where old *Cam* foft paces o'er the lea
In penfive mood, and tunes his *Doric* reeds,
The whilft his flocks at large the lonely fhepherd feeds.

XXII.

Yet the fine arts were what he finifh'd leaft.
For why? They are the quinteffence of all,
The growth of labouring time, and flow increaft;
Unlefs, as feldom chances, it fhould fall,
That mighty patrons the coy fifters call
Up to the fun-fhine of uncumber'd eafe,
Where no rude care the mounting thought may thrall,
And where they nothing have to do but pleafe:
Ah! gracious God! thou know'ft they afk no other fees.

XXIII.

But now, alas! we live too late in time:
Our patrons now even grudge that little claim,
Except to fuch as fleek the foothing rhyme;
And yet, forfooth, they wear Mæcenas' name,
Poor fons of puft-up vanity, not fame.
Unbroken fpirits, chear! ftill, ftill remains
Th' *Eternal Patron*, Liberty; whofe flame,
While fhe protects, infpires the nobleft ftrains.
The beft, and fweeteft far, are toil-created gains.

* Conftantinople.

XXIV.

When as the knight had fram'd, in BRITAIN-LAND,
A matchlefs form of glorious government,
In which the fovereign laws alone command,
Laws ftablifh'd by the public free confent,
Whofe majefty is to the fceptre lent;
When this great plan, with each dependent art,
Was fettled firm, and to his heart's content,
Then fought he from the toilfome fcene to part,
And let life's vacant eve breathe quiet thro' the heart.

XXV.

For this he chofe a farm in *Deva*'s vale,
Where his long alleys peep'd upon the main.
In this calm feat he drew the healthful gale,
Here mix'd the chief, the patriot, and the fwain.
The happy monarch of his fylvan train,
Here, fided by the guardians of the fold,
He walk'd his rounds, and chear'd his bleft domain:
His days, the days of unftain'd Nature, roll'd,
Replete with peace and joy, like patriarch's of old.

XXVI.

Witnefs, ye lowing herds, who gave him milk;
Witnefs, ye flocks, whofe woolly veftments far
Exceed foft *India*'s cotton, or her filk;
Witnefs, with autumn charg'd, the nodding car,
That homeward came beneath fweet evening's ftar,
Or of *September*-moons the radiance mild.
O hide thy head, abominable war!
Of crimes and ruffian idlenefs the child!
From heaven this life yfprung, from hell thy glories vild!

XXVII.

Nor from his deep retirement banifh'd was
Th' amufing care of rural induftry.
Still, as with grateful change the feafons pafs,
New fcenes arife, new landfkips ftrike the eye,
And all th' enliven'd country beautify:
Gay plains extend where marfhes flept before;
O'er recent meads th' exulting ftreamlets fly;
Dark frowning heaths grow bright with *Ceres'* ftore,
And woods imbrown the fteep, or wave along the fhore.

XXVIII.

As nearer to his farm you made approach,
He polifh'd Nature with a finer hand:
Yet on her beauties durft not Art incroach;
'Tis Art's alone thefe beauties to expand.
In graceful dance immingled, o'er the land,
Pan, Pales, Flora, and *Pomona* play'd:
Here too brifk gales the rude wild common fand
An happy place; where free, and unafraid,
Amid the flowering brakes each coyer creature ftray'd.

XXIX.

But in prime vigour what can laft for ay?
That foul-enfeebling wizard INDOLENCE,
I whilom fung, wrought in his works decay:
Spread far and wide was *his* curs'd influence;
Of public virtue much *he* dull'd the fenfe,
Even much of private; ate our fpirit out,
And fed our rank luxurious vices: whence
The land was overlaid with many a lout;
Not, as old Fame reports, wife, generous, bold, and ftout.

XXX.

A rage of pleafure madden'd every breaft,
Down to the loweft lees the ferment ran:
To his licentious wifh each muft be bleft,
With joy be fever'd; fnatch it as he can.
Thus *Vice* the ftandard rear'd; her arrier-ban
Corruption call'd, and loud fhe gave the word,
" Mind, mind yourfelves! why fhould the vulgar man,
" The lacquey be more virtuous than his lord?
" Enjoy this fpan of life! 'tis all the gods afford."

XXXI.

The tidings reach'd to where in quiet hall,
The good old knight enjoy'd well-earn'd repofe.
" Come, come, Sir Knight! thy children on thee call:
" Come, fave us yet, ere ruin round us clofe!
" The demon INDOLENCE thy toils o'erthrows."
On this the noble colour ftain'd his cheeks,
Indignant, glowing thro' the whitening fnows
Of venerable eld; his eye full-fpeaks
His ardent foul, and from his couch at once he breaks.

XXXII.

I will, (he cry'd) fo help me, God! deftroy
That villain Archimage.—His page then ftrait
He to him call'd, a fiery-footed boy,
Benempt *Difpatch*. " My fteed be at the gate;
" My bard attend; quick, bring the net of fate."
This net was twifted by the fifters three;
Which when once caft o'er harden'd wretch, too late
Repentance comes: replevy cannot be
From the ftrong iron grafp of vengeful Deftiny.

XXXIII.

He came, the bard, a little druid-wight,
Of withered afpect; but his eye was keen,
With fweetnefs mix'd.   In ruffet brown bedight,
As is his fifter * of the copfes green,
He crept along, unpromifing of mien.
Grofs he who judges fo.   His foul was fair,
Bright as the children of yon azure fheen.
True comelinefs, which nothing can impair,
Dwells in the mind: all elfe is vanity and glare.

XXXIV.

Come (quoth the knight), a voice has reach'd mine ear:
The demon INDOLENCE threats overthrow
To all that to mankind is good and dear:
Come, PHILOMELUS; let us inftant go,
O'erturn his bowers, and lay his caftle low.
Thofe men, thofe wretched men! who *will* be flaves,
Muft drink a bitter wrathful cup of woe:
But fome there be, thy fong, as from their graves,
Shall raife. Thrice happy he! who without rigour faves.

XXXV.

Iffuing forth, the knight beftrode his fteed,
Of ardent bay, and on whofe front a ftar
Shone blazing bright: fprung from the generous breed
That whirl of active day the rapid car,
He pranc'd along, difdaining gate or bar.
Meantime, the bard on milk-white palfrey rode;
An honeft fober beaft, that did not mar
His meditations, but full foftly trode:
And much they moraliz'd as thus yfere they yode.

* The Nightingale.

XXXVI.

They talk'd of virtue, and of human blifs.
What elfe fo fit for man to fettle well?
And ftill their long refearches met in this,
This *Truth of Truths*, which nothing can refel:
" From virtue's fount the pureft joys out-well,
" Sweet rills of thought that chear the confcious foul;
" While vice pours forth the troubled ftreams of hell,
" The which, howe'er difguis'd, at laft with dole
" Will, through the tortur'd breaft, their fiery torrent
      roll."

XXXVII.

At length it dawn'd, that fatal valley gay,
O'er which high wood-crown'd hills their fummits
      rear.
On the cool height awhile our palmers ftay,
And fpite even of themfelves their fenfes chear;
Then to the vizard's wonne their fteps they fteer.
Like a green ifle, it broad beneath them fpred,
With gardens round, and wandering currents clear,
And tufted groves to fhade the meadow bed,
Sweet airs and fong; and without hurry all feem'd glad.

XXXVIII.

" As God fhall judge me, knight, we muft forgive
(The half-enraptur'd PHILÓMELUS cry'd)
" The frail good man deluded here to live,
" And in thefe groves his mufing fancy hide.
" Ah! nought is pure. It cannot be deny'd,
" That virtue ftill fome tinÆture has of vice,
" And vice of virtue. What fhould then betide,
" But that our charity be not too nice?
" Come, let us thofe we can to real blifs entice."

XXXIX.

" Ay, ficker (quoth the knight), all flefh is frail,
" To pleafant fin and joyous dalliance bent;
" But let not brutifh vice of this avail,
" And think to 'fcape deferved punifhment.
" *Juftice* were cruel weakly to relent;
" From *Mercy*'s felf fhe got her facred glaive:
" Grace be to thofe who can, and will, repent;
" But penance long, and dreary, to the flave,
" Who muft in floods of fire his grofs foul fpirit lave."

XL.

Thus, holding high difcourfe, they came to where
The curfed carle was at his wonted trade;
Still tempting heedlefs men into his fnare,
In witching wife, as I before have faid.
But when he faw, in goodly geer array'd,
The grave majeftic knight approaching nigh,
And by his fide the bard fo fage and ftaid,
His countenance fell; yet oft his anxious eye
Mark'd them, like wily fox who roofted cock doth fpy.

XLI.

Nathlefs, with feign'd refpect, he bade give back
The rabble-rout, and welcom'd them full kind;
Struck with the noble twain, they were not flack
His orders to obey, and fall behind.
Then he refum'd his fong; and unconfin'd,
Pour'd all his mufic, ran through all his ftrings:
With magic duft their eyne he tries to blind,
And virtue's tender airs o'er weaknefs flings.
What pity bafe his fong who fo divinely fings!

XLII.

Elate in thought, he counted them his own,
They liften'd fo intent with fix'd delight:
But they inftead, as if tranfmew'd to ftone,
Marvel'd he could with fuch fweet art unite
The lights and fhades of manners, wrong and right.
Mean time, the filly crowd the charm devour,
Wide-preffing to the gate. Swift, on the knight
He darted fierce, to drag him to his bower,
Who backning fhunn'd his touch, for well he knew its
     power.

XLIII.

As in throng'd amphitheatre, of old,
The wary *Retiarius* * trap'd his foe;
Even fo the knight, returning on him bold,
At once involv'd him in the *Net of Woe*,
Whereof I mention made not long ago.
Inrag'd at firft, he fcorn'd fo weak a jail,
And leapt, and flew, and flounced to and fro;
But when he found that nothing could avail,
He fet him felly down and gnaw'd his bitter nail.

XLIV.

Alarm'd, th' inferior demons of the place
Rais'd rueful fhrieks and hideous yells around;
Black ftormy clouds deform'd the welkin's face,
And from beneath was heard a wailing found,
As of infernal fprights in cavern bound;
A folemn fadnefs every creature ftrook,
And lightnings flafh'd, and horror rock'd the ground:
Huge crowds on crowds out-pour'd, with blemifh'd
     look,
As if on time's laft verge this frame of things had fhook.

* A gladiator, who made ufe of a net, which he threw over his adverfary.

XLV.

Soon as the ſhort-liv'd tempeſt was yſpent,
Steam'd from the jaws of vext Avernus' hole,
And huſh'd the hubbub of the rabblement,
Sir Industry the firſt calm moment ſtole.
" There muſt (he cry'd), amid ſo vaſt a ſhoal,
" Be ſome who are not tainted at the heart,
" Not poiſon'd quite by this ſame villain's bowl:
" Come then, my bard, thy heavenly fire impart;
" Touch ſoul with ſoul, till forth the latent ſpirit ſtart."

XLVI.

The bard obey'd; and taking from his ſide,
Where it in ſeemly ſort depending hung,
His *Britiſh* harp, its ſpeaking ſtrings he try'd,
The which with ſkilful touch he deftly ſtrung,
Till tinkling in clear ſymphony they rung.
Then, as he felt the muſes come along,
Light o'er the chords his raptur'd hand he flung,
And play'd a prelude to his riſing ſong:
The whilſt, like midnight mute, ten thouſands round
    him throng.

XLVII.

Thus, ardent, burſt his ſtrain.———
                    " Ye hapleſs race,
" Dire-labouring here to ſmother reaſon's ray,
" That lights our Maker's image in our face,
" And gives us wide o'er earth unqueſtion'd ſway;
" What is th' ador'd supreme Perfection, ſay?
" What, but eternal never-reſting ſoul,
" Almighty power, and all-directing day;
" By whom each atom ſtirs, the planets roll;
" Who fills, ſurrounds, informs, and agitates the whole.

Q 3

XLVIII.

" Come, to the beaming GoD your hearts unfold!
" Draw from its fountain life! 'Tis thence, alone,
" We can excel.   Up from unfeeling mold,
" To feraphs burning round th' ALMIGHTY's throne,
" Life rifing ftill on life, in higher tone,
" Perfeftion forms, and with perfeftion blifs.
" In univerfal Nature this clear fhewn,
" Not needeth proof: to prove it were, I wis,
" To prove the beauteous world excels the brute abyfs.

XLIX.

" Is not the field, with lively culture green,
" A fight more joyous than the dead morafs?
" Do not the fkies, with aftive ether clean,
" And fann'd by fprightly Zephyrs, far furpafs
" The foul November-fogs, and flumberous mafs,
" With which fad Nature veils her drooping face?
" Does not the mountain-ftream, as clear as glafs,
" Gay-dancing on, the putrid pool difgrace?
" The fame in all holds true, but chief in human race.

L.

" It was not by vile loitering in eafe,
" That GREECE obtain'd the brighter palm of art,
" That foft yet ardent ATHENS learn'd to pleafe,
" To keen the wit, and to fublime the heart,
" In all fupreme! complete in every part!
" It was not thence majeftic ROME arofe,
" And o'er the nations fhook her conquering dart:
" For fluggard's brow the laurel never grows;
" Renown is not the child of indolent repofe.

LI.

" Had unambitious mortals minded nought,
" But in loofe joy their time to wear away;
" Had they alone the lap of dalliance fought,
" Pleas'd on her pillow their dull heads to lay,
" Rude Nature's ftate had been our ftate to-day;
" No cities e'er their towery fronts had rais'd,
" No arts had made us opulent and gay;
" With brother-brutes the human race had graz'd;
" None e'er had foar'd to fame, none honour'd been,
    none prais'd.

LII.

" Great HOMER's fong had never fir'd the breaft
" To thirft of glory and heroic deeds;
" Sweet MARO's mufe, funk in inglorious reft,
" Had filent flept amid the *Mincian* reeds:
" The wits of modern time had told their beads,
" And monkifh legends been their only ftrains;
" Our MILTON's *Eden* had lain wrapt in weeds,
" Our SHAKESPEAR ftroll'd and laugh'd with *War-
    wick* fwains,
" Ne had my mafter SPENSER charm'd his *Mulla's* plains.

LIII.

" Dumb too had been the fage hiftoric mufe,
" And perifh'd all the fons of ancient fame;
" Thofe ftarry lights of virtue, that diffufe
" Thro' the dark depth of time their vivid flame,
" Had all been loft with fuch as have no name.
" Who then had fcorn'd his eafe for others' good?
" Who then had toil'd rapacious men to tame?
" Who in the public breach devoted ftood,
" And for his country's caufe been prodigal of blood?

Q 4

LIV.

" But fhould to fame your hearts unfeeling be,
" If right I read, you pleafure all require:
" Then hear how beft may be obtain'd this fee,
" How beft enjoy'd this Nature's wide defire.
" Toil, and be glad! let Induftry infpire
" Into your quicken'd limbs her buoyant breath!
" Who does not act is dead; abforpt entire
" In miry floth, no pride, no joy he hath:
" O leaden-hearted men, to be in love with death!

LV.

" Ah! what avail the largeft gifts of HEAVEN,
" When drooping health and fpirits go amifs?
" How taftelefs then whatever can be given!
" Health is the vital principle of blifs,
" And exercife of health. In proof of this,
" Behold the wretch, who flugs his life away,
" Soon fwallow'd in difeafe's fad abyfs;
" While he whom toil has brac'd, or manly play,
" Has light as air each limb, each thought as clear as day.

LVI.

" O who can fpeak the vigorous joys of health!
" Unclogg'd the body, unobfcur'd the mind:
" The morning rifes gay, with pleafing ftealth,
" The temperate evening falls ferene and kind.
" In health the wifer brutes true gladnefs find.
" See! how the younglings frifk along the meads,
" As *May* comes on, and wakes the balmy wind;
" Rampant with life, their joy all joy exceeds:
" Yet what but high-ftrung health this dancing plea-
        faunce breeds?

LVII.

" But here, inftead, is fofter'd every ill, .
" Which or diftemper'd minds or bodies know.
" Come then, my kindred fpirits! do not fpill
" Your talents here. This place is but a fhew,
" Whofe charms delude you to the den of woe:
" Come, follow me, I will direct you right,
" Where pleafure's rofes, void of ferpents, grow,
" Sincere as fweet; come, follow this good knight,
" And you will blefs the day that brought him to your
      fight.

LVIII.

" Some he will lead to courts, and fome to camps;
" To fenates fome, and public fage debates,
" Where, by the folemn gleam of midnight-lamps,
" The world is pois'd, and manag'd mighty ftates;
" To high difcovery fome, that new-creates
" The face of earth; fome to the thriving mart;.
" Some to the rural reign, and fofter fates;
" To the fweet mufes fome, who raife the heart;
" All glory fhall be yours, all nature, and all art.

LIX.

" There are, I fee, who liften to my lay,
" Who wretched figh for virtue, but defpair.
" All may be done, (methinks I hear them fay)
" Even death defpis'd by generous actions fair;
" All, but for thofe who to thefe bowers repair,
" Their every power diffolv'd in luxury,
" To quit of torpid fluggifhnefs the lair,
" And from the powerful arms of floth get free.
" 'Tis rifing from the dead——Alas!—It cannot be!

LX.

" Would you then learn to diffipate the band
" Of thefe huge threatning difficulties dire,
" That in the weak man's way like lions ftand,
" His foul appall, and damp his rifing fire?
" Refolve, refolve, and to be men afpire.
" Exert that nobleft privilege, alone,
" Here to mankind indulg'd: controul defire:
" Let godlike Reafon, from her fovereign throne,
" Speak the commanding word—*I will!*—and it is done.

LXI.

" Heavens! can you then thus wafte, in fhameful wife,
" Your few important days of trial here?
" Heirs of eternity! yborn to rife
" Thro' endlefs ftates of being, ftill more near
" To blifs approaching, and perfection clear,
" Can you renounce a fortune fo fublime,
" Such glorious hopes, your backward fteps to fteer,
" And roll, with vileft brutes, thro' mud and flime?
" No! no!—Your heaven-touch'd hearts difdain the
        fordid crime!"

LXII.

" Enough! enough!" they cry'd—ftrait, from the
        crowd,
The better fort on wings of tranfport fly:
As when amid the lifelefs fummits proud
Of *Alpine* cliffs, where to the gelid fky
Snows pil'd on fnows in wintry torpor lie,
The rays divine of vernal *Phœbus* play;
Th' awaken'd heaps, in ftreamlets from on high,
Rous'd into action, lively leap away,
Glad-warbling thro' the vales, in their new Being gay.

LXIII.

Not lefs the life, the vivid joy ferene,
That lighted up thefe new-created men,
Than that which wings th' exulting fpirit clean,
When, juft deliver'd from his flefhly den,
It foaring feeks its native fkies agen:
How light its effence! how unclogg'd its powers,
Beyond the blazon of my mortal pen!
. Even fo we glad forfook thefe finful bowers,
Even fuch enraptur'd life, fuch energy was ours.

LXIV.

But far the greater part, with rage inflam'd,
Dire-mutter'd curfes, and blafphem'd high Jove.
" Ye fons of hate! (they bitterly exclaim'd)
" What brought you to this feat of peace and love?
" While with kind Nature, here amid the grove,
" We pafs'd the harmlefs fabbath of our time,
" What to difturb it could, fell men, emove
" Your barbarous hearts? Is happinefs a crime?
" Then do the fiends of hell rule in yon heaven fublime.

LXV.

" Ye impious wretches," (quoth the knight in wrath)
. " Your happinefs behold!"—Then ftrait a wand
He wav'd, an anti-magic power that hath,
True from illufive falfhood to command.
Sudden the landfkip finks on every hand;
. The pure quick ftreams are marfhy puddles found;
On baleful heaths the groves all blacken'd ftand;
And, o'er the weedy foul abhorred ground,
Snakes, adders, toads, each loathfome creature crawls
    around.

LXVI.

And here and there, on trees by lightning fcath'd,
Unhappy wights who loathed life yhung;
Or, in frefh gore and recent murder bath'd,
They weltering lay; or elfe, infuriate flung
Into the gloomy flood, while ravens fung
The funeral dirge, they down the torrent rowl'd:
Thefe, by diftemper'd blood to madnefs ftung,
Had doom'd themfelves; whence oft, when night
        controul'd
The world, returning hither their fad fpirits howl'd.

LXVII.

Meantime a moving fcene was open laid;
That lazar-houfe, I whilom in my lay
Depeinted have, its horrors deep-difplay'd,
And gave unnumber'd wretches to the day,
Who toffing there in fqualid mifery lay.
Soon as of facred light th' unwonted fmile
Pour'd on thefe living catacombs its ray,
Thro' the drear caverns ftretching many a mile,
The fick up-rais'd their heads, and dropp'd their woes
        awhile.

LXVIII.

" O Heaven! (they cry'd) and do we once more fee
" Yon bleffed fun, and this green earth fo fair?
" Are we from noifome damps of peft-houfe free?
" And drink our fouls the fweet ethereal air?
" O thou! or Knight, or God! who holdeft there
" That fiend, oh keep him in eternal chains!
" But what for us, the children of defpair,
" Brought to the brink of hell, what hope remains?
" Repentance does itfelf but aggravate our pains."

LXIX.

The gentle Knight, who faw their rueful cafe,
Let fall adown his filver beard fome tears.
" Certes (quoth he) it is not even in grace,
" T' undo the paft, and eke your broken years:
" Nathlefs, to nobler worlds repentance rears,
" With humble hope, her eye; to her is given
" A power the truly contrite heart that chears;
" She quells the brand by which the rocks are riven;
" She more than merely foftens, fhe rejoices HEAVEN.

LXX.

" Then patient bear the fufferings you have earn'd,
" And by thefe fufferings purify the mind;
" Let wifdom be by paft mifconduct learn'd:
" Or pious die, with penitence refign'd;
" And to a life more happy and refin'd,
" Doubt not, you fhall, new creatures, yet arife.
" Till then, you may expect in me to find
" One who will wipe your forrow from your eyes,
" One who will foothe your pangs, and wing you to the
    fkies."

LXXI.

They filent heard, and pour'd their thanks in tears.
" For you (refum'd the Knight with fterner tone)
" Whofe hard dry hearts th' obdurate demon fears,
" That villain's gifts will coft you many a groan;
" In dolorous manfion long you muft bemoan
" His fatal charms, and weep your ftains away;
" Till, foft and pure as infant goodnefs grown,
" You feel a perfect change: then, who can fay,
" What grace may yet fhine forth in Heaven's eternal
    day?"

LXXII.

This faid, his powerful wand he wav'd anew:
Inftant, a glorious angel-train defcends,
The Charities, to-wit, of rofy hue;
Sweet love their looks a gentle radiance lends,
And with feraphic flame compaffion blends.
At once, delighted, to their charge they fly:
When lo! a goodly hofpital afcends;
In which they bade each lenient aid be nigh,
That could the fick-bed fmoothe of that fad company.

LXXIII.

It was a worthy edifying fight,
And gives to human kind peculiar grace,
To fee kind hands attending day and night,
With tender miniftry, from place to place.
Some prop the head; fome, from the pallid face
Wipe off the faint cold dews weak Nature fheds;
Some reach the healing draught: the whilft, to chafe
The fear fupreme, around their foften'd beds,
Some holy man by prayer all opening heaven difpreds.

LXXIV.

Attended by a glad acclaiming train,
Of thofe he refcu'd had from gaping hell,
Then turn'd the Knight; and, to his hall again
Soft-pacing, fought of peace the moffy cell:
Yet down his cheeks the gems of pity fell,
To fee the helplefs wretches that remain'd,
There left thro' delves and deferts dire to yell;
Amaz'd, their looks with pale difmay were ftain'd,
And fpreading wide their hands they meek repentance
    feign'd.

LXXV.

But ah! their fcorned day of grace was paft:
For (horrible to tell!) a defert wild
Before them ftretch'd, bare, comfortlefs, and vaft;
With gibbets, bones, and carcafes defil'd.
There nor trim field, nor lively culture fmil'd;
Nor waving fhade was feen, nor fountain fair;
But fands abrupt on fands lay loofely pil'd,
Thro' which they floundering toil'd with painful care,
Whilft *Phœbus* fmote them fore, and fir'd the cloudlefs
air.

LXXVI.

Then, varying to a joylefs land of bogs,
The fadden'd country a grey wafte appear'd;
Where nought but putrid fteams and noifome fogs
For ever hung on drizzly *Aufter*'s beard;
Or elfe the ground by piercing *Caurus* fear'd,
Was jagg'd with froft, or heap'd with glazed fnow:
Thro' thefe extremes a ceafelefs round they fteer'd,
By cruel fiends ftill hurry'd to and fro,
Gaunt *Beggary*, and *Scorn*, with many hell-hounds moe.

LXXVII.

The firft was with bafe dunghill rags yclad,
Tainting the gale, in which they flutter'd light;
Of morbid hue his features, funk, and fad;
His hollow eyne fhook forth a fickly light;
And o'er his lank jaw-bone, in piteous plight,
His black rough beard was matted rank and vile;
Direful to fee! an heart-appalling fight!
Meantime foul fcurf and blotches him defile;
And dogs, where-e'er he went, ftill barked all the while.

LXXVIII.

The other was a fell defpightful fiend:
Hell holds none worfe in baleful bower below:
By pride, and wit, and rage, and rancour, keen'd;
Of man alike, if good or bad, the foe:
With nofe up-turn'd, he always made a fhew
As if he fmelt fome naufeous fcent; his eye
Was cold, and keen, like blaft from boreal fnow;
And taunts he caften forth moft bitterly.
Such were the twain that off drove this ungodly fry.

LXXIX.

Even fo thro' *Brentford* town, a town of mud,
An herd of brifly fwine is prick'd along;
The filthy beafts, that never chew the cud,
Still grunt, and fqueak, and fing their troublous fong,
And oft they plunge themfelves the mire among:
But ay the ruthlefs driver goads them on,
And ay of barking dogs the bitter throng
Makes them renew their unmelodious moan;
Ne ever find they reft from their unrefting fone.

A

P O E M,

SACRED TO THE

M E M O R Y

OF

SIR ISAAC NEWTON.

INSCRIBED TO

THE RIGHT HONOURABLE

SIR ROBERT WALPOLE.

Vol. I.   R

TO THE

MEMORY

OF

SIR ISAAC NEWTON.

SHALL the great foul of NEWTON quit this earth,
   To mingle with his ftars; and every Mufe,
Aftonifh'd into filence, fhun the weight
Of honours due to his illuftrious name?
But what can man?—Even now the fons of light,
In ftrains high-warbled to feraphic lyre,
Hail his arrival on the coaft of blifs.
Yet am not I deterr'd, tho' high the theme,
And fung to harps of angels; for with you,
Ethereal flames! ambitious, I afpire
In nature's general fymphony to join.

   And what new wonders can ye fhew your gueft!
Who, while on this dim fpot, where mortals toil
Clouded in duft, from Motion's fimple laws,
Could trace the fecret hand of Providence,
Wide-working thro' this univerfal frame.

   Have ye not liften'd while he bound the Suns,
And Planets, to their fpheres! th' unequal tafk
Of human-kind till then.   Oft had they roll'd
O'er erring man the year, and oft difgrac'd

The pride of fchools, before their courfe was known
Full in its caufes and effects to him,
All-piercing fage! who fat not down and dream'd
Romantic fchemes, defended by the din
Of fpecious words, and tyranny of names;
But, bidding his amazing mind attend,
And with heroic Patience years on years
Deep-fearching, faw at laft the Syftem dawn,
And fhine, of all his race, on him alone.

What were his raptures then! how pure! how ftrong!
And what the triumphs of old *Greece* and *Rome*,
By his diminifh'd, but the pride of boys
In fome fmall fray victorious! when inftead
Of fhatter'd parcels of this earth ufurp'd
By violence unmanly, and fore deeds
Of cruelty and blood, Nature herfelf
Stood all-fubdu'd by him, and open laid
Her every latent glory to his view.

All intellectual eye, our folar round
Firft gazing thro', he by the blended power
Of *Gravitation* and *Projection* faw
The whole in filent harmony revolve.
From unaffifted vifion hid, the moons
To chear remoter planets numerous form'd,
By him in all their mingled tracts were feen.
He alfo fix'd our wandering queen of night,
Whether fhe wanes into a fcanty orb,
Or, waxing broad, with her pale fhadowy light,
In a foft deluge overflows the fky.
Her every motion clear-difcerning, He
Adjufted to the mutual Main, and taught
Why now the mighty mafs of water fwells
Refiftlefs, heaving on the broken rocks,
And the full river turning: till again

The tide revertive, unattracted, leaves
A yellow wafte of idle fands behind.

   Then breaking hence, he took his ardent flight
Thro' the blue infinite; and every ftar,
Which the clear concave of a winter's night
Pours on the eye, or aftronomic tube,
Far-ftretching, fnatches from the dark abyfs;
Or fuch as farther in fucceffive fkies
To fancy fhine alone, at his approach
Blaz'd into funs, the living centre each
Of an harmonious fyftem: all combin'd,
And rul'd unerring by that fingle power,
Which draws the ftone projected to the ground.

   O unprofufe magnificence divine!
O wifdom truly perfect! thus to call
From a few caufes fuch a fcheme of things,
Effects fo various, beautiful, and great,
An univerfe compleat! And O belov'd
Of Heaven! whofe well-purg'd penetrative eye,
The myftic veil tranfpiercing, inly fcann'd
The rifing, moving, wide-eftablifh'd frame,

   He, firft of men, with awful wing purfu'd
The Comet thro' the long elliptic curve,
As round innumerous worlds he wound his way;
Till, to the forehead of our evening fky
Return'd, the blazing wonder glares anew,
And o'er the trembling nations fhakes difmay.

   The heavens are all his own; from the wild rule
Of whirling *vortices*, and circling *fpheres*,
To their firft great fimplicity reftor'd.
The fchools aftonifh'd ftood; but found it vain
To combat ftill with demonftration ftrong,
And, unawakened, dream beneath the blaze
Of truth. At once their pleafing vifions fled,

With the gay fhadows of the morning mix'd,
When NEWTON rofe, our philofophic fun.

 Th' aërial flow of Sound was known to him,
From whence it firft in wavy circles breaks,
Till the touch'd organ takes the meffage in.
Nor could the darting beam of fpeed immenfe,
Efcape his fwift purfuit, and meafuring eye.
Even Light itfelf, which every thing difplays,
Shone undifcover'd, till his brighter mind
Untwifted all the fhining robe of day;
And, from the whitening undiftinguifh'd blaze,
Collecting every ray into his kind,
To the charm'd eye educ'd the gorgeous train
Of Parent-colours. Firft the flaming Red
Sprung vivid forth; the tawny Orange next;
And next delicious Yellow; by whofe fide
Fell the kind beams of all-refrefhing Green.
Then the pure Blue, that fwells autumnal fkies,
Ethereal play'd; and then, of fadder hue,
Emerg'd the deepened Indico, as when
The heavy-fkirted evening droops with froft.
While the laft gleamings of refracted light
Dy'd in the fainting Violet away.
Thefe, when the clouds diftil the rofy fhower,
Shine out diftinct adown the watery bow;
While o'er our heads the dewy vifion bends
Delightful, melting on the fields beneath.
Myriads of mingling dyes from thefe refult,
And myriads ftill remain; infinite fource
Of beauty, ever-blufhing, ever-new!

 Did ever poet image aught fo fair,
Dreaming in whifpering groves, by the hoarfe brook!
Or prophet, to whofe rapture Heaven defcends!
Even now the fetting fun and fhifting clouds,

Seen, *Greenwich*, from thy lovely heights, declare
How juft, how beauteous the *refractive law*.
    The noifelefs tide of time, all bearing down
To vaft eternity's unbounded fea,
Where the green iflands of the happy fhine,
He ftemm'd alone: and to the fource (involv'd
Deep in primeval gloom) afcending, rais'd
His lights at equal diftances, to guide
Hiftorian, wilder'd on his darkfome way.
    But who can number up his labours? who
His high difcoveries fing? when but a few
Of the deep-ftudying race can ftretch their minds
To what he knew: in fancy's lighter thought,
How fhall the mufe then grafp the mighty theme?
    What wonder thence that his devotion fwell'd
Refponfive to his knowledge! For could he,
Whofe piercing mental eye diffufive faw
The finifh'd univerfity of things,
In all its order, magnitude, and parts,
Forbear inceffant to adore that Power
Who fills, fuftains, and actuates the whole?
    Say, ye who beft can tell, ye happy few,
Who faw him in the fofteft lights of life,
All unwithheld, indulging to his friends
The vaft unborrow'd treafures of his mind,
Oh fpeak the wondrous man! how mild, how calm,
How greatly humble, how divinely good;
How firm eftablifh'd on eternal truth;
Fervent in doing well, with every nerve
Still preffing on, forgetful of the paft,
And panting for perfection: far above
Thofe little cares, and vifionary joys,
That fo perplex the fond impaffion'd heart
Of ever-cheated, ever-trufting man.

R 4

And you, ye hopelefs gloomy-minded tribe,
You who, unconfcious of thofe nobler flights
That reach impatient at immortal life,
Againft the prime endearing privilege
Of Being dare contend, fay, can a foul
Of fuch extenfive, deep, tremendous powers,
Enlarging ftill, be but a finer breath
Of fpirits dancing thro' their tubes awhile,
And then for ever loft in vacant air?

But hark! methinks I hear a warning voice,
Solemn as when fome awful change is come,
Sound thro' the world—*'Tis done!*—*The meafure's full*;
And I refign my charge.——Ye mouldering ftones,
That build the towering pyramid, the proud
Triumphal arch, the monument effac'd
By ruthlefs ruin, and whate'er fupports
The worfhip name of hoar antiquity,
Down to the duft! what grandeur can ye boaft
While NEWTON lifts his column to the fkies,
Beyond the wafte of time.   Let no weak drop
Be fhed for him.   The virgin in her bloom
Cut off, the joyous youth, and darling child,
Thefe are the tombs that claim the tender tear,
And elegiac fong.   But NEWTON calls
For other notes of gratulation high,
That now he wanders thro' thofe endlefs worlds
He here fo well defcrib'd, and wondering talks
And hymns their Author with his glad compeers.

O BRITAIN's boaft! whether with angels thou
Sitteft in dread difcourfe, or fellow-bleft,
Who joy to fee the honour of their kind;
Or whether, mounted on cherubic wing,
Thy fwift career is with the whirling orbs,
Comparing things with things, in rapture loft,

And grateful adoration, for that light
So plenteous ray'd into thy mind below,
From Light *himfelf*; Oh look with pity down
On human-kind, a frail erroneous race!
Exalt the fpirit of a downward world!
O'er thy dejected country chief prefide,
And be her *Genius* call'd! her ftudies raife,
Correct her manners, and infpire her youth.
For, tho' deprav'd and funk, fhe brought thee forth,
And glories in thy name; fhe points thee out
To all her fons, and bids them eye thy ftar:
While in expectance of the fecond life,
When time fhall be no more, thy facred duft
Sleeps with her kings, and dignifies the fcene.

A

P O E M,

TO THE

M E M O R Y

OF

THE RIGHT HONOURABLE THE

LORD TALBOT,

LATE CHANCELLOR OF GREAT BRITAIN.

TO THE

M E M O R Y

OF

THE RIGHT HONOURABLE THE

LORD TALBOT.

ADDRESSED TO HIS SON.

WHILE, with the Public, you, my Lord, lament
  A friend and father loft; permit the Mufe,
The Mufe affign'd of old a double theme,
To praife dead worth and humble living pride,
Whofe generous tafk begins where int'reft ends,
Permit her on a TALBOT's tomb to lay
This cordial verfe fincere, by truth infpir'd,
Which means not to beftow but borrow fame.
Yes, fhe may fing his matchlefs virtues now—
Unhappy that fhe may.—But where begin?
How from the diamond fingle out each ray,
Where all, tho' trembling with ten thoufand hues,
Effufe one dazzling undivided light?
    Let the low-minded of thefe narrow days
No more prefume to deem the lofty tale
Of ancient times, in pity to their own,
Romance. In TALBOT we united faw
The piercing eye, the quick enlighten'd foul,
The graceful eafe, the flowing tongue of *Greece*,
Join'd to the virtues and the force of *Rome*.

ETERNAL WISDOM, that all-quick'ning fun,
Whence every life, in juft proportion, draws
Directing light and actuating flame,
Ne'er with a larger portion of its beams
Awaken'd mortal clay.   Hence fteady, calm,
Diffufive, deep, and clear, his reafon faw,
With inftantaneous view, the truth of things;
Chief what to human life and human blifs
Pertains, that nobleft fcience, fit for man:
And hence, refponfive to his knowledge, glow'd
His ardent virtue.   Ignorance and vice,
In confort foul, agree; each heightening each;
While virtue draws from knowledge brighter fire.
    What grand, what comely, or what tender fenfe,
What talent,. or what virtue was not his;
What that can render man or great, or good,
Give ufeful worth, or amiable grace?
Nor could he brook in ftudious fhade to lie,
In foft retirement, indolently pleas'd
With felfifh peace.   The Syren of the wife,
(Who fteals th' *Aonian* fong, and, in the fhape
Of virtue, wooes them from a worthlefs world)
Tho' deep he felt her charms, could never melt
His ftrenuous fpirit, recollected,. calm,
As filent night, yet active as the day.
The more the bold, the buftling, and the bad,
Prefs to ufurp the reins of power, the more
Behoves it virtue, with indignant zeal,
To check their combination.   Shall low views
Of fneaking int'reft or luxurious vice,
The villain's paffions, quicken more to toil,
And dart a livelier vigour thro' the foul,
Than thofe that, mingled with our trueft good,
With prefent honour and immortal fame,

Involve the good of all? An empty form
Is the weak virtue, that amid the fhade
Lamenting lies, with future fchemes amus'd,
While Wickednefs and Folly, *kindred powers,*
Confound the world. A TALBOT's, different far,
Sprung ardent into action: action, that difdain'd
To lofe in deathlike floth one pulfe of life,
That might be fav'd; difdain'd for coward eafe,
And her infipid pleafures, to refign
The prize of glory, the keen fweets of toil,
And thofe high joys that teach the truly great
To live for others, and for others die.

    Early, behold! he breaks benign on life.
Not breathing more beneficence, the fpring
Leads in her fwelling train the gentle airs:
While gay, behind her, fmiles the kindling wafte
Of ruffian ftorms and winter's lawlefs rage.
In him *Aftrea,* to this dim abode
Of ever-wandering men, return'd again:
To blefs them his delight, to bring them back,
From thorny error, from unjoyous wrong,
Into the paths of kind primeval faith,
Of happinefs and juftice. All his parts,
His virtues all, collected, fought the good
Of human-kind. For *that* he, fervent, felt
The throb of patriots, when they model ftates:
Anxious for *that,* nor needful fleep could hold
His ftill-awaken'd foul; nor friends had charms
To fteal, with pleafing guile, one ufeful hour;
Toil knew no languor, no attraction joy.
Thus with unwearied fteps, by Virtue led,
He gain'd the fummit of that facred hill,
Where rais'd above black envy's dark'ning clouds,
Her fpotlefs temple lifts its radiant front.

Be nam'd, victorious ravagers, no more!
Vanish, ye human comets! shrink your blaze!
Ye that your glory to your terrors owe,
As, o'er the gazing desolated earth,
You scatter famine, pestilence, and war;
Vanish! before this vernal sun of fame;
Effulgent sweetness! beaming life and joy.

How the heart listen'd, while he, pleading, spoke!
While on the enlighten'd mind, with winning art,
His gentle reason so persuasive stole,
That the charm'd hearer thought it was his own.
Ah! when, ye studious of the laws, again
Shall such enchanting lessons bless your ear?
When shall again the darkest truths, perplext,
Be set in ample day? when shall the harsh
And arduous open into smiling ease?
The solid mix with elegant delight?
His was the talent with the purest light
At once to pour conviction on the soul,
And warm with lawful flame th' impassion'd heart.
That dangerous gift with him was safely lodg'd ,
By Heaven—He, sacred to his country's cause,
To trampled want and worth, to suffering right,
To the lone widow's and her orphan's woes,
Reserv'd the mighty charm.   With equal brow, .
Despising then the smiles or frowns of power,
He all that noblest eloquence effus'd,
Which generous passion, taught by reason, breathes:
Then spoke the man; and, over barren art,
Prevail'd abundant nature.   Freedom then
His client was, humanity and truth.

Plac'd on the seat of justice, there he reign'd,
In a superior sphere of cloudless day,

A pure intelligence. No tumult there,
No dark emotion, no intemp'rate heat,
No paffion e'er difturb'd the clear ferene
That round him fpread. A zeal for right alone,
The love of juftice, like the fteady fun,
Its equal ardor lent;· and fometimes rais'd
Againft the fons of violence, of pride,
And bold deceit, his indignation gleam'd,
Yet ftill by fober dignity reftrain'd.
As intuition quick, he fnatch'd the truth,
Yet with progreffive patience, ftep by ftep,
Self-diffident, or to the flower kind,
He thro' the maze of falfehood trac'd it on,
Till, at the laft, evolv'd, it full appear'd,
And even the lofer own'd the juft decree.
   But when, in fenates, he, to Freedom firm,
Enlighten'd Freedom, plann'd falubrious laws,
His various learning, his wide knowledge, then,
His infight deep into BRITANNIA's weal,
Spontaneous feem'd from fimple fenfe to flow,
And the plain patriot fmooth'd the brow of law.
No fpecious fwell, no frothy pomp of words
Fell on the cheated ear; no ftudy'd maze
Of declamation, to perplex the right,
He darkening threw around: fafe in itfelf,
In its own force, all-powerful Reafon fpoke;
While on the great the ruling point, at once,
He ftream'd decifive day, and fhow'd it vain
To lengthen farther out the clear debate.
Conviction breathes conviction; to the heart,
Pour'd ardent forth in eloquence *unbid*,
The heart attends: for let the *Venal* try
Their every hard'ning ftupifying art,

Truth muſt prevail, zeal will enkindle zeal,
And Nature, ſkilful touch'd, is honeſt ſtill.

   Behold him in the councils of his prince,
What faithful light he lends? How rare, in courts,
Such wiſdom! ſuch abilities! and join'd
To virtue ſo determin'd, public zeal,
And honour of ſuch adamantine proof,
As even Corruption, hopeleſs, and o'er-aw'd,
Durſt not have *tempted!* Yet of Manners mild,
And winning every heart, he knew to pleaſe,
Nobly to pleaſe; while equally he ſcorn'd
Or adulation to receive, or give.
Happy the ſtate, where wakes a ruling eye
Of ſuch inſpection keen, and general care!
Beneath a guard ſo vigilant, ſo pure,
Toil may reſign his carcleſs head to reſt,
And ever-jealous Freedom ſleep in peace.
Ah! loſt untimely! loſt in downward days!
And many a patriot counſel with him loſt!
Counſels, that might have humbled *Britain*'s foe,
Her native foe, from eldeſt time by fate
Appointed, as did once a *Talbot*'s arms.

   Let learning, arts, let univerſal worth,
Lament a patron loſt, a friend and judge.
Unlike the ſons of vanity, that, veil'd
Beneath the patron's proſtituted name,
Dare ſacrifice a worthy man to pride,
And fluſh confuſion o'er an honeſt cheek.
When he conferr'd a grace, it ſeem'd a debt
Which he to merit, to the Public, paid,
And to the great all-bounteous Source of good.
His ſympathizing heart itſelf receiv'd
The generous obligation he beſtow'd.

This, this indeed, is patronizing worth.
Their kind protector him the Mufes own,
But fcorn with noble pride the boafted aid
Of taftelefs vanity's infulting hand.
The gracious ftream, that chears the letter'd world,
Is not the noify gift of fummer's noon,
Whofe fudden current, from the naked root,
Wafhes the little foil which yet remain'd,
And only more dejects the blufhing flowers:
No, 'tis the foft-defcending dews at eve,
The filent treafures of the vernal year,
Indulging deep their ftores, the ftill night long;
Till, with returning morn, the frefhen'd world,
Is fragrance all, all beauty, joy, and fong.
    Still let me view him in the pleafing light
Of private life, where pomp forgets to glare,
And where the plain unguarded foul is feen.
There, with that trueft greatnefs he appear'd,
Which thinks not of appearing; kindly veil'd
In the foft graces of the friendly fcene,
Infpiring focial confidence and eafe.
As free the converfe of the wife and good,
As joyous, difentangling every power,
And breathing mix'd improvement with delight,
As when amid the various-bloffom'd fpring,
Or gentle-beaming autumn's penfive fhade,
The philofophic mind with Nature talks.
Say ye, his *Sons*, his dear remains, with whom
The father laid fuperfluous ftate afide,
Yet rais'd your filial duty thence the more,
With friendfhip rais'd it, with efteem, with love,
Beyond the ties of blood, oh! fpeak the joy,
The pure ferene, the chearful wifdom mild,

The virtuous fpirit, which his vacant hours,
In femblance of amufement, thro' the breaft
Infus'd.   And thou, O *Rundle*!* lend thy ftrain,
Thou darling friend! thou brother of his foul!
In whom the head and heart their ftores unite:
Whatever fancy paints, invention pours,
Judgment digefts, the well-tun'd bofom feels,
Truth natural, moral, or divine, has taught,
The Virtues dictate, or the Mufes fing.
Lend me the plaint, which, to the lonely main,
With memory converfing, you will pour,
As on the pebbled fhore you, penfive, ftray,
Where *Derry*'s mountains a bleak crefcent form,
And mid their ample round receive the waves,
That from the frozen pole, refounding, rufh,
Impetuous.   Tho' from native fun-fhine driven,
Driven from your friends, the fun-fhine of the foul,
By flanderous zeal, and politics infirm,
Jealous of worth; yet will you blefs your lot,
Yet will you triumph in your glorious fate,
Whence *Talbot*'s friendfhip glows to future times,
Intrepid, warm; of kindred tempers born;
Nurs'd, by experience, into flow efteem,
Calm confidence unbounded, love not blind,
And the fweet light from mingled minds difclos'd,
From mingled chymic oils as burfts the fire.
    I too remember well that chearful bowl,
Which round his table flow'd.   The ferious there
Mix'd with the fportive, with the learn'd the plain;
Mirth foften'd wifdom, candour temper'd mirth;
And wit its honey lent, without the fting.
Not fimple Nature's unaffected fons,

---

* Dr. *Rundle*, late Bifhop of *Derry* in *Ireland*.

The blamelefs *Indians*, round the foreft-chear,
In funny lawn or fhady covert fet,
Hold more unfpotted converfe: nor, of old,
Rome's awful confuls, her dictator-fwains,
As on the product of their *Sabine* farms
They far'd, with ftricter virtue fed the foul:
Nor yet in *Athens*, at an *Attic* meal,
Where *Socrates* prefided, fairer truth,
More elegant humanity, more grace,
Wit more refin'd, or deeper fcience reign'd.
   But far beyond the little vulgar bounds
Of family, or friends, or native land,
By juft degrees, and with proportion'd flame,
Extended his benevolence: a friend
To human kind, to parent Nature's works.
Of free accefs, and of engaging grace,
Such as a brother to a brother owes,
He kept an open judging ear for all,
And fpread an open countenance, where fmil'd
The fair effulgence of an open heart;
While on the rich, the poor, the high, the low,
With equal ray, his ready goodnefs fhone:
For *nothing human foreign was to him.*
   Thus to a dread inheritance, my Lord,
And hard to be fupported, you fucceed:
But kept by virtue, as by virtue gain'd,
It will, thro' lateft time, enrich your race,
When groffer wealth fhall moulder into duft,
And with their authors in oblivion funk
Vain titles lie, the fervile badges oft
Of mean fubmiffion, not the meed of worth.
True genuine honour its large patent holds
Of all mankind, thro' every land and age,

Of univerfal Reafon's various fons,
And even of God himfelf, fole perfect Judge!
Yet knows thefe nobleft honours of the mind
On rigid terms defcend: the high-plac'd heir,
Scann'd by the public eye, that, with keen gaze,
Malignant feeks out faults, cannot thro' life,
Amid the namelefs infects of a court,
Unheeded fteal: but, with his fire compar'd,
He muft be glorious, or he muft be fcorn'd.
This truth to you, who merit well to bear
A name to *Britons* dear, th' officious Mufe
May fafely fing, and fing without referve.

Vain were the plaint, and ignorant the tear
That fhould a *Talbot* mourn. Ourfelves, indeed,
Our country robb'd of her delight and ftrength,
We may lament. Yet let us, grateful, joy,
That we fuch virtues knew, fuch virtues felt,
And feel them ftill, teaching our views to rife
Thro' ever-bright'ning fcenes of future worlds.
Be dumb, ye worft of zealots! ye that, prone
To thoughtlefs duft, renounce that generous hope,
Whence every joy below its fpirit draws,
And every pain its balm: a *Talbot*'s light,
A *Talbot*'s virtues claim another fource,
Than the blind maze of undefigning blood;
Nor when that vital fountain plays no more,
Can they be quench'd amid the gelid ftream.

Methinks I fee his mounting fpirit, freed
From tangling earth, regain the realms of day,
Its native country, whence, to blefs mankind,
Eternal Goodnefs, on this darkfome fpot,
Had ray'd it down a while. Behold! approv'd
By the tremendous Judge of heaven and earth,

And to th' Almighty Father's prefence join'd,
He takes his rank, in glory, and in blifs,
Amid the human worthies.   Glad around
Crowd his compatriot fhades, and point him out
With joyful pride, *Britannia*'s blamelefs boaft.
Ah! who is he, that with a fonder eye
Meets thine enraptur'd?—'Tis the beft of fons!
The beft of friends!——Too foon is realiz'd
That hope, which once forbad thy tears to flow!
Mean-while the kindred fouls of every land,
(Howe'er divided in the fretful days
Of prejudice and error) mingled now,
In one felected never-jarring ftate,
Where GOD himfelf their only monarch reigns,
Partake the joy; yet, fuch the fenfe that ftill
Remains of earthly woes, for us below,
And for our lofs they drop a pitying tear.
But ceafe, prefumptuous Mufe, nor vainly ftrive
To quit this cloudy fphere that binds thee down:
'Tis not for mortal hand to trace thefe fcenes,
Scenes, that our grofs ideas grovelling caft
Behind, and ftrike our boldeft language dumb.

    Forgive, immortal fhade! if aught from earth,
From duft low-warbled, to thofe groves can rife,
Where flows celeftial harmony, forgive
This fond fuperfluous verfe.   With deep-felt voice,
On every heart imprefs'd, thy deeds themfelves
Atteft thy praife.   Thy praife the widow's fighs,
And orphan's tears embalm.   The good, the bad,
The fons of juftice and the fons of ftrife,
All who or freedom or who intereft prize,
A deep-divided nation's parties all,
Confpire to fwell thy fpotlefs praife to heaven.

Glad heaven receives it, and feraphic lyres
With fongs of triumph thy arrival hail.
How vain this tribute then! this lowly lay!
Yet nought is vain which gratitude infpires
The Mufe, befides, her duty thus approves
To virtue, to her country, to mankind,
To ruling Nature, that, in glorious charge,
As to her prieftefs, gives it her, to hymn
Whatever good and excellent fhe forms.

P O E M S

ON

SEVERAL OCCASIONS.

VERSES

OCCASIONED BY THE

DEATH of Mr. AIKMAN,

A PARTICULAR FRIEND OF THE AUTHOR'S.

AS thofe we love decay, we die in part,
  String after ftring is fever'd from the heart;
Till loofen'd life, at laft, but breathing clay,
Without one pang is glad to fall away.
Unhappy he, who lateft feels the blow,
Whofe eyes have wept o'er every friend laid low,
Dragg'd lingering on from partial death to death,
Till, dying, all he can refign is breath.

O D E.

I.

TELL me, thou foul of her I love,
　　Ah! tell me, whither art thou fled;
To what delightful world above,
　　Appointed for the happy dead?

II.

Or doft thou, free, at pleafure, roam,
　　And fometimes fhare thy lover's woe;
Where, void of thee, his chearlefs home
　　Can now, alas! no comfort know?

III.

Oh! if thou hover'ft round my walk,
　　While, under ev'ry well-known tree,
I to thy fancy'd fhadow talk,
　　And every tear is full of thee;

IV.

Should then the weary eye of grief,
　　Befide fome fympathetic ftream,
In flumber find a fhort relief,
　　Oh vifit thou my foothing dream!

EPITAPH

ON

MISS STANLEY.

HERE, STANLEY, reft, efcap'd this mortal ftrife,
Above the joys, beyond the woes of life.
Fierce pangs no more thy lively beauties ftain,
And fternly try thee with a year of pain:
No more fweet patience, feigning oft relief,
Lights thy fick eye, to cheat a parent's grief:
With tender art, to fave her anxious groan,
No more thy bofom preffes down its own:
Now well-earn'd peace is thine, and blifs fincere:
Ours be the lenient, not unpleafing tear!

O born to bloom, then fink beneath the ftorm;
To fhow us Virtue in her faireft form;
To fhow us artlefs Reafon's moral reign,
What boaftful Science arrogates in vain;
Th' obedient paffions knowing each their part;
Calm light the head, and harmony the heart!

Yes, we muft follow foon, will glad obey,
When a few funs have roll'd their cares away,
Tir'd with vain life, will clofe the willing eye:
'Tis the great birth-right of mankind *to die*.
Bleft be the bark! that wafts us to the fhore,
Where death-divided friends fhall part no more:
To join thee there, here with thy duft repofe,
Is all the hope thy haplefs mother knows.

TO

The Rev. Mr. MURDOCH,

RECTOR OF STRADDISHALL IN SUFFOLK.

MDCCXXXVIII.

THUS fafely low, my friend, thou can'ft not fall:
    Here reigns a deep tranquillity o'er all;
No noife, no care, no vanity, no ftrife;
Men, woods and fields, all breathe untroubled life.
Then keep each paffion down, however dear;
T'ruft me, the tender are the moft fevere.
Guard, while 'tis thine, thy philofophic eafe,
And afk no joy but that of virtuous peace;
That bids defiance to the ftorms of fate:
High blifs is only for a higher ftate.

A

PARAPHRASE

ON THE

LATTER PART OF THE SIXTH CHAPTER OF
St. MATTHEW.

WHEN my breaſt labours with oppreſſive care,
 And o'er my cheek deſcends the falling tear;
While all my warring paſſions are at ſtrife,
O, let me liſten to the words of life!
Raptures deep-felt his doctrine did impart,
And thus he rais'd from earth the drooping heart:

 Think not, when all, your ſcanty ſtores afford,
Is ſpread at once upon the ſparing board;
Think not, when worn the homely robe appears,
While, on the roof, the howling tempeſt bears;
What farther ſhall this feeble life ſuſtain,
And what ſhall clothe theſe ſhiv'ring limbs again.
Say, does not life its nouriſhment exceed?
And the fair body its inveſting weed?

 Behold! and look away your low deſpair——
See the light tenants of the barren air:
To them, nor ſtores, nor granaries, belong,
Nought, but the woodland, and the pleaſing ſong;

Yet, your kind heavenly Father bends his eye
On the leaft wing, that flits along the fky.
To him they fing, when Spring renews the plain,
To him they cry, in Winter's pinching reign;
Nor is their mufic nor their plaint in vain:
He hears the gay, and the diftrefsful call,
And with unfparing bounty fills them all.

 Obferve the rifing lily's fnowy grace,
Obferve the various vegetable race;
They neither toil, nor fpin, but carelefs grow,
Yet fee how warm they blufh! how bright they glow!
What regal veftments can with them compare!
What king fo fhining! or what queen fo fair!

 If, ceafelefs, thus the fowls of heaven he feeds,
If o'er the fields fuch lucid robes he fpreads;
Will he not care for you, ye faithlefs, fay?
Is he unwife? or, are ye lefs than they?

S O N G.

ONE day the God of fond defire,
　　On mifchief bent, to Damon faid,
Why not difclofe your tender fire,
　　Not own it to the lovely maid?

The fhepherd mark'd his treacherous art,
　　And, foftly fighing, thus reply'd:
'Tis true you have fubdu'd my heart,
　　But fhall not triumph o'er my pride.

The flave in private only bears
　　Your bondage, who his love conceals;
But when his paffion he declares,
　　You drag him at your chariot-wheels.

S O N G.

HARD is the fate of him who loves,
　　Yet dares not tell his trembling pain,
But to the fympathetic groves,
　　But to the lonely liftening plain.

Oh! when fhe bleffes next your fhade,
　　Oh! when her footfteps next are feen
In flowery tracks along the mead,
　　In frefher mazes o'er the green;

VOL. I.　　　　　　　T

Ye gentle fpirits of the vale,
　To whom the tears of love are dear,
From dying lilies waft a gale,
　And figh my forrows in her ear.

Oh tell her what fhe cannot blame,
　Tho' fear my tongue muft ever bind;
Oh tell her that my virtuous flame
　Is as her fpotlefs foul refin'd.

Not her own guardian angel eyes
　With chafter tendernefs his care,
Not purer her own wifhes rife,
　Not holier her own fighs in prayer.

But if, at firft, her virgin fear
　Should ftart at love's fufpefted name,
With that of friendfhip footh her ear——
　True love and friendfhip are the fame.

S O N G.

U NLESS with my Amanda bleft,
　In vain I twine the woodbine bower;
Unlefs to deck her fweeter breaft,
　In vain I rear the breathing flower:

Awaken'd by the genial year,
　In vain the birds around me fing;
In vain the frefhening fields appear:
　Without my love there is no fpring.

S O N G.

FOR ever, Fortune, wilt thou prove
　　An unrelenting foe to love,
And when we meet a mutual heart,
Come in between, and bid us part:

Bid us figh on from day to day,
And wifh, and wifh the foul away;
Till youth and genial years are flown,
And all the life of life is gone?

But bufy bufy ftill art thou,
To bind the lovelefs joylefs vow,
The heart from pleafure to delude,
To join the gentle to the rude.

For once, O Fortune, hear my prayer,
And I abfolve thy future care;
All other bleffings I refign,
Make but the dear Amanda mine.

S O N G.

COME, gentle God of foft defire,
　　Come and poffefs my happy breaft,
Not fury-like in flames and fire,
　　Or frantic folly's wildnefs dreft;

But come in friendfhip's angel-guife:
　　Yet dearer thou than friendfhip art,
More tender fpirit in thy eyes,
　　More fweet emotions at the heart.

O come with goodnefs in thy train,
    With peace and pleafure void of ftorm,
And wouldft thou me for ever gain,
    Put on Amanda's winning form.

O D E.

O Nightingale, beft poet of the grove,
    That plaintive ftrain can ne'er belong to thee,
Bleft in the full poffeffion of thy love:
    O lend that ftrain, fweet Nightingale, to me!

'Tis mine, alas! to mourn my wretched fate:
    I love a maid who all my bofom charms,
Yet lofe my days without this lovely mate;
    Inhuman Fortune keeps her from my arms.

You, happy birds! by Nature's fimple laws
    Lead your foft lives, fuftain'd by Nature's fare;
You dwell wherever roving fancy draws,
    And love and fong is all your pleafing care:

But we, vain flaves of int'reft and of pride,
    Dare not be bleft, left envious tongues fhould blame:
And hence in vain I languifh for my bride;
    O mourn with me, fweet bird, my haplefs flame.

O D E,

TO SERAPHINA.

THE wanton's charms, however bright,
Are like the falfe illufive light,
Whofe flattering unaufpicious blaze
To precipices oft betrays:
But that fweet ray your beauties dart,
Which clears the mind, and cleans the heart,
Is like the facred queen of night,
Who pours a lovely gentle light
Wide o'er the dark, by wanderers bleft,
Conducting them to peace and reft.
    A vicious love depraves the mind,
'Tis anguifh, guilt, and folly join'd;
But Seraphina's eyes difpenfe
A mild and gracious influence;
Such as in vifions angels fhed
Around the heav'n-illumin'd head.
To love thee, Seraphina, fure
Is to be tender, happy, pure;
'Tis from low paffions to efcape;
And woo bright virtue's faireft fhape;
'Tis ecftacy with wifdom join'd;
And heaven infus'd into the mind.

O D E

ON

Æ O L U S's   H A R P *.

ÆThereal race, inhabitants of air,
 Who hymn your God amid the fecret grove;
Ye unfeen beings to my harp repair,
 And raife majeftic ftrains, or melt in love.

Thofe tender notes, how kindly they upbraid,
 With what foft woe they thrill the lover's heart!
Sure from the hand of fome unhappy maid,
 Who dy'd of love, thefe fweet complainings part.

But hark! that ftrain was of a graver tone,
 On the deep ftrings his hand fome hermit throws;
Or he the facred Bard †; who fat alone,
 In the drear wafte, and wept his people's woes.

Such was the fong which Zion's children fung,
 When by Euphrates' ftream they made their plaint;
And to fuch fadly folemn notes are ftrung
 Angelic harps, to footh a dying faint.

Methinks I hear the full celeftial choir,
 Thro' heaven's high dome their awful anthem raife;
Now chanting clear, and now they all confpire
 To fwell the lofty hymn, from praife to praife.

Let me, ye wand'ring fpirits of the wind,
 Who, as wild fancy prompts you, touch the ftring,
Smit with your theme, be in your chorus join'd,
 For till you ceafe, my Mufe forgets to fing.

* *Æolus's Harp* is a mufical inftrument which plays with the
wind, invented by Mr. *Ofwald*; its properties are fully defcribed in
the *Caftle of Indolence*.

† Jeremiah.

H Y M N

O N

S O L I T U D E.

HAIL, mildly pleafing Solitude,
    Companion of the wife and good;
But from whofe holy, piercing eye,
The herd of fools, and villains fly.

  Oh! how I love with thee to walk,
And liften to thy whifper'd talk,
Which innocence, and truth imparts,
And melts the moft.obdurate hearts.

  A thoufand fhapes you wear with eafe,
And ftill in every fhape you pleafe.
Now wrapt in fome myfterious dream,
A lone philofopher you feem;
Now quick from hill to vale you fly,
And now you fweep the vaulted fky.
A fhepherd next, you haunt the plain,
And warble forth your oaten ftrain,
A lover now, with all the grace
Of that fweet paffion in your face:
Then, calm'd to friendfhip, you affume
The gentle-looking HARFORD's bloom,
As, with her MUSIDORA, fhe
(Her MUSIDORA fond of thee)
Amid the long withdrawing vale,
Awakes the rival'd nightingale.

  Thine is the balmy breath of morn,
Juft as the dew-bent rofe is born;

And while Meridian fervors beat,
Thine is the woodland dumb retreat;
But chief, when evening fcenes decay,
And the faint landfkip fwims away,
Thine is the doubtful foft decline,
And that beft hour of mufing thine.

Defcending angels blefs thy train,
The virtues of the fage, and fwain;
Plain Innocence in white array'd,
Before thee lifts her fearlefs head:
Religion's beams around thee fhine,
And chear thy glooms with light divine:
About thee fports fweet Liberty;
And rapt Urania fings to thee.

Oh, let me pierce thy fecret cell!
And in thy deep recefses dwell;
Perhaps from Norwood's oak-clad hill,
When Meditation has her fill,
I juft may caft my carelefs eyes
Where London's fpiry turrets rife,
Think of its crimes, its cares, its pain,
Then fhield me in the woods again.

END OF THE FIRST VOLUME.

O

www.ingramcontent.com/pod-product-compliance
Lightning Source LLC
Chambersburg PA
CBHW020951030726
47496CB00005B/1454